FIONA GRAPH lives in
That Bounded, was publishe
is her second novel.

C000293222

Beloved Ghost

FIONA GRAPH

SilverWood

Published in 2022 by SilverWood Books

SilverWood Books Ltd
14 Small Street, Bristol, BS1 1DE, United Kingdom
www.silverwoodbooks.co.uk

Cover painting 'Aquamarine' by Henry Scott Tuke is reproduced with
thanks to the Tuke Collection, Royal Cornwall Polytechnic Society,
Falmouth.

This is a work of fiction. With the exception of public figures, any
resemblance to persons living or dead is coincidental. The roles played by
Alan Turing and Guy Burgess in this narrative are fictional but consistent
with the known facts of their lives.

ISBN 978-1-80042-211-7 (paperback)

British Library Cataloguing in Publication Data
A CIP catalogue record for this book is
available from the British Library

Typesetting by SilverWood Books with the author's artistic direction

For all those who suffered under the ban on homosexuals in
the diplomatic service (1952-1991)

1940–1945: This was the most important decision we would make in our lives

1

We had another air raid during my last night in the hospital. They were becoming regular, and this was a bad one. From my ward window, I could see fires burning all over Bristol. The enemy planes danced and darted in the spotlights like metallic dragonflies. It had a strange, savage beauty, until you remembered people were suffering and dying.

As I stood watching, I felt numb. The last year had been so tumultuous, so confronting, that I was drained of emotion. I had gone from being a healthy man, at the start of his life, to someone who was a cripple with no apparent future, stumbling through the darkest days of the war. If I tried to look more than a few weeks ahead, I saw myself going back to finish university and then – a vacuum of nothingness that haunted me in the small hours.

I thought of Daniel, newly ordained as a vicar after deciding to walk away from his nature and our love. I wished him well, but his image felt dim, as if glimpsed through the smoke curling up towards me. My mind turned inevitably to Zac, hoping he was safe.

The following afternoon, I saw the doctor and physiotherapist, said my goodbyes to the nurses, and walked out clutching my belongings in a paper bag – to find Zac waiting for me. I hadn't been sure he could get away from the station, and my face must have shown my delight. He smiled back at me and said, 'Show me your new home, Theo.'

I had spent several days walking around Bristol to find a flat, making a virtue of the need to break in my new boot. Some places were dirty or depressing, while others had no privacy. Finally, I'd found a decent flat with a bathroom, small kitchenette and large front room with a bed in the corner. The landlord lived upstairs, a widower in his seventies who seemed a nice old chap. When he told me the price, I raised my eyebrows and he said, 'For an injured soldier I'll do you a special price, sonny.' We shook on something slightly less eye-watering. But it had a telephone, and it was walking distance from Zac's place.

When I picked up the keys, the landlord eyed Zac, smart in his uniform, with grudging approval. Zac made all the right noises about the flat, then went out to the car and brought in some food and a portable wireless. How generous and thoughtful, how typical of the man. 'Come on, Theo,' he said. 'Let's go out to celebrate your escape from hospital and your new home.'

We went to our usual pub by the port and talked as readily as always. I had known Zac barely a year, in the midst of battle and while we both struggled through injuries. In one way, I knew so little about him, yet I trusted him with my life. To the outside world he might appear reserved, but I knew the kind, honourable man behind that facade and considered myself fortunate to be his friend.

'What are you thinking about?'

I realised Zac had been watching me. I'd been in a world of my own, a habit of mine from childhood. How many times had I been told I lived too much in my head? I shrugged, irritated with myself, and smiled over at him. 'Do you know, Zac, I never asked you about your name. Is it short for Zachary?'

'Afraid so. "Beloved by God", I believe it means. My parents were religious. What about you – does your name come from anywhere?'

'I was named after an uncle who died in the Great War. My stepfather insists on calling me "Theodore" in his pompous way.'

'He seems that sort of man – but didn't I hear your mother call you "Teddy"? Is that your childhood nickname?' Zac had recently met my mother and stepfather when they visited me in the hospital.

I laughed. 'God, how embarrassing. I managed to lose it when I went to university. I suppose it must sound childish.'

He looked at me from under his eyelashes. 'Teddy. No, I like it. It's sweet. It suits you. OK, it's my round.' He disappeared off to the bar.

It felt as though a weight had lifted from me. I'd spent five months in hospital after Dunkirk, although I don't remember much about the first weeks. Apparently, the doctors had argued whether my leg should be amputated but decided to try and save it. I'd endured several operations and infections in the wound. The pain had been relentless, clouding everything I did. I'd survived from day to day, one set of painkillers to the next. Scars covered my leg and I had to wear an orthopaedic boot because the operations had shortened it. But it seemed churlish to complain. Everyone kept telling me how fortunate I was to still have two legs. My situation had improved dramatically a month earlier, when Zac found me in a makeshift military hospital in Kent and arranged my transfer to Bristol. I had a further operation, which gave me more mobility, and the pain started to recede. His friendship had made such a difference.

In every way, not just at Dunkirk, Zac had pulled me from the shadows and saved my life.

I hadn't realised until then how oppressive my long hospital stay had been. When I told Zac on his return from the bar he said, 'Poor old Theo, you've been through a bloody hard time, haven't you? What are your plans now?'

'I'll be going to outpatients three times a week for treatment on my leg. And I need to start revising before I go back to Cambridge in January. There's enough to keep me busy.'

'It must feel like a return to some sort of normality for you.'

'Hmm ... that reminds me, the army's discharging me tomorrow, so I have to do some shopping. All my clothes are at my mother's and I've got nothing to wear once I hand back my uniform.'

'It seems mad to buy things if it's just a case of waiting to collect your own. Why don't you borrow some of my clothes? I hardly get to use them, and we're much the same size, after all.'

Zac was slightly taller, but I didn't mind trousers flapping around my ugly boots. I grinned and said, 'Thanks, I'd appreciate it.' His cheerful mood must have infected me. I started feeling hopeful for the first time in ages.

Back at his place, he made up the fire while I fixed the blackout. His room was austere and full of books. I loved to be there. It had felt like a refuge on my visits from the hospital. When he got out his clothes, I teased him about how impeccable they were. Everything about him was tidy, his movements brisk and graceful. He'd once mentioned he was captain of the fencing team at his school.

'That'll do nicely,' he said as he held up a shirt against me. 'I think your shoulders are a bit broader because of the swimming, but they should fit.'

'You're far too generous to me, Zac. I don't deserve it.'

He turned and fiddled with a shirt. 'You know, Theo, you could still swim. Why don't you try the lido in Clifton?'

That hadn't occurred to me and I brightened at the thought. Of course, he wanted to give me far too many clothes and we bickered amiably. In the end, I agreed to take two shirts, one jumper and some trousers. He had only one overcoat and I refused to take it.

Zac made some sandwiches and we sat in front of the fire to eat. After a while he asked, 'What is it, Theo? Are you thinking about Daniel? Have you heard from him again?' So often, he seemed to read my mind. Shadows shifted on his face in the firelight, his eyes darker than usual.

I admitted, 'Yes, I've had another letter. He doesn't understand why I want to stay in Bristol. He said he'd find me a room somewhere in his village. I suppose he'd see me when his parish duties permit.'

'He's not reconsidered his decision?'

'No. He still believes our relationship was a sin. He loves me "platonically". He loves me for my soul.' I couldn't help smiling bitterly.

'It seems to me he just wants the best of both worlds. He'd have you dangling on a string, at his beck and call, while he denies who he is. Does he plan to hide you away, like a married man with his mistress, and sneak over to hold your hand?' He sounded impatient. Who could blame him – how many times had I maundered on about Daniel? Always, Zac had listened patiently, but there was a limit.

I made a half-hearted shrug. Zac gave me one of his penetrating looks, then said in a lighter voice, 'Talking about married men, did I tell you about the time I was sheep shearing in Australia?'

Zac had travelled the world since he was seventeen – working on sheep and cattle farms in Canada, Australia and Argentina, going on trawlers around Southeast Asia. He had a warm speaking voice and told marvellous stories, which he wrote down in a journal. He didn't lose his thread or umm and aah – he was a natural storyteller.

When he finished his anecdote, he said, 'You look pale, my dear. Is your leg hurting? Do you need a painkiller?'

'Oh, it's not too bad. It just aches a bit now.' I didn't like to talk about my injury. 'How about your hand – are you doing the exercises?'

'Yes, the exercises, the cream, the whole lot. And I have to admit, it seems to be working. All thanks to your physiotherapist – you must thank her from me. Look, I can move my fingers better, and I've got more grip in my hand.'

He rolled up his sleeve to show how he could partly bend and straighten the fingers on his left hand. The angry burns running along his hand and arm were less vivid, and he looked pleased when I told him this. 'We're slowly healing up, Theo.' He smiled over at me. 'Come on, let's get you home.'

The following day, I was formally discharged from the army. Here are your papers, sorry about your crippled leg. Have a nice life. But I held no bitterness. We were in a desperate fight for survival, and we did what was needed. I left in Zac's civilian clothes, thinking: *this is a new chapter in my life.* Theoretically, I was free to do whatever I wanted. But I felt a deep bond with Zac, and never once contemplated being anywhere else.

The next days settled into a routine. I went for treatment at the hospital and started swimming in the lido. My breaststroke was clumsy, but I could do the front crawl. My leg became stronger and more flexible. I spent hours in the library, feeling my brain stutter back to life. Each afternoon, I fell into a deep slumber, my body demanding recompense for a hefty bill of sleep-starved nights. I had energy and a sense of my strength returning, physically and mentally. Finally, I could think clearly about Daniel.

By the time I left school, I'd known my nature for some time. A series of crushes on other boys had made me understand there was a reason I felt different. I was attracted to my own sex. I knew this was considered wrong and disgusting. It was completely out of the question I could talk to anyone about it. The closest I came was when my mother spoke about me living in the family house in the future "with your wife". The house was rented to tenants, but technically mine after she'd remarried. When I told her I would never marry, she looked startled and changed the subject. If she'd asked me why, I would have told her. But it was for the best, really. She was loving, but never could deal with unpleasantness. Anything nasty was swept under the carpet.

I think having to work this out for myself meant I got tied up in knots about things. Sometimes I felt I was trying to follow a map in the dark without a torch or any instructions. I began to learn how to live a double life, wearing a cloak of false identity and knowing what I must keep hidden. I'd been a contented child, but this was a time of great unhappiness and confusion.

When I went up to Cambridge in 1936 and met Daniel, a theology student, I was elated to find someone like me. For the first time in years, I didn't feel alone. In my idealistic imaginings we were soulmates, like David and Jonathan. We read Plato to each other, agreeing our love was on a higher plane than just the physical.

But in the months before the war, Daniel's religious belief deepened and he started to say our love was wrong. His manner became increasingly cold. We had ferocious arguments – he criticised me for saying I accepted I was homosexual; he lectured me if he thought I behaved in a way that was not "manly" or "normal". If I wanted to make love, he would flinch and push me away, or was consumed by remorse afterwards. He talked of dedicating himself to God. When university broke up for the summer holidays, he took himself off to a religious retreat in Norfolk while I planned for my final Cambridge year without him.

Then war was declared – and the world as we knew it turned upside down. I was conscripted while Daniel took the path of ordination.

The manner of his rejection had been a seam of grief running through the last year. It seemed I'd lost my only chance of happiness – of feeling I belonged somewhere. I'd decided I would live a celibate life and keep my sexual preference to myself. I would put my energy into work and friendships.

Now, for the first time, I realised I had compromised my identity for Daniel. I'd suffered repeated insults in the hope he would come back to me. I'd let him spend hours telling me our love was wrong, that we were wicked in the eyes of God, then clinging to me with urgent kisses. I had allowed myself to be used as a whipping boy for his self-rejection. This would never happen with Zac. He challenged you to see things clearly and to hold to what is right. Meeting Zac had confirmed my hope that, as homosexuals, we could meet life with dignity. Daniel now seemed irrelevant, a part of my past. I was sorry he was tormented by his nature, but his emotional hold over me had gone.

2

Zac and I spent every evening together unless he had to work a late shift. He'd been offered a medical discharge after Dunkirk, but had chosen to move into Military Intelligence and worked at a nearby station. We would walk by the port, then go to the pub. One of these nights, we saw two drunk men walk straight into the water because it was so dark with the blackout. Once we saw they were safe, we couldn't stop laughing. God knows, you needed reasons to laugh in the war.

On Zac's rare days off work, we went out to the countryside. The trees were a brawl of red and gold in the November sunlight. I scuffed through the leaves like a child, pretending, as they covered my boots, that I was still the Theo who could run and dance. We walked until my leg ached or we got too cold, found a pub and came back in the dark. We were different in so many ways. He was three years older and had done so much in his life. I felt like a sheltered schoolboy in comparison. And yet we would talk for hours, absorbed and with an instinctive understanding.

One evening in the pub, I asked, 'You went to boarding school when you were ten, didn't you?'

'It's too young, I know,' Zac said with a grimace. 'But it was an improvement on my home life, although I missed my sister.'

'What was it like at home?'

Zac hesitated. I could see he was battling his innate

reserve. 'It's all ancient history now, Theo. Are you really interested? Well, if you must know … my parents were fanatically religious, particularly my mother. She came from an evangelical background where the Bible was considered the literal truth. Nearly everything was a sin to her. If we did anything she considered wrong, she'd freeze us out and give us the silent treatment, part of what she called "discipline". I know your father died when you were young, and your stepfather is a bit of a prig, but you have a loving mother. You were lucky.'

'What about your father? Is he French?'

'Oh, you mean my name? That goes back generations – our ancestors were French Huguenots. No,' he added with a twist of his lips, 'he's a perfect English gentleman.'

I thought that would explain Zac's looks: the striking green eyes and dark hair, the skin that tanned so easily in the sun. He seemed caught up in his memories. I prompted him, 'Did you get on with your father?'

'Him! He never paid us attention. He just hid behind his newspaper and deferred in everything to my mother. She ran the house like a little tyrant. They never praised us, never gave us hugs. We were punished over the smallest things … I don't talk about this to anyone. Are you sure you want to hear this drivel?'

'It's not drivel, Zac. You've asked me enough questions about my life.' For all our long conversations over the last year, it was the first time I'd managed to get him to talk properly about his childhood. He stared into his beer and I waited, secretly thrilled he was opening up to me like this.

'If my mother decided I'd committed some transgression, she'd tell my father to get his strap out. He did as she said. In a way, I blame him more, for being so weak. I got quite

17

a few beatings. At best, there was grudging acceptance if we did something good. I can barely remember seeing my mother smile or appear to like our company. She was a cruel person – she should never have had children. Oh, Theo, don't look at me like that. It's all in the past.'

'Did they always plan to send you to boarding school so young?'

'Who knows?' he replied. 'But then I committed a monstrous crime that put me beyond the pale, so I was cast out like that chap in the Bible. Ironic, really, because we weren't rich, far from it, but I managed to get a full scholarship. So, I made possible my own exile.'

'What happened to make them send you away?'

'Oh …' He hesitated, appearing to debate something internally. 'My younger brother died when I was ten, and I was blamed for it.'

'But – why?'

'Isaac was six when it happened. I was often put in charge of him and Ruth. My mother spent most of her time with her Bible group – she wasn't too interested in looking after us. We were out playing in the woods one day and … well, there was a railway crossing on the way home. I was holding onto both of them, but Isaac pulled his hand out of mine and ran onto the tracks. He was killed instantly by a train. My parents told me I was responsible …' His voice faltered.

Instinctively, I put my hand on his. 'But, Zac – you were only a child! How could they say that?' I was outraged on his behalf.

Zac gave me a crooked smile. 'Well, yes … but at the time I took on all the guilt, especially as I was sent away soon after.'

'Were you close to your sister?'

'She's six years younger, so we didn't really have a proper relationship before I was sent away. But we became close when she got older. I always tried to protect her from the worst with my parents. We spent every moment together in the school holidays. Those are my happiest family memories,' he added.

'What's she doing now?'

'Bloody hell, Theo, you're full of questions today! The short answer is, I don't know. My parents threw me out when I was seventeen, with the words "wicked pervert" ringing in my ears. I haven't seen her since then. We wrote regularly, but she stopped replying a few months before the war. I hope she's all right. She'd be twenty now.'

I looked at him, shocked. 'Zac – you never told me your parents threw you out of home. What happened?'

'Why don't you just shine a light on me and interrogate me properly?' he muttered with an attempt at humour. I waited patiently, sensing sadness behind his light manner. 'They found me in bed with another boy. I hitched to London and spent a few weeks on the streets, then got myself sorted out. No big story. Now, drink up and I'll get a refill.'

I watched him as he stood at the bar, feeling deep compassion. No wonder he was so self-sufficient and kept people at a distance. No wonder he'd left England and travelled all over. I was struck by the realisation of how alone he was in the world, apart from his friend Claude. And his injury at Dunkirk had stopped him from active duty. I knew he was dying to contribute to the fight against the Nazis. But he never complained or felt sorry for himself. To me, he was the benchmark for courage and integrity.

Over the following days, Zac spoke more freely about his past.

Most evenings we would have a quick drink in the pub then go back, usually to my place, and sit in front of the gas fire. We talked or listened to the wireless in an easy companionship. During these days, my thoughts of Daniel grew steadily dimmer.

I was in the kitchen once, making coffee and humming a Bach cantata to myself. I turned to see Zac leaning against the doorframe. 'I can't remember the last time I heard someone sing Bach. You play the piano, too, don't you?' I nodded, smiling at him. 'A man of many talents.' At times like this, it seemed we were the only people in the world.

But sometimes we visited the queer pub in Bristol to meet Zac's oldest friend. Claude was a clever man with a ready line in sardonic quips, who had recently qualified as a doctor. I knew they'd been best friends at boarding school, and guessed they gave each other a sense of family. Claude's mother had arrived from India as a young bride, disowned by her family for marrying an English Christian. Both parents had died before the war and he was an only child, like me.

On this particular evening, Claude's boyfriend was present when we arrived. I'd met Gordon once before and found him superficial and gossipy. He seemed to be in a brittle mood when we sat down. Almost immediately, he started goading Zac.

'My dear Zac, whatever has happened to Ricky? I thought you two were in the throes of mad passion?'

Zac was curt. 'He's history.'

Claude opened his mouth to speak, but Gordon gave a small laugh and went on, 'Of course, that was last month. I suppose he's old news. Talk about "love them and leave them" – you take it to a whole new level, you butch thing. Even poor old Claude didn't get more than a few months out of you. Well, there's a long line of queers dying to get into your bed. Although

I suspect your interest lies closer to home—'

Zac spoke angrily across him. 'You're talking complete bollocks.' He got up abruptly and walked off, Claude following him.

I was uncomfortable, but conscious of a wild curiosity as well. I'd often wondered, but Zac had never really spoken about his romantic life.

Gordon fiddled with his bracelets. 'Well, Theo, how are you and Zac getting along?'

I was cautious. 'Fine. He's a good friend.'

'Of course, you're flavour of the month right now. Can't you see all the attention you're getting? Make the most of it, ducky. You won't always be a dish. One day those looks will fade.' I gaped at him. Unmistakeable hostility crackled in his eyes. 'Oh, you needn't play the innocent with me, although I'm sure it works a treat with Zac. Playing hard to get can be quite effective. You really are a spoilt little urning, hmm?'

I said angrily, 'What the hell are you talking about?'

'Do you think Zac just came across you in the hospital? He'd been searching for you for months. Do you think he's taking all this care of you out of the goodness of his heart?'

Zac and Claude returned at that moment. I took the opportunity to grab my cane and go to the loo, my thoughts stumbling in confusion. By the time I refused someone's offer of a drink and got back to our table, Gordon was nowhere in sight.

'Theo, I apologise for Gordon's behaviour. The thing is, we had an argument before you arrived and … well, he was in a bitchy mood.' I could see concern on Claude's face.

I made myself smile and said, 'It doesn't matter at all.' Claude then entertained us with hospital stories and the conversation was not mentioned again.

Zac was quiet on the way home. 'Come in for a drink?' he suggested. I agreed, my head full of speculation.

We sat down in front of the fire and Zac got straight to the point. 'That bloody Gordon is really too much. I don't know how Claude puts up with him.' He glanced over at me. 'I hope you didn't pay any attention to the crap he was coming out with.'

I asked curiously, 'What does Claude see in him?'

'Oh, Theo, that's the question. It's such an obvious mismatch. I suppose he's good in bed. Sometimes it's a case of being with someone who's not right, rather than being alone. Loneliness can be a killer for queers, you know.'

'I've been wondering how he managed to avoid conscription.'

'Don't get me started on that!' Zac replied, contempt jagging at his voice. 'There's a black market in buying exemptions. I daresay he claimed to have terrible asthma, or whatever. Why should he put his body on the line? We're only fighting for our survival, after all.'

I hesitated, but the temptation to ask was too strong for my usual shyness. 'Were you and Claude lovers once?'

'Yes.' Zac was looking at me intently and I reddened for some reason. 'That was in my last year at school. I told you we were best friends. We realised we were queer at more or less the same time. I thought it was just an amazing coincidence, but of course, I worked out later there was a reason we felt comfortable together from the start. It seemed to make sense to try each other out. But it wasn't right for us – we're much better suited as friends. Does it worry you?'

I felt tense without comprehending why. 'Of course not. Anyway, it's nothing to do with me.'

Zac kept on looking at me. 'What did Gordon say to you?

Something has upset you.'

I didn't want to touch on certain things, so said only, 'He made it pretty obvious he dislikes me. I'm not sure what I've done to him.'

'Oh, Theo. You're completely without conceit. You really don't notice how every queer in Bristol is eyeing you up. Gordon's jealous, of course. Why wouldn't he be? You have everything he lacks: brains, talent, sweetness – and you're a very lovely man.'

I fixed my eyes on the fire, unable to respond. The clock ticking on the mantelpiece crashed like drumbeats in the silence.

Zac's voice was quiet. 'Theo. Is your heart still with Daniel?'

'Oh, he – no, no, I …' Words piled up in a heap to escape my mouth, but my tongue was a surly gatekeeper.

His tone still soft, disturbing, Zac asked, 'Have you never thought of finding someone else? A lot of men would be interested.'

Out of a barrage of emotions, anger was the easiest one to grasp. 'Do you think I don't know I'm useless at all the queer games? It's not for me. I don't want any part of it. I thought I'd found someone to love, but it didn't work out. I've turned my back on it all. I thought you, as my friend—' I stood, frothing myself up into a rage. 'I don't need you patronising me! I'm sure you think I'm a complete idiot.'

I went to the door. Zac started to follow, exclaiming, 'My dear – I didn't mean it like that. Please don't go. Teddy—'

I shook my head at him, banged the door and clumped down the stairs. At home, I sat in front of my gas fire for a long time, brooding over the conversation, wanting to cry without fully understanding why. This was the point when something shifted for me. Self-knowledge was knocking at the doors of my mind, but I refused to let it in.

3

The following morning, I decided I'd become too dependent on Zac, especially as things had now become complicated. After throwing myself through the water at the lido, I went to the library. I got talking to a discharged serviceman who suggested we go for a drink, and we ended up having dinner with a group of his friends. They were pleasant enough, but the evening dragged in a yawn of tedium. I couldn't help thinking how I could talk to Zac about anything, and wondered what he was doing. When I got home, I was disappointed to find no message or phone call. I felt dreary and hopeless.

As I was getting ready to go out the following morning, the doorbell rang. When I opened the door to Zac, I was aware of an involuntary blush. He began to say, 'I want to apologise—'

But, this time, the words jumped out of my mouth. 'No, Zac, it's I who should apologise. I acted like an ill-mannered brat the other evening. I feel quite ridiculous now.'

'Oh, Theo, it was never my intention to patronise you. I just expressed myself clumsily – like a schoolboy.' He smiled ruefully.

'I hope we're still friends?'

'Friends? Why – of course.'

We were standing awkwardly in my room. I was conscious of my unmade bed, the cup of half-drunk tea. Always, his place was spotless. 'Good friends can argue and it doesn't change anything.' I knew I was talking nervously. 'I see you as the older brother I always wanted. I'd hate us to fall out.'

A shadow crossed his face and he looked down, fiddling with the braid on his cuff. 'Brothers ... yes.'

I suddenly remembered his dead brother and was mortified into silence. *You blathering fool, Theo Lawder.* Zac cleared his throat. 'Well, I have to do a late shift today, but we could do something tomorrow night?'

'I won't be here. I'm going to my mother's place.'

'Sorry? Did you say you were going?' He stared with a quick frown.

'Tomorrow. I have to pick up my clothes. I've been using yours far too long. And I need my textbooks. I'll be back Sunday.'

'Oh, yes, of course.' He grinned. 'About time you got your things. That'll help you feel more settled. I tell you what, I'll swap my late shift and we can meet up tonight.'

'If it's not going to cause a problem with you at work, yes, I'd like that.' We smiled at each other in increasing relief. 'Why don't you come here? I'll provide the food.'

'It's a deal.' He turned to go, then added, 'Did you have a nice time, whatever you did last night?'

I shrugged. 'I just saw some people. It was all right.' As he was going, I said impulsively, 'Zac, thank you. I'm glad you came around.'

He briefly gripped my arm. 'So am I.'

I found myself humming as I tidied up.

I fixed a meal of bread, cheese and ham, a rare treat that had used up all my rationing coupons. We sprawled on the rug in front of the gas fire to eat, but our usual easy communication was replaced by stilted talk. As I looked at him, the face of my friend seemed that of a stranger. After dwelling overlong on the latest war news, our conversation dried up. I rushed to fill the silence with an inane comment about my studies. Zac asked what had made me decide to do psychology at Cambridge.

'I suppose I'm just interested in people,' I replied, falling thankfully on another neutral topic. 'It probably comes from this feeling I've always had of being on the outside, observing others.'

'But didn't you once say you'd started with philosophy?'

'I chose philosophy because of Plato,' – glancing at him self-consciously – 'but the endless rhetorical discussions on how do we know we exist, what is life, what is a dream and so on, really got on my nerves. I agree with Socrates that the unexamined life isn't worth living, but I'd rather do the examination through people, rather than metaphysically. I want to understand what makes people tick, how our experiences change us. That's why I switched to psychology and statistics.'

'Well, you're certainly good at listening to people. Everyone seems to want to tell you their life stories. You've even got me at it.'

He smiled at me, but I was overcome with self-disgust. 'I'd make the worst psychologist, Zac. Look at how I've been so stupid about things, completely lacking any self-knowledge—'

'You're much too hard on yourself, Theo. You need to cut yourself some slack.' The wireless was playing a medley of popular tunes in the background. Zac went on in the same mild tone, 'This ham is delicious. There's no doubt, simple food is the best.'

That reminded me of something I'd been turning over in my head. 'Zac, how did you get money to eat when your parents threw you out?'

I heard his sharp intake of breath. 'I didn't beg on the

streets, if that's what you're thinking.'

'I wasn't thinking anything,' I muttered defensively, wondering what I'd started.

After a hush that stretched my nerves taut, Zac said abruptly, 'I sold my body.' He looked closely at me, I think to see if I looked shocked.

I could only say, 'Go on.'

He gave a sigh and looked down. 'I spent the first night in Piccadilly Circus. I don't mind admitting, I felt scared and lost. On the second night, a man approached me and I thought a blow job was at least a way to get some money. I went around restaurants and shops every day looking for work, but it was impossible. Don't forget, this was the height of the Depression. Hunger would force me back to work as a rent boy.'

He paused and I nodded encouragingly. 'At first, I met decent enough men. Sometimes I'd get a bed for a night, or a bath. But the encounters started getting rougher. I was living on my nerves – afraid of the police – afraid of what the next punter might demand. This is where I fell way down into a cesspit, Theo. Just days before, I'd been at school, with university ahead of me – now I was a Dilly boy on the streets.' He shook his head quickly in an involuntary gesture. 'Anyway … I came to my senses one night. The whole scene disgusted me. I hitched to the coast and got onto a trawler going over to France. That's how I started my travels. I picked up jobs where I could and kept moving on.'

'Did something happen to make you leave London?'

Zac hesitated. 'Let's just say it was one nasty experience too far.' He looked over at me. 'Does this shock you, Theo? I suppose you've lost any respect for me now.' His tone was flippant, but I sensed the feeling behind it. I also knew that the barrier between us had come down.

'No, it doesn't shock me, Zac. I'm just sad you went through that on your own. If only I'd known you then! I would have done anything to help you.'

I saw tears come into his eyes. He tried to make light of it. 'I last cried when I was ten, but since I met you ... What must you think of me? A right old camp idiot—'

I was overwhelmed with compassion and something much stronger. I leaned over, covering his burnt hand with mine. 'We can be and say anything with each other, Zac. Do you know that?'

'I do.'

A smoochy Cole Porter ballad came on the wireless. The words of love seemed to burn themselves on my forehead. My nerve endings felt raw, exposed.

'What is it, Theo?'

Did I even know, myself? A frenzy of words flung themselves at me. I hesitated, opened my mouth – and the air raid warning went off. Zac swore. We usually ignored the siren. Zac was so brave it didn't occur to him others might be nervous about bombs falling from the sky. But I knew he was on fire watch that night.

He said, 'It can wait.'

I'd already lost my nerve. 'It's nothing Zac. You'd better go.' We were both obviously emotional. I saw him to the door and said, 'Be careful.'

'See you Sunday, Theo. Have a nice time with your mother.'

We stood facing each other as the ack-ack guns began their juddering song. Then he left.

My mother looked well. My stepfather always seemed puzzled by me – he adopted a bluff, hearty tone when I was around. Relations were cordial at best. I put up with him because he adored my mother. She chatted about village gossip and I made an effort to look interested. When they retired to bed, I sat in front of the fire, rain beating on the window. Finally, I made myself think about what Zac meant to me.

When war was declared, everything in my life changed. I was sent to a training camp in Sussex and met Zac, one of the instructors, on my second day there. I liked his friendly, direct manner. When we'd passed in a corridor afterwards, we smiled at each other and I felt slightly less adrift.

He would often stop to talk to me after that. Everyone in my unit liked him – the general opinion was that he was kind and didn't put on any airs. One of the men, a tough cockney from Spitalfields, went to see him about some problem and afterwards wouldn't hear a word against him. When we finished drills, a group of us would sometimes drive to the coast and muck about on the beach. It was a mild, sunny autumn and I would sit with Zac while I dried off after a swim. He'd tell me stories of his travels or we talked about books.

The change in our friendship happened after I'd met Daniel on a day off. We were in the pub when I felt a hand on my shoulder and looked up to see Zac. I introduced Daniel, he chatted pleasantly and went on his way. That evening, he saw me brooding on my own and came over to talk. He let me know he was homosexual and guessed I was the same. We became increasingly close. In public we were Lieutenant Bonneval and Sergeant Lawder, but between us the army hierarchy disappeared. We met most evenings and I found an incredible release in our conversations. Partly it was because I could say anything to Zac – I didn't have to hold back in the way I did with everyone else. Partly it was because he was so intelligent and perceptive. But it was more. He might challenge or disagree with something I said, but he really listened and seemed to care.

I found Zac's calm acceptance of his sexuality refreshing after Daniel's self-hatred and my own struggles. 'It's just a difference, Theo. It's not good or bad. It happens in nature everywhere. There's nothing wrong with being queer. Don't let Daniel tell you otherwise. The important thing is to be true to yourself and not get hung up on what society says. We're human beings first. We have as much rights as anyone else.'

The others in my unit noticed our friendship and I was teased about being "teacher's pet", but fortunately no one guessed about us.

Our company was sent over to France in December and we were immediately embroiled in the fighting. We had to struggle through snowdrifts and could never get warm – the cold dug right into our bones. The German army was better equipped and better trained, and we were soon in trouble. It was hard and it was bloody. I did my share of killing, and I saw men around me die. Zac and I had few opportunities for private conversations, but we spent all day together and he was always close by when we were in battle. Just knowing he was there – being able to give each other a private smile or have the occasional chat – gave me great comfort, and I sensed he felt the same.

After some months, we were surrounded and in a proper retreat. The enemy snarled at our heels like daemons from the underworld. All this time, rumours were going around the troops: the Nazis were marching on Paris; Belgium had surrendered. We put on an air of bravado to keep up our spirits. I wanted to show courage for my fellow soldiers, but most of all, I wanted to be brave for Zac. He was magnificent, a natural leader. By this time our unit had been decimated. We were grimy and exhausted, dropping to sleep for a few hours in a field before having to retreat further. He kept up our spirits, he looked after each man and he made it possible for us to go on.

By the end of May, we were trapped on a strip of ground by the sea. Soldiers blundered around, helpless and directionless, as the Luftwaffe attacked us, their Stukas a cacophony of screeching and wailing as they dived. It was a nightmare of chaos. There was no escape from the carnage – we were all going to be slaughtered if they couldn't get us out. I could hear the shrieks of men in pain. One soldier near me was slowly dying and crying out for his mother. Corpses surrounded us and the stench of death glued into my nostrils. Some faint wisp of memory would come into my mind – punting on the Cam with Daniel, or swimming in the river near my home – as if it had happened to someone else in another life.

It was in one of these machine-gun attacks that my left kneecap was shattered, as well as getting some bullets in my side. My memories after that are dreamlike. I was mostly out of it on morphine and steadily losing blood. Zac bandaged my wounds and didn't leave me. I accepted I would probably die, but his presence made it easier.

During my last night on the beach, I drifted in and out of consciousness. I came to at first light, the soldiers around us sleeping, to find Zac leaning over me. 'Stay with me, Theo. We'll get you home safe in a few hours. You're strong. You'll make it.' He leant down and gave me a simple kiss.

I have a vague recall of being taken onto a fishing boat

by stretcher, forcing myself not to scream with the pain. The next time I came to, it was days later and I was in an emergency hospital in Kent.

Over the following months, I was unable to get news of Zac and feared the worst. A soldier from my unit turned up with a head wound and told me the rest of the men had been bombed as they were getting onto a ship. I responded minimally to conversation. I surfed the waves of pain and reminded myself of reasons to go on living.

And then, on a late September day, Zac walked into the ward. I looked at him in stupefied delight, breath suspended in my throat. When his eyes came to me, he stood unmoving before a wide smile spread over his face. In the end, Matron had to shoo him out as we didn't stop talking. Within days, he'd arranged for me to be transferred to Bristol and I had the final operation that greatly improved my leg.

Thinking about him now, the truth I'd been fighting all along could no longer be denied. I had convinced myself no one could come after Daniel. I had pretended my deep bond with Zac was one of pure friendship. I had told myself the pleasure I took from gazing at him came from admiration. But really, it had always been Zac for me, from the moment we met. Fragments of erotic dreams about him, long buried in the shamed swamps of my mind, exploded into my consciousness. *I'm in love with him!* Sitting there, I cursed my stupidity out loud and banged my fist on the chair.

Now I understood my feelings, I needed to tell Zac how I felt. If he offered only friendship, I would have to accept it – but I could no longer stand back passively and let the chance of a life with this man pass me by.

4

The next morning, I told my mother I needed to return to Bristol. I arrived home in the evening, awkward on the cobblestones with my load of clothes and books. As soon as I dumped my bags, I rang Zac to say I'd come back early. When he replied that he was about to meet Claude in the queer pub, I asked if I could come along.

'Of course, my dear, but Gordon will be there. I know he's not your favourite person.'

'That doesn't matter.'

'Good. I've got some petrol in the car for a change. Shall I pick you up?'

'No, thanks. You go ahead. I'll see you there in about an hour.'

I ran a bath and unpacked, pleased to see how my books embellished the plain sitting room. I had a strong drink for courage and put on my favourite shirt. Grabbing my overcoat and scarf, I glanced in the mirror. My flushed face stared back, half scared and half determined.

Gordon must have been given a ticking off, because he was on his best behaviour. We had a pleasant time – chat, chat as you do – but my mind wasn't really on the conversation. At one point, I glanced over and caught Gordon raising an eyebrow at Claude, who seemed to be keeping an interested eye on us.

The evening loitered on. Claude and Gordon got talking to friends. Zac told me the colour of my shirt suited me.

I smiled at him, then we were just looking at each other. All I wanted was to get out of there so we could talk. I'd been thinking about it all day and knew what I wanted to say.

But then, he went over to the bar and got into a lengthy conversation with a man. Watching them, I could not deny a fearful realisation. *That man will be Zac's next lover. I've missed my chance.* Why had I hoped he might feel the same? He probably thought of me as a naive fool who needed support. Sick with jealousy, I couldn't bear to stay there. I grabbed my coat. As I walked out, a man put his hand on my arm and said, 'Don't rush off, dolly boy,' but I pushed angrily past him.

When I turned into a quieter street, I could no longer hold back my despair. I walked along cursing, whacking my cane against the wall. Passers-by gave me startled looks, but I was beyond caring. It was a clear, frosty night, just past the full moon – the sort of conditions the Luftwaffe loved. I decided to find another pub, unable to contemplate going home on my own.

Just then, a car slowed down next to me. I heard Zac's voice saying, 'Get in the car, Theo.'

I hadn't expected that. I stopped and looked over at him, a shadowy outline in the blackout. He said again, more forcefully, 'Get in.' I did, and he drove off.

'You don't need to take me home. I don't want to drag you away from your friends.' I knew my voice sounded stiff and sulky.

'Don't be a bloody idiot.' But he said this quite calmly. He didn't seem angry I'd interrupted his flirtation.

I decided I still wanted to tell him how I felt, even though my chance had clearly passed. I owed it to myself to at least be honest. I stated, 'We need to talk.'

'Yes.' He didn't sound surprised.

When he stopped the car, I turned to him but he said, 'Not here, let's go inside. You're freezing, aren't you?'

It was true, I was trembling from a combination of cold and nerves. His voice was kind. *He's going to let me down gently.*

Once in my flat, Zac said, 'We need a drink,' and went over to the cupboard. I switched on the gas fire and a lamp and gulped the drink he handed me. He sat on the floor near the chair. I felt too nervous to face him. I stared at the fire and started talking. Maybe it was the drink, maybe because I'd given up hope, but the gatekeeper had been breached.

'It's pretty obvious I've been in a state of confusion since I met you. I've been so stupid! It's taken me till now to work out how I feel about you.'

'Theo—'

'Please, Zac, let me finish. I need to say this. Just hear me out.' From the edge of my eye, I saw him stir for a moment then be still.

I continued, 'I finally understand why I decided to be celibate after Daniel. He made me feel there was something evil or sick about my nature. But I know who I am, and I know I want more than anything in the world to be with you. I'm in love with you, Zac. And now I've left it too late. You've obviously found someone else. Who can blame you when—'

'It's not too late, Theo. I'd wait my whole life for you.'

A noise escaped me, somewhere between a groan and a laugh. Zac came and knelt up in front of me, putting his hands on my shoulders.

'Oh, my dear – I loved you the moment I saw you. I wanted so many times to tell you! But the timing was always wrong, then you were injured and in such a bad way. I was terrified you'd back away if I said something. How I've longed for this ...'

We grinned at each other like crazy fools. His eyes were jade flints, blazing mineral. He said, 'You darling thing.' We were half laughing and half breathless. He held me tight and gently rubbed his cheek against mine. The simplicity of that gesture touched me as almost unbearably sweet. We spoke in broken sentences, then not at all. We started kissing and it quickly became passionate. After a few minutes, he moved me down onto the rug. We lay wrapped in each other's arms. All my ceaseless observing and analysing just stopped. I was simply there in the moment, kissing and touching Zac, my body pressed against his, feeling our arousal. After a while he said in my ear, 'Let's go to bed.'

Even then, he folded his clothes neatly, while I left mine in a heap. He stood naked waiting for me. My lovemaking with Daniel had only ever been in the dark. To see Zac in front of me was an undeniable truth of who and what we were. His body was as magnificent as I'd imagined – lithe yet strong. It could be the body of a dancer or an athlete. As I stood there, just taking him in, the words came into my head: *this will change everything*. I hesitated, looking inwards. My lifetime defences – keeping people at a distance, running away from my nature – were there, waiting to claim me. But I could no more resist him than a starving man could turn his back on food. I came out of my thoughts to find understanding in Zac's eyes.

'Come here, Theo.'

I limped towards him, shivering with anticipation.

That night did change everything. I found a response in myself I never knew I had. My sexual experience before this had been crumbs at a table, and now an exquisite banquet was laid before me. I found a generosity and tenderness in him that quite overwhelmed me. But it was clear this was not just about sex. This was longing, this was passion; but, above all, this was love.

Sometime in the night, Zac asked why I'd thought he'd met someone else. When I mentioned the man he'd been talking to, he threw back his head and laughed. 'He's married with children! He's one of the boffins at the station. All he does is talk about work.'

'But he was in a queer pub?'

'I don't think he even realised. Anyway, he's not my type.'

Of course, I had to ask. 'What is your type?'

'You, you, you,' with his face close to mine.

I woke up the next morning as Zac was getting ready to leave. We agreed to meet at his place when he finished work. But he didn't want to go. 'Just one more kiss, Theo.' In the end I had to push him out the door.

I was dizzy with rejoicing. Life could not be better. At the lido, I floated, gazing up at the pale sky, my thoughts full of him, sighing and smiling. An ode of exaltation thrummed through my mind and body. When I got to the library, I tried to concentrate on the book in front of me, before falling asleep with my head on my arms. I was woken by the porter ringing the bell for closing time and sleepily went down the steps to the street.

The warning siren sounded as I emerged. Dazzled by flares dropping from the sky, I knew they held a deadly beauty. Wardens ordered me into a shelter and I was arguing with them when we heard an unmistakeable noise. We froze, straining our eyes upwards. Enemy planes were heading towards us, little silver toys buzzing in the searchlights. The wardens started shouting and I was pushed into the shelter as the attack started.

It seemed endless, wave after wave of incendiary bombs. The sounds of explosions and shouting washed over us. We were all crammed in, mostly women, children and old people. How bitterly I regretted my lame leg – desperate to be out there doing something useful, desperate to see Zac. Eventually, I slipped out when the wardens were occupied.

I walked through the gates into hell. Fires bloomed around me, an apocalyptic flower garden under a blood-red sky. The roaring of the flames competed with the crash of collapsing buildings and screams of trapped people. I watched, mesmerised, as the spire of a church crashed into its burning bowels. The fire wardens' puny jets of water appeared futile against the bellowing inferno, like a toddler pummelling an adult's legs. Then I looked up to the sky and saw more bombers coming over.

All I knew was that I had to get to Zac. I set off to his place, crunching over broken glass and debris. Dust stuck in my throat and my face burned from the ferocity of the flames. I thought then of Dunkirk – but this was happening to ordinary people, in the place where they lived, worked, loved. A bomb landed close to me, bricks and objects flying in all directions. Something hit me on the head and I was thrown to the ground, knocked out cold. I came around to find an elderly warden bending over me.

'Are you all right?' he asked, and I nodded, dazed.

'I've got to get on. People are dying here. Get into a shelter.' He ran off.

Something warm was on my face. When I put up my hand, I saw blood. I struggled to my feet and noticed a young boy nearby, lying at an awkward angle. As I went closer,

I realised to my horror that half his head was missing. I staggered away, sobbing. There was nothing I could do for him.

I saw several fires in Zac's street as I limped along to his building. But my brain would not tell me what my eyes could see. I had to stand and stare before I could comprehend there was a space where his building had been. My legs went from under me. I fell on the ground, retching. I heard moaning and crying, and realised it was me. This was when I understood Zac must be lying in the ruins of the building in front of me. This was when I believed I had lost my love – that my happiness was now over, just when it had begun.

No one noticed me. They had more important things to do. Sparks landed on my scarf, which started smouldering. I clumsily flung it off.

I don't know how long I lay there. I lost all track of time. Finally, I used my cane to lever myself upright. My feet took me in the direction of my flat. I had no plan in mind, no hope, just a primordial need for shelter. The street was quieter here with no fires, but shrouded in smoke. The blood from my head wound had glued my left eye shut and, as I rubbed my face, slivers of glass came away. I could hear myself whimpering quietly, like an injured dog.

As I came closer to my place, I could spot the dim outline of a figure through the smoke. I squinted my right eye and there, out of the gloom, like a ghost, was Zac. I blinked my eye, thinking he was a vision I had conjured up. Then he called, 'Theo, Teddy,' and I knew it really was him. We clung to each other wordlessly, not caring who saw us.

Zac said, 'Come inside. Come home, Teddy.' We went into my flat. I stood vacantly. 'Sit down in front of the fire.'

He put me in the chair and disappeared. I could hear him

running the bath. Convulsive judders ran through my body and my teeth chattered, as if I were a rag doll being shaken in a giant hand. Zac came back and pulled me up, saying, 'Let's get you washed.'

All this time I had not said a word. He undressed me and sat me on the edge of the bath, bending my head over the sink. He scooped water onto my head and started washing the wound, picking out pieces of glass from cuts on my face and talking soothingly. 'It's just a cut. The thing is, head wounds can bleed a lot. There, that's not too bad.'

He helped me into the bath and gently washed me. Slowly, I started to come out of a sort of trance, I suppose caused by shock. I started responding to his conversation and looking at him properly. Then Zac said, 'I'm going to join you.' He took off his clothes and came into the bath with me. We fitted our legs around each other. He had to shift to avoid the tap, and we started laughing. I found my voice.

'Zac – I thought I'd lost you. I love you so much. I want to spend my life with you.' We were serious, looking at each other.

He said, 'I will spend my life loving you, Theo.'

This was our pledge. That is why we always celebrated our anniversary on the twenty-fourth of November, because that is the day we made a full and conscious commitment. I suppose it must seem comical really, two men sitting in a bath pledging their lives to each other while bombs fell around us. We would laugh about it in later years and call it our bathtub vow. But we both knew. This was the most important decision we would make in our lives.

After drying off, we curled up in the armchair, the noise of the raid continuing outside. I took painkillers for my leg and

41

Zac gently massaged it. Our voices were hushed. I said, 'They'll destroy us.'

Zac hugged me closer. 'We won't give up, we can't. We must believe we can win this.'

We started to talk about the night. Just as I had feared Zac died in his building, he had thought me lost there as well. After standing in terror and despair, he had come to my flat and waited, more in hope than anything else. 'Then I saw you coming towards me through the smoke, like a ghost,' he told me.

I stared at that, because those had been just my thoughts. We were young – soon our energy moved to a more instinctive level. We were in bed, making love, when the all-clear sounded after midnight.

We spent most of the following morning in bed. The station agreed Zac could have time off to sort out his accommodation. When he got off the phone I said, 'But, Zac, you must stay here. You can take over the flat when I go to Cambridge. I'll sort it out with the landlord. He can't complain when you've been made homeless.'

'Are you sure it won't be too crowded for you?' he asked.

'Of course not. Poor you, you've lost everything. Your journals with all your stories, your books and photos—'

'No, I've won everything. What are possessions when we have each other?' I don't know why he maintained he wasn't romantic.

When we went into town, the smell of smoke and death assailed us. Buildings were destroyed or half standing, and many fires were still burning. The church at the top of Castle Street was a ruin, the street itself unrecognisable. People wandered along in shock, mostly silent, some with clear marks of grief on their faces. 'We're near the hospital. Let's check on Claude,' I suggested.

We found Claude alone in the doctors' room having a cup of tea, sagging with fatigue. He squinted his eyes at us and remarked, 'It's obvious what you've been up to! You're bloody well glowing. It's indecent.'

Zac laughed, while I ducked my head. 'We wanted to make sure you were all right,' I explained.

'I'm fine. Dead on my feet. I've been on duty for twenty hours. We've been deluged with emergencies. Mostly crush and burn injuries.' He spoke in brusque sentences, as though to expend the least amount of energy. 'How was it for you?'

'My place has been flattened, luckily not when I was in it.'

'Zac, you say that as casually as if you'd lost a glove. Do you need somewhere to stay?'

'Thanks, but I'll be stopping with Theo.' He smiled at me.

'Really, you two, just get a room! Theo, let me look at that.' Claude got up stiffly and examined my head wound. 'It could do with a stitch,' he said with his professional voice, but I was looking at Zac and hardly noticed.

When we got up to go, I turned back and kissed his cheek, saying, 'Claude, thank you for being such a good friend.' His umber eyes looked back at me, inscrutable.

Out on the street, Zac said, 'At least those shops still standing will welcome my business.' He bought clothes and insisted on buying a blue scarf for me. We saw a sign on one shop declaring "Business as usual, we can take it", and silently acknowledged the brave defiance in those words.

5

We had six more weeks before I was due to go up to Cambridge. The Luftwaffe came back nearly every night and it was a grim, fearful time. It became a familiar sight to walk past bodies being removed from the rubble of destroyed buildings. Fires sometimes burned for days before they could be extinguished. The odour of dust and phosphorus enveloped the air. We kept up a public pretence that we would get through this, we would win the war – but privately, many believed we were doomed and the invasion would happen soon. Winter also set in with a vengeance, delivering freezing temperatures and snow blizzards. Sometimes, it seemed the whole world was against us.

And yet, in our private bubble, it was a time of such sweetness and joy. This was the start of a voyage of self-discovery for me. I'd always kept people at a distance – even Daniel, even my mother. But, with Zac, all my defences tumbled. I could put on a front with others, but not with him. He held up a mirror to my eyes so I could see myself, and I did the same for him. Having Zac by my side, loving me unconditionally, gave me a fundamental confidence and belief. More than that – for the first time I felt there was meaning to my life. Everything now had a purpose, because I wanted Zac to be proud of me, because he cared about everything I did.

Being able to talk with such an intrinsic understanding was bliss. We would trawl over our lives, fascinated about every small detail in the way only lovers can be. He opened up his heart about his childhood, and wanted to know everything about mine. He already knew my father had died when I was eight. After that it was just my mother, me and my dog, Patch, until my mother married again when I was eleven.

'Do you remember much about your father?' Zac asked me one evening when we were curled lazily in bed.

'Not really. He'd been gassed in the Great War and his lungs were bad. That's what killed him in the end. My grandparents would tell me stories of him as a young man, nothing like the distant stranger who lived in our house. I realised later he was never the same after the war. I was a toddler when he came home and I suppose our world seemed insignificant after the suffering he'd been through. I wish I could have known how he was before.'

'There's a whole traumatised generation from that time, Theo. And we're going through the same thing again. But at least now there's a reason why we're fighting.'

We'd often talked about this. We agreed war was ugly. It was always better to look for a peaceful solution. But we were threatened with a fascist dictatorship and had, seemingly, no other option than to fight.

He went on, 'It sounds like you were a happy child?'

'Very much so, although I lived a lot in my own head or in a book. I think only children tend to be content with their own company, don't you? But always I had this sense of being different, somehow on the edge of things.'

'I imagine your stepfather didn't help with that.'

'Ha, there's a story about that. I insisted on calling him Henry, which created quite a rumpus. I refused to play rugby, and he was horrified when he heard I'd asked for dancing lessons. I was always singing and dancing around the house. He told my mother I was too soft and she'd made me into a "cissy". The final straw came when he found me doing pirouettes in the garden with daisies in my hair.'

Zac laughed. 'I can just see you! How old were you then?'

I rubbed my cheek on his shoulder as I thought. 'I must have been twelve. Anyway, there were family discussions and he said I should go to boarding school. It was supposed to make a "man" of me. It's the only time I can remember my mother standing up to him, although I had to stop the dancing. I learned to monitor my behaviour, and at least he approved when I won school prizes in swimming and piano. But that was the time I started putting up a wall between me and the rest of the world.'

'Imagine if you'd come to my school, Teddy! But he didn't need to worry. You're all man …' and we got distracted for a while.

We revisited everything that had happened since we met, agreeing it was the most incredible luck we'd ended up in the same army squadron.

'I actually applied for the navy,' Zac said one day. 'I love to be on the water and thought at least I'd have that compensation. I was disappointed they put me into the army instead. Until the day you turned up, of course.'

'But Zac – I applied for the air force!' We started laughing.

'God, Teddy, what a miracle we found each other.' Always, we came back to this.

Very early on, Zac asked me, 'How on earth did you plan to lead a celibate life, when you're so damned sexy?' Daniel had always been conflicted about sex, so I had decided it wasn't important. With Zac, I quickly discovered how wrong that was. I learned to overcome my shyness and talk to him about this as easily as about everything else. Zac unlocked the door to my desires and they came flooding out.

I hadn't expected I could feel such intense sensuality and desire. Sitting in the pub, I would feel weak with passion merely from seeing the outline of Zac's chest and stomach through his shirt. I'd lie in bed watching as he got dressed for work, my eyes aching with delight. It was a feast for my senses to look at him naked, to touch and kiss him. And I could spend hours gazing at his face. I loved to muss up his thick hair, to trace my finger along his cheekbones and his mouth. The curves and planes, the hollows, folds and secrets of our bodies became an endlessly fascinating playground. I was obsessed, entranced by him. I wanted to dive into his eyes and swim through his body. I wanted to breathe through his pores.

We were suspended in an alternate world, both dreamlike yet brilliantly sharp. We were creating a butterfly in our chrysalis, putting down foundations for the rest of our life together. The snow and air raids were only an excuse not to go out or see others, although sometimes we made it out to the country to walk. As far as we could see there were white fields, the River Avon semi-frozen. Even the ruined parts of the city looked enchanted in the snow.

One evening I told Zac, 'I'm not going back to Cambridge. It seems pointless with the war going on, and I don't want to leave you.'

Zac listened in his usual careful way. 'It's only a few months, and you'll be glad of your degree after the war. I've always regretted I lost the chance to finish my education. Don't make the same mistake, Theo. The war took you away from university and nearly took your life – it's time for you to get something back.' So that convinced me.

We did have our first argument on New Year's Eve.

Gordon came over in the pub with a snide look. 'So, you finally got your fair-haired boy into bed! Are you bored yet? We're laying bets it won't last until Easter.' Zac made an angry movement towards him and Gordon walked off laughing.

I felt my humiliation had been exposed to the world and told Zac, 'I want to leave.' When we got home, I picked a quarrel, telling him he was an arrogant bastard, and started to storm out.

But he was so much wiser in these things. He stood in front of the door, his voice calm. 'Please don't leave, Theo, let's sort this out. We're having an argument, that's all. We haven't stopped loving each other.'

I stood and glared at him. Then we talked. I confessed my fear that he would one day stop loving me. By this time, I knew all about his numerous affairs. I'd got the impression he moved on from them very easily.

'I told you, Teddy, I want no one but you in my life. Always before – I was never in love. I thought maybe I wasn't capable of it. But from the first day I saw you, it was completely different. You are my first and last love, my only love.' The way Zac looked at me, I could not doubt him. Always, he was so honest.

Afterwards, in bed, he murmured, 'I think we're feeling emotional because you're going soon.' Of course, it made sense. I'd been waking up thinking: *only six more days; only five days.*

I was due back at Cambridge for the Hilary term, and the sirens went off while I was packing. We didn't want to spend our last night together in a shelter, so we checked the blackout and stayed put. The bombing went on, without break, until the dawn. We lay in each other's arms – *if we have to die, at least let us go together.* But we were safe. Zac said, 'We're leading a charmed life at the moment.'

We walked to the station the next morning past the now-familiar fires and destruction. Few buildings were left standing in the city centre. Icicles hung in crazy shapes from where the firefighters had aimed their hoses.

'Why am I going to Cambridge when the world is going to hell?' I asked despairingly.

'Teddy, we'll get through this. I know it seems like the end right now, but we will win this war. There'll be time enough for you to do your bit.'

Only eighteen months had passed since I'd left Cambridge, but it was like stepping into another world. The town suffered the occasional bombing raid, but the university had escaped and was serene, and somehow unreal, after the devastation we'd come from. We had a long embrace in my room, then I walked with Zac back to the station. He gave a cheery wave and off he went. I confess, I was very low that first night.

In the end, I enjoyed Cambridge more than I'd expected. I'd dreaded going back to cloistered academia, so redundant to the way our lives had changed, but external appearances had been misleading. Most of the students were like me, discharged soldiers or service cadets, and there were many more women students. Some of the colleges were used for officer training or to house government departments. I enjoyed my studies and it was wonderful to get back to singing in a choir. There were sandbags around the Bridge of Sighs, and RAF training planes overhead, but the absence of air raids made me realise the suffocation of living under continual bombardment.

There was one telephone in my college. I had to queue for a short, public conversation with Zac. Sometimes we went several days without speaking and I became twitchy, knowing

Bristol was still being bombed. We compressed everything into the weekends. He'd meet me at the station on the Friday and we'd go straight home. We didn't move much from the flat on the first day – we'd make love and catch up with each other's news. I wanted to know everything about his life, and he was the same with me. Then we would resurface, get out for a walk, and meet Claude for a drink. He'd finished with Gordon but was still entangled in the resulting scenes and threats of suicide. When Zac asked why he didn't just walk away, Claude said he couldn't live with his conscience if Gordon did something stupid.

We looked forward to Easter as a time when we could spend more than two snatched days together. On Good Friday we went high up in the Mendips, overlooking the River Avon and the gorge. Early daffodils opened their faces to the pale sunshine. We walked for several hours and Zac said, 'Theo, do you realise how much your leg has improved?' I had little pain now, usually just an ache in the evening. I was still slow and clumsy on stairs, and I still hated my ugly boots. Zac's burns had healed up well, and he had a lot more strength in his hand.

The warning siren went off late that evening. At times, it seemed to be raining incendiaries. We lay in bed, waiting tensely for the next bomb. After one loud explosion, Zac muttered, 'Maybe it's time to make for the shelter,' which meant it really was serious.

We got dressed and went out to the street. We could see our planes in the searchlights, engaging the Luftwaffe. 'They've hit the gasometer.' Zac was looking at an immense flame shooting up in the air.

I saw my landlord peering out of his window and went up

to check on him. He would tell me stories from the Great War and left us alone, for which we'd been grateful. I'd just come back when we heard a whistling noise. Zac pulled me down and a bomb fell twenty yards away. To our astonishment, it didn't explode. We could see, in the moonlight, the crater in the road. We started laughing with relief and probably a touch of hysteria.

'We really are charmed,' Zac said.

We lay on the road looking at each other, then got up and went back inside to each other's arms. Life felt fragile and beautiful – we needed to celebrate it.

The next day, we couldn't reach Claude at the hospital and agreed to check on him. Outside, we found a team of men around the crater. One warden, grimy with dust, looked at us through red-rimmed eyes. He said to Zac, 'Morning, Lieutenant,' then asked me, 'Get that at Dunkirk, did you, matey?' I nodded, used to this. Sometimes strangers would stop me in the street to ask. I knew it was well meant.

He rubbed his weary face, smearing more ash in the process. 'My youngest got taken there. The wife still ain't over it. But you have to get on with things, don't you?'

I looked at him with a new respect. 'I'm sorry to hear that, sir.'

He told us there had been a few unexploded bombs, which they needed to defuse quickly. I said something about it being a bad night, and he spat off to one side. 'Don't you worry, we'll sort those buggers out in no time. I've got a bet on with my mates we'll be done by Christmas.'

We walked on to the hospital in a chastened mood. *What am I doing at Cambridge when this is going on?* Zac remarked, 'I know what you're thinking, my dear. But you'll have time enough to get involved. This won't be finished by Christmas.'

The hospital was in uproar. Doctors and nurses dashed through corridors crammed with stretchers. We found a doctor who told us Claude was at the mortuary. Seeing our faces, he asked, 'Didn't you hear? His friend Gordon was killed last night.'

We found Claude talking to Gordon's mother. As she wept, I ached with a deep melancholy for the quiet day-to-day courage, for families like her, grieving their loved ones. She asked us, 'You were his friends. Will you come to the funeral?' We promised we would.

That evening, Claude was full of remorse, exclaiming, 'Why did I make his last weeks so unhappy?'

I said, 'You obviously had reasons to finish it. What were they?'

Claude sighed, replying, 'It was never really serious for me, and he suffocated me with his jealousy. I knew our relationship wasn't healthy for either of us. Seeing you two together made me realise that.'

I tried not to look at Zac. *Theo Lawder, never take this for granted.* I gave Claude a hug. 'You're a lovely man, my dear. There's someone special out there for you.' And I wished it with all my heart.

I came back the following weekend for the funeral. The ceremony was short – they had a lot of funerals to get through. So many deaths, too many. That evening Claude was able to cry for the first time and we all raised a glass to Gordon. I had my own private thoughts. I hadn't liked the man, but his comments that evening had been the trigger forcing me to acknowledge my feelings about Zac. In a strange way, I owed him everything.

But life is constant change. By the end of April, the air raids had stopped. When we celebrated Zac's twenty-seventh birthday, we could hear birdsong instead of warning sirens.

Claude started to recover from his grief and guilt, and there were small hints of hope in the air.

6

I dedicated myself to my studies and lived for the weekends. Somehow, I scraped a first. Zac was so proud – that gave me the greatest pleasure. My mother came to the graduation ceremony and fussed over me in my subfusc. Afterwards, we took her for tea then walked her to the station, before going for a final punt along with a bottle of champagne Zac had obtained on the black market.

It was a shining day just past the summer solstice, one that made you purr with delight at being alive. Zac had picked some wildflowers and weaved them together as we drifted along. Evening sunlight glinted on the water's surface, while the darker depths sparked with emerald flashes. We had a lot to discuss. He'd been offered a transfer to Military Intelligence in London, while I'd been approached about working at Bletchley Park. Our conversation was mainly about how it would affect us.

Zac was sanguine. 'We're going to be separated enough with this bloody war, Theo. It could be a lot worse. Bletchley isn't far from London – we'll be closer than we are now. And I can take a more active part against Hitler. Let's just take our happiness while we can. We have the rest of our lives in front of us.'

I agreed, unable to contemplate taking an ordinary job. Soldiering had not been my strength, so I welcomed the thought of fighting the Nazis by using my brain.

We stopped at the Backs and lay on the grass to drink the champagne. Zac placed the crown of flowers on my head. 'My

Ganymede,' he said with a tender smile.

After packing up our place in Bristol, we drove to London where Zac had found a third-floor flat above shops in Highgate. It was shabby and plain, but with impressive views over London, that essential telephone and no landlord to frown over my visits.

Zac had managed, through a work colleague, to get the use of a cottage in a village outside Chichester. We dumped our things and caught the train to the south coast. Ever since Dunkirk, we'd never been together for more than a few days – always work or hospital, or Cambridge, had intervened. Two weeks on our own was a sumptuous gift.

The cottage was in a quiet lane running down to the sea. We found someone in the harbour who rented us a small yacht and Zac taught me to sail. Our days were spent exploring the coast, then we'd drop the anchor somewhere quiet. I would strip off and dive under the surface. I'd always loved swimming, but water now held an extra attraction for me. It was the only place where I could be freed from the earthbound constraints of my leg – where I could move and dance as gracefully as in my dreams.

We spent nearly every daylight hour out of doors. When it rained on a couple of days, we lay on the sofa doing the crossword or reading, saying the sweet nothings of lovers. There were no air raids. Despite the barrage balloons and fortifications around the coast, we almost forgot about the war. I told Zac it was the best holiday I'd had in my life.

In the evenings, we strolled by the harbour and tried out the different pubs, sometimes taking the bus into Chichester. One evening, I was smiling at Zac in a pub there when he murmured, 'Be careful, Teddy.'

Soon after, a man walked by and said loudly, 'Fuck off,

you disgusting poofs.'

We left, and nothing further happened. But when we got home, Zac fell into a very dark mood. He sat out the back, smoking and drinking. I asked what was wrong but he didn't respond. After a couple of attempts, I left him in peace and retreated inside to read a book. He came to bed around midnight, wrapped his arms around me and all was well.

I asked in the morning what had been wrong. 'Sorry, Theo, a stupid mood. Please forget it.' I shrugged it off. I was aware of my unattractive tendency to sulk, so he had a right to his moods.

I'd always known I couldn't be open with my identity. I had to be wary with everyone and cover up my real thoughts and feelings. It made me feel lonely and isolated. But now, I was realising two men didn't fade into the background so easily. I needed to constantly censor and dampen down my behaviour with Zac in public. If I looked at him too long, or with my feelings showing; if we sat or walked together too closely – sooner or later we attracted suspicious looks and comments. I hated the ongoing vigilance. I wanted to shout to the skies I was in love with the most magnificent man in the world. Yet, if this was the price to pay for being with Zac, I accepted it.

Once again, we had to say our goodbyes and make plans to meet in a week. The partings seemed to get harder. This time, we held each other tight in my room for several minutes. I missed him that night with a physical ache.

In the first weeks, I spent most of my spare time looking for new lodgings in Bletchley. The landlady was giving us hostile looks and pointedly referred to "no overnight guests". I found a place with a phone and a deaf landlord that suited us well enough. The only drawback was the small bed. The first time we fell off it, I said to Zac, 'Ooh, I felt the earth move,' and we got a fit of giggles. We became used to sleeping crammed together. For the next four years, the work at Bletchley was so demanding I think I could have slept anywhere. But we stayed in London as much as possible to enjoy Zac's double bed.

We're allowed to talk about Bletchley now, but it's strange to break the habit of so many years. We signed the Official Secrets Act and had to give a cover story, although Zac and I always told each other everything about our work. We knew we could trust each other with our lives.

At Bletchley, we deciphered all the German communications coming in. They'd already made the main breakthrough on the code, although it took most of 1942 before we cracked the naval code. Most of us worked in huts in the grounds. They were stuffy in summer and freezing in winter, when we'd work in fingerless gloves and blankets. Other than half an hour for lunch, we remained bent over papers, working out the cipher. It needed enormous concentration; by the end of the shift we felt sucked dry. But there was an urgency about our work, because we knew it made a vital difference to the war. That's what made the work bearable, as well as the people. We formed a strong team, helped by countless cups of tea, cigarettes and increasingly black humour. We used to howl with laughter sometimes, but we were all so tired we'd probably laugh at anything.

I was in Hut Eight. The others were maths whizzes, but my statistics knowledge seemed to help. I liked them all, but became closest to Alan, our team leader. He'd done physics and mathematics at Cambridge, and he invented the machine at Bletchley that broke the code. It took some months to get to know Alan because he seemed unaware of how social niceties help you rub along. He didn't do small talk, and would walk past with his head down without saying good morning. He was quite scruffy – his nails were bitten right down and he never seemed to comb his hair. Actually, he had a nice face and big, expressive eyes.

The breakthrough came one evening, when Zac and I were in the pub. It would have been the end of November, because we'd just celebrated our first anniversary. Alan came over; by then, he seemed to like me and seek me out. He sat down with a beer, I introduced Zac, and he said, 'You're lovers, aren't you?'

I was taken aback but said, 'Yes.' I had resolved I would never deny what I had with Zac, no matter what the consequences.

Alan beamed at us. 'I'm homosexual, too.'

To be honest, I hadn't picked it up. He'd been engaged to a woman when I arrived at Bletchley, although they'd broken it off soon after. And Alan always had this vague, distracted manner, if he wasn't completely ignoring you. When I told Zac this later, he laughed. 'Typical Theo! You never notice when people fancy you.'

I don't know if that was the case, but there seemed to be no harm done. I came to realise Alan was a lovely man, just shy and socially inept. He lived mostly in his own head and I could certainly identify with that. Sometimes, I could only understand half of what he was saying. He would explain a way to use machines to solve a problem, how everything could be broken down to mathematics, and I'd try to follow him.

I explained this once to Zac and he said, 'Poor Alan, he must feel lonely.'

'I think he really wants to find someone. He deserves to be loved.'

'But it's more than that, Theo. Imagine how isolating it must feel, to find even intelligent people can't keep up with your mind – to have to explain your thoughts, in what to you are simple terms. And then, to be queer on top of that …'

Alan occasionally told me how lucky Zac and I were to have found each other. I heard about Christopher, his first love, who had died suddenly in the last year of school. Alan had not met anyone to compare with him, and saw the work he was doing as somehow a dedication. I shuddered when I thought how close I'd come to losing Zac at Dunkirk. If only Christopher had lived, or Alan had found someone else to love – how differently it might have turned out. That does still break my heart.

The work was relentless. Every two days we went from the morning shift to the afternoon, then the overnight shift. We had one day free before we started the routine again. Zac tried to arrange his day off at the same time, but this didn't often happen. Petrol rationing meant we had to use an irregular train service, which further ate into our precious hours together. An entire day off together was a luxury we looked forward to all week. We spent most of it in bed – we would talk, make love, sleep and eat, then start again. We'd make it out sometime in the afternoon for a walk or to go to the pub.

We knew we were fortunate to be only fifty miles apart – many had their loved ones far away, for months at a time – but we were greedy with love and craved more time together. Zac also went on several overseas missions for Military Intelligence. I would hear nothing for weeks and knew he was in danger. My nerves jangled out a staccato of dread at these times, but I hid this, knowing it was important for him to be part of the fight against Hitler. There were social activities and good friends at Bletchley to keep me occupied. At least we managed to speak most days. We would catch up on our news and have the usual talk between lovers. Sometimes we just listened to each other's breathing, the crackling and buzzing of the telephone line a mournful counterpoint.

We got one week's holiday a couple of times a year. If he couldn't get the same time off, I would stay in his Highgate flat. The National Gallery put on free lunchtime concerts, and I enjoyed exploring the city until Zac finished work. We walked around the destroyed streets in the blackout, the sun or winter fog, discovering the vibrancy and changing character of London's different villages: Hampstead Heath and the men's swimming pond, the secret lanes, the different immigrant communities, the queer pubs in Soho. Then we would go home to each other's arms.

Several times I suggested we go to Bristol to see Claude, but he was always busy. Zac said, 'Maybe it's for the best. He needs some breathing space.' I thought seeing us must remind him of Gordon, so I didn't insist. Claude sounded cheerful enough in his letters. Then he transferred to the hospital in Liverpool and was even further away.

If we got leave at the same time, we always went back to the cottage on the south coast. We'd spend the days sailing and walking – relishing the open air after being confined so much indoors – and the nights recharging our bond. I sometimes woke up to find Zac sitting by the bed, watching me. He would make a joke, saying he needed to remind himself what I looked like, but the emotion was plain on his face. He was the most loving, generous man I could have hoped to find.

7

I was finishing my lunch break one day, about two years after I'd arrived in Bletchley, when I heard someone call out, 'Ruth, over here,' and turned to see a young Wren join a group of friends. The name could have been a coincidence, but there was a resemblance to Zac – the same glossy dark hair, the same firm mouth and chin. After that, I looked out for her every day.

My chance came a couple of weeks later, when I saw her eating on her own. I grabbed a sandwich, went over and asked, 'Is this seat free?' She smiled, so I sat down, introduced myself and started chatting in a way most unlike me.

I started with the usual work gossip, and she described daily life in the "hell hole" (the hut with the bombe, the noisy machine that decoded Enigma). Then I started working in questions about her family: where she grew up, did she have brothers or sisters, that sort of thing. She gave me a coolly appraising look that reminded me of Zac, but responded cheerfully enough. When she said she had to get back to work, I asked, 'Can we meet for lunch again soon?' She looked puzzled, probably because I hadn't been flirting, but agreed.

I'd obtained enough information in those few minutes to make me fairly certain she was Zac's sister, but I wasn't ready to tell him. I wanted to check she would not be someone who would reject Zac. Perhaps her parents had poisoned her mind against him?

The next time we met, I wasted no time in enquiring

about her brother. When she told me he'd left home, I asked, 'Why do you think he left?'

'I don't know and I don't care. As far as I'm concerned, he's the best brother in the world. That's all that matters,' she responded curtly, in a manner so similar to Zac I wanted to laugh.

I said, 'I think I know your brother. Would you like to meet Zac again?'

Ruth looked at me with wide eyes, aware that she hadn't given me his name, then grabbed my arm. 'Yes, yes!'

I couldn't wait to tell Zac when he rang that evening. He was silent at first, then said, 'Oh, Teddy … my little sister!' I told him about the part when she'd said it didn't matter what he'd done. Zac was excited, but I could sense his nervousness. It was my fear as well – if Ruth rejected him when she found out he was homosexual, it might be worse than never seeing her again.

We arranged to meet in a cafe in Bletchley on Zac's next visit. He took extra care with his appearance, polishing his shoes and combing his hair carefully, before turning to me. 'Let's go and find my sister,' he said. His tone was brisk, but the hurt boy inside him peeked out anxiously.

He kept up a determined chat as we walked to the cafe, but as soon as he saw Ruth, the tension fled his face. They hugged and laughed and spoke over each other, and all was well.

Zac and Ruth spent the evening catching up on news and exclaiming over the changes in each other. I offered to leave them alone, but they both wanted me there and I was glad to stay. At some point, Zac put his left hand on the table and I saw Ruth's look of shock, which was quickly masked. The burns had faded by then to a duller red and I barely noticed them, but for a moment I saw the injury with Ruth's eyes.

Zac was casual. 'I know it's no beauty, but I'm used to it by now.'

'How did it happen, Zac?'

'It was when we were being evacuated from Dunkirk. Theo had gone some hours before and I was with the rest of my unit. We were wading out to the ship when it took a direct hit. There was petrol on the water and it caught alight …' His voice wavered, then he went on. 'I was lucky. Most of the men died. But it's improved a lot. I can do quite a bit with this hand now.' He gave me a quick wink and I had to look down.

As we were parting, Ruth exclaimed, 'Zac, I can't tell you how glad I am we've found each other! I don't feel alone any more.'

I got into the habit of having lunch with Ruth at Bletchley. She was a clever and strong-minded woman; even if she hadn't been Zac's sister, I would have liked her. There were a couple of awkward moments early on. She teased us that we must have left a trail of broken hearts and asked if we had girlfriends. Zac made a joke and changed the subject.

And once, we were having lunch when Alan came over. After glancing at her in a vaguely curious way, he said, 'You must be Zac's sister.'

Her face lit up. 'Oh, do you know Zac too?'

'Oh yes, he's—'

I kicked his ankle and he seemed to realise he should shut up. You never knew with Alan – he could be oblivious to social clues.

Shortly before Christmas, Ruth came down to London after we all managed to arrange the same day off. We collected her at the station and took her out for lunch. It didn't take her long to look

63

around when we got back to Zac's place, then we settled down comfortably to talk. She started speaking about their parents in a rush of words.

'They became a lot worse after you left, Zac. Everything I did seemed to be wrong. My mother would slap me for the slightest thing. She called me a "slut" if she saw me with a boy – even though we were just talking! I got home from school one day to find she'd burned all your letters. I thought I'd hidden them so well … She refused to speak to me during my last weeks at home, I suppose because I'd committed the "sin" of communicating with you. That's why I couldn't write back to you.'

'I should have known they were the cause,' Zac said, looking at her with sympathy.

'Oh, Zac – it was as if she hated us! I counted the days until I could escape. When I left home, I told my parents they'd never see me again. I feel no love or duty towards them.' I realised she was trying not to cry.

Zac held her hand consolingly. 'I'm sorry you had to deal with them on your own, Ruthie.'

'You couldn't help that. I was glad you were free of them. But I loved your letters! Do you know, Theo,' she added, looking at me in her sweet way, 'Zac used to write to me about the adventures of made-up people, like little novels. I got so much pleasure from them. Once he'd left home, his letters were the only warm thing in my life.'

We moved onto happier memories. I told them about my imaginary childhood friend, Pip, and heard their stories of exploring the countryside in the school holidays, or going out in Zac's dinghy on the nearby Somerset coast. 'At least they didn't consider sailing a mortal sin,' he said with a rueful grin.

Zac had bought a bottle to celebrate Ruth's visit and said to me after a while, 'Come and help me open the wine.' We went into the small kitchen where I gave him a quick embrace. I could see he was emotional after the conversation about his parents.

When we came back into the sitting room, Ruth said abruptly, 'You're together, aren't you?'

We froze. I felt Zac, next to me, tense up. He replied quietly, 'Yes, Ruth. We're in love. We're lovers.'

I held my breath. I couldn't bear for Zac to be rejected by his sister. But Ruth jumped out of her chair and came over to us with open arms and countenance. 'Now I have another brother!' she declared.

We stood hugging. All I cared about was Zac being accepted by his sister, but I also hoped we could be some sort of a family. In the end, we talked so much we had to run for her train back to Bletchley.

Afterwards, Zac and I lay in bed discussing the turn of events. It was clear Ruth filled a void that Zac had carried around for years. She gave him something I couldn't – a link to his family and his past, even if that included painful memories. His smile was peaceful. 'Teddy, you found my sister. I can't tell you what this means to me.' I would do anything to make him happy, but it meant a hell of a lot to me, too.

Ruth and I became increasingly close. She told me she'd realised that the public stereotypes of queer men and women were all wrong, adding, 'Now I've started questioning things, I can't stop. I've started seeing how much mindless prejudice is out there.'

I loved to hear her stories of Zac as a boy. I enjoyed seeing the family resemblance and little similarities. They both had a way of frowning and narrowing their eyes when thinking;

they both tapped their fingers when irritated. It was funny and endearing.

We had one break from the routine when we celebrated Zac's thirtieth birthday. He'd persuaded Claude to make the trip down from Liverpool and we met in a smart cafe in the West End. Claude looked exhausted, as we all did. After five years of war, short of sleep and decent food, we were living on our reserves.

Claude was pleased to meet Ruth again, but at first his manner seemed brittle. Ruth knew Zac and I had been in the army together, but we'd omitted the full story. Claude wasted no time on filling her in.

'So, you don't know how they got together?' Ruth shook her head, smiling. Claude continued, with some relish, 'When Zac was brought into the hospital in Bristol, he didn't know if Theo had survived. As soon as they discharged him, he spent weeks ringing all the hospitals in the south of England, thinking Theo was dead. God, he was a mess! He was pining for Theo and a bloody misery to be around—'

Zac interrupted, 'This must be boring for Ruth.'

'Not at all! Go on, Claude. What happened then?'

'Zac finally found him in some godforsaken hospital in the wilds of Kent, so they had the big reunion. He got Theo transferred to a proper hospital and we sorted out the mess they'd made of his leg. Zac was hanging off his every word. But Theo still carried a torch for his old love and all he could do was talk about Daniel,' Claude continued in his sardonic way.

Ruth turned to me. 'Who's Daniel?'

'Oh, no one important,' I replied hastily, then realised what I had said. The words echoed in my head. Zac looked at me with such a tender expression that I felt my heart move. We gazed at each other and I lost the conversation for a moment.

Ruth was saying, 'You don't know the security it gives me, being around you two. It's really opened my eyes. Gosh, most women count themselves lucky if their husbands bring their pay packet home and don't beat them. It's rare to find a relationship as equal as yours. I've decided I won't settle for anything less from a man.'

She looked around the table, bright-eyed and determined, and I squeezed her hand. Zac smoothly changed the subject and Claude seemed to relax after that.

When we took him to the station at the end of the day, I asked Claude, 'Why have you stayed away so long? We've missed you.'

'Oh, I've been far too busy having wild affairs,' he responded flippantly.

'Promise me you'll keep in touch. You're a dear friend.'

Zac said, 'Theo's right, Claude. We have a bond. We mustn't lose it.'

Claude looked at us, suddenly serious, and nodded. The platform was packed so we shook hands and I gripped his arm. He waved from the train, looking back at us forlornly.

As Zac and I were drifting off to sleep, he murmured, 'So here I am: thirty. I haven't achieved much with my life. The war has stolen five years from me.' He kissed me and added, 'But I wouldn't change anything. I have you, and that's all that counts.'

Our talk with Claude must have worked, because he obtained a post at the Royal Free Hospital. He found rooms in Gray's Inn Road and started work in the autumn of 1944. We welcomed him warmly and fell back into our easy camaraderie.

Time leached away from us into a fog of fatigue. We were weary of the restrictions, with "make do and mend". Our clothes were as threadbare as our energy. I think, because we were working such long hours, the days just bled into each other – but we didn't complain because we were winning the war. Air raids became less frequent, apart from a burst of attacks in the final months. Zac and I spent a few evenings in his armchair, lights out and the blackout down, watching the bombs transform London into a black and crimson patchwork. It seemed the whole world was on fire, but there was an air of hopeful anticipation. I no longer protested when Zac got some luxury on the black market. Once, he somehow found us olives. The salty bitterness was an explosion of taste after our bland diet.

I still remember the day Zac told me about the Nazi concentration camps, set up for the mass murder of Jews and other groups of people. I stared at him in horror. In spite of all we had gone through – the unspeakable cruelties of war – it had not occurred to us such evil could exist. We were to hear and see a lot more about these atrocities, but that was when I realised this really had been a battle for a way of life.

We kept on with our work, hanging on for an end to the war. Each time, our separations got harder, not easier. I would remember with incredulity how I'd stopped myself from acknowledging my feelings for him. I could not see my life without Zac now. Everything seemed more intense, better – I felt more alive. I had found myself, come home, with him.

1945–1951: Waking up with him every morning is the greatest gift possible

8

The war was all but won. The Germans were pinned back between the Allies on one side and Russians on the other. Hitler had killed himself in his bunker and we were waiting for the official surrender. Work at Bletchley Park had slowed to a trickle. For the first time in years, we were planning a future without war.

I was on the late shift when the ceasefire was signed. Alan had moved to work in a nearby station, but was back on a visit. Those still working in Hut Eight had gone early. We were drinking tea and reminiscing when the announcement came on the wireless: the war was over and the next day would be a holiday. We looked at each other with a grin of weary satisfaction.

The deputy director put his head around the door. 'Turing, Lawder, what are you still doing here? Go and celebrate for God's sake – we've bloody done it!'

I gave Alan a hug and went straight to the station. The train was heaving with people in a party spirit, bottles of gin being passed around, and there was a communal sing-song. On the bus to Zac's flat, we passed groups of revellers. My dislike of crowds prevented me from joining them, but it was more than that. *So here we are. The war is finished.* Why did it feel like an anticlimax? Everyone else seemed so clear about their plans. Ruth had applied to London colleges to train as a teacher on a one-year course offered to the armed forces. Claude was specialising in paediatrics at the Royal Free, while Alan was working on an electronic machine that he said would work like a human brain. I'd had a job offer, but didn't seem to have the energy to decide.

The flat was empty. I stood for a moment, looking vaguely around, then kicked off my boots and collapsed on the bed. I slept through the singing and car horns, only to be woken by a kiss on my lips. Zac was sitting on the bed smiling down at me. 'Hello, sleeping beauty,' he said. I opened my arms wordlessly and we melted into each other.

Then it was VE day. So: we were all ecstatic, dancing on the streets, happy and carefree, right? Only it wasn't like that for everyone. While there was relief, quite a few of us weren't jumping up and down. We'd lost loved ones, been injured, lost our homes. Our lives had been put on hold for too many years. The country was nearly bankrupt. Rationing was still in place and, although we didn't know it then, would be for years. I think we were just too damned tired.

Zac suggested we get out of London for the day. As we drove to Broadstairs I stared out the window, unable to work out why I felt so flat. The sun was shining as we walked along the clifftops – yet there was an unspoken tension between us. We commented on the scenery like polite acquaintances.

After a couple of hours, I could no longer ignore the ache in my leg and said, 'I think I need to take a rest.'

'Do you mind if I go on for a bit?'

'Of course not.'

Once on my own, I turned my face to the ground and wept bitterly. Part of it was grief at my lame leg, how it stopped me doing what I wanted, and part of it was less clear. I felt weighed down by the eternal conundrum of humanity – how our imperfections stopped us from achieving happiness. How we seemed doomed to go through life making mistakes, destroying the planet and each other. I had a deep, generalised melancholy.

After a while I stopped crying and lay on my back, drifting along in my thoughts. Then I sat up and looked around, taking pleasure from the view and the perky daffodils jostling for attention. As I watched the play of sunlight and cloud on the sea below, something resembling serenity crept into me.

I heard, 'Hello, Theo,' as Zac returned. He sat down next to me and said, 'I have some thoughts about our future. Can we talk?'

'Of course.' I couldn't help feeling anxious at his serious manner.

'We need to make a decision about our living arrangements. I don't know if you've thought about it, but I'd like us to live together.' I looked at him, astounded. He plucked clumps of grass, looking down, and went on, 'There's no denying we'll be more exposed, as two men sharing a home—'

I could no longer remain silent. 'But, Zac, of course I want to live with you! If anything, I thought you might want to take off from England again.'

'I know I can be bossy. I know you're used to your own space. I thought you might not want to live with me. As for leaving England – no, those days are gone. I had nothing to keep me anywhere. Now, my home is wherever you are. I was waiting for you, Teddy, you know that. I will love only you. That's my promise.' We grinned at each other and we were as always, best companions.

Two women in their forties, walking past with linked

arms, said hello. We all agreed it was wonderful the war was at an end. They went on their way with a warm smile. *This is normal life. We are in peacetime.* A sudden lightening of my spirit made me look up to see a kestrel hovering over us.

I heard Zac say, 'I wish I could marry you, darling. I wish we could make a formal commitment.'

I glanced over to make a joke – because the idea of two men marrying was of course absurd, impossible – but stopped when I saw his wistful expression. There were times when love for Zac flooded my body and left me washed up on his beach, defenceless and trusting. That we had found each other and survived Dunkirk – I still marvelled at my luck.

I took his burnt hand in mine and kissed it. 'We don't need a ceremony, Zac. We know our commitment. Anyway, we have our bathtub vow.' There was no one else around. We lay close together.

Zac murmured in my ear, 'Come live with me and be my love.' I could hear the kestrel calling. After a while he asked, 'Where shall we live?'

I looked back up at the sky, smiling with a rush of joy. After years of war, when our lives had been sublimated to a greater cause, freedom tasted delicious. I started to feel carefree in a way I hadn't for years. We could make decisions. We could control our own destiny. I suggested, 'Hmm, I hear the South Pacific is rather nice?'

Then we got serious. I quickly ruled out my family home. It was too close to my stepfather, and on my last visits I had found the village claustrophobic. As we talked, we seemed to be concentrating on the benefits of London. Zac reminded me there was a lot more to offer us as homosexuals, and more possibility to keep our lives private. We'd be close to Ruth and

Claude. That was it. We agreed to start our life together in London.

Our walk back was light-hearted. We stopped to eat in a pub. Everyone was in the bar loudly toasting the end of the war, and we had our corner to ourselves. I mentioned that the Foreign Office had offered me a job and Zac said, 'Good for you! It sounds like a good fit. Why the hesitation?'

'I'm worried about the overseas postings. After all our separations during the war – I don't want to be parted from you again like that.'

'Oh, don't let that stop you, Teddy. We'll find a way not to be separated too long, trust me.'

Well then, that was my decision clear. Zac had more of a dilemma. The army would go on employing him, but he'd also been approached by the Secret Intelligence Service.

I suggested, 'Have you thought of going to university? Don't forget, the army's helping people with grants. You gave years of your life to the war. Why shouldn't you get something back?'

Zac looked thoughtful but, after discussing it for a while, decided, 'I can't see myself as a student now. I think I'll take up the SIS offer.' We raised our glasses to our new life together.

Later, in his Highgate flat, I said, 'How strange my mood seems now!'

Zac's contented face was close to mine. 'I know, my dear. But don't forget, we've only ever been lovers during wartime. We've had so many separations. Our time together has always felt snatched. We've had no real control about where we worked and lived. Everything is changing now. It's bound to make us feel slightly off kilter.' His eyes gleamed, verdant pools of light. 'Now, we can really make a life for ourselves.'

Zac had to work out his notice with Military Intelligence, and Foreign Office bureaucracy was wheezing along. One day, I got talking to one of the old regulars at the men's pond on the Heath, who said his neighbour had a small house to rent in Hampstead village. By the end of the day, we had signed the lease. We bought basic furniture and moved in soon after.

I remember that house so fondly. We were welcomed by our neighbour Monica, an artist in her late forties who became a friend. Hampstead had been bombed during the war, but our immediate area was untouched. At night it was so quiet we could hear foxes calling on the Heath, just minutes away. After a few months, we could not imagine living anywhere else.

I needed to learn the various ruses I must adopt to hide the fact I lived with another man. With acquaintances and work colleagues, I pretended I lived on my own. Whenever I was asked a question about my life, my response had to be internally monitored, with pronouns turned to singular and a necessary vagueness added, before I could open my mouth. I knew I was seen as some sort of celibate neuter, or else the charade was that I hadn't met the "right woman". I'd been a useless liar as a child – far too transparent – but now my sexuality taught me the hard way how to maintain a facade of deceit. I hated all of it. But the most bitter lesson, about the downside of our living arrangements, came early on.

Not long after my twenty-eighth birthday, I visited my mother. I'd seen her infrequently during the war, jealously preserving my free time for Zac. Henry was at work, no doubt annoying his secretary. My mother looked a little plumper, her fair hair more mixed with grey. She made tea and we had the usual "how wonderful the war is over" conversation. But when I told her Zac and I had found a house in Hampstead, her expression changed. She looked away from me.

I asked, 'Is something wrong?'

'Oh, darling … It will send out the wrong message to be living with Zac. Why don't you come back to live in your house? If money is a problem, I'm sure we can help …' Her voice mizzled away damply.

'I live with Zac because I want to. You must know we're extremely close.'

She turned down her mouth and fluttered her hands. 'Soon you'll meet a nice girl and get married. It's nice to have a friend, but surely, Theo, you're old enough to see how it might be interpreted?'

I knew then that Henry must have guessed. I'd thought he'd glared suspiciously at Zac that time they met. No doubt he'd informed my mother in the most lurid way. Watching her closely, I said, 'I'll never get married. I've told you that already. Anyway, you should be grateful to Zac. Don't forget, he saved my life at Dunkirk.'

My mother blurted, 'Perhaps it would have been better if you'd died then, rather than—'

She stopped abruptly, looking shocked, her mouth in a little "o" of surprise that her thoughts had escaped. She snapped her lips shut, but it was too late. The words had bolted and hovered in the air, jeering at me.

For some reason, I recalled a childhood picnic, the summer before my mother remarried. I swam in the river and threw sticks for Patch; we ate sandwiches and drank my mother's homemade lemonade. We sang silly songs all the way home in the bus. She'd always been warm and loving.

I kept this memory in my head and my voice as steady as

possible. 'I don't think you really mean that, mother. Let's say no more now. I wish you every happiness.' When I walked to the front door, I expected her to call me back. She didn't.

I told Zac in the evening. He looked at me, frowning. 'Your mother didn't mean it. She's a kind woman. It's that bloody man. I'm sorry, Teddy.'

'There's nothing to be sorry about. I know who I am and I've made my choice. Anyone who doesn't accept that can go to hell.'

All the same, he must have seen something on my face because he held me close. 'Don't worry, she'll come round. Just give her time.'

The next day, a letter arrived from Henry. Don't contact your mother again; you're dead to her. Don't bring your depravity into our household. There were several more pages about "the abominable crime". Zac read it through, his mouth a tight line, and said, 'Well, you always did think the man was a complete loser. Don't despair, Teddy. Your mother has a mind of her own. This will change.'

I tore the letter into pieces and threw it in the bin. But we ended up having a stupid argument. Zac became monosyllabic and sat smoking in the garden. I asked him what was wrong and he said in a dull voice, 'Best to leave me alone, Theo.'

I shouted, 'You're a selfish bastard. I'm the one needing support!' He just bent his head, unresponsive as a stone, ossified by his private Medusa.

I banged the front door and went to the pub, letting the talk wash around me. After a while, I calmed down and thought about it rationally. The Zac I knew seemed to have vanished, replaced by some interloper. To have him withdraw from me like that had shocked me. I knew my response to him had been unfair – if he was troubled, he needed my understanding. I couldn't wait to get back to him.

He opened the front door to me and, once inside, we hugged tightly. He was the same Zac as ever, although with a sombre layer.

'What happened, darling?'

'Oh, Theo, I get these moods sometimes. They come on me and I can't seem to do anything. It's nothing to do with you, please believe me. I'm afraid I'm just a moody bastard. And now your mother has rejected you, thanks to me—'

I stared at him in consternation. 'But, Zac, you can't take the blame for that! My mother has decided she'd rather have me dead than queer. Well, that's her decision.'

He smiled fretfully and said, in what was meant to be a light voice, 'I suppose you must be sorry you ever agreed to live with me.'

I kissed him consolingly. Regret was the furthest thing from my mind.

I started in the Foreign Office in July and Zac moved to the SIS the following week. The FO building in King Charles Street looked imposing, but inside the scene was one of faded grandeur. The building had been full to the rafters during the war, and the walls and ceilings were grubby from the coal fires. Durbar Court, an Italian-style courtyard, apparently had a beautiful marble floor but it was hidden beneath pallets and pigeon droppings. The building was a maze, with corridors and stairs everywhere. But you could still see signs of past glories: the ornate wooden doorways to the ministerial offices; the intricate carvings on the staircases.

I was placed on the North America desk, working on

post-war reconstruction efforts. I was expected to put in the hours, and didn't mind because the work was interesting; but the downside was an increase of the pain in my leg. I told myself I would have this all my life. *Just get on with it.*

London was full of demobbed soldiers, and the bomb sites were being cleared. Rationing continued. Day to day life was still hard – but I was full of optimism. This was a time of great change for us. Within a few weeks, we'd moved from the restrictions of wartime to new careers and a peaceful future. Our energy was centred on our life together, and the outside world hardly intruded. Claude said sarcastically one evening, 'Look at you two lovebirds, all cosy in your nest! You're blossoming like bloody great roses or something.' But we just laughed. We were ecstatic to be making a home together.

9

Claude turned up at the pub one evening in the autumn accompanied by a colleague, who seemed to look intently at me when I was introduced. The mystery was soon explained by Claude. 'Theo, you and Huw have met before, although you won't remember it.'

I looked at Huw enquiringly, who explained in his soft Welsh accent that he had been a medical student helping out when soldiers were brought back from Dunkirk. 'I noticed some corpses laid out and decided to check them. I walked along the row and thought I saw a slight movement. I stopped, looked closer, and realised your eyes were fluttering.' I heard Zac gasp. Huw went on, 'I could feel a faint heartbeat, so I pumped your chest and we sent you straight off to hospital. I knew your name, because you had a toe tag, and wondered if you'd survived. I couldn't believe it when Claude and I got talking about the war and he said he knew you.'

I looked at him, lost for words. A spiteful voice whispered in my ear that my mother almost had her wish.

'Another few minutes and you may not have survived,' Huw said, adding with a laugh, 'You look damned healthy for a corpse.' Zac made a convulsive movement but remained silent.

I recovered from my shock. 'I owe you my life. All I can do is thank you.' It seemed inadequate, but what do you say to someone who saved your life?

The conversation moved on. Zac recovered and got into

a discussion with Huw about sailing. An idea occurred to me and I said, 'Huw, I'd like to invite you for a meal to thank you properly. Do you have a wife or girlfriend you can bring?'

Huw shook his head. 'Afraid not. Work is controlling my life at the moment.'

'What are you doing this Sunday? Could you come for dinner?' This was agreed.

Zac was subdued on the bus home. After we got in, I put my arms around him. He said, 'Oh, Teddy, you nearly died …'

But I was cradling my elation at how fortunate I was to have this wonderful life, and responded flippantly, 'Sorry, Zac. You're stuck with me now!'

He replied, as if the words were ripped out of him, 'I nearly lost you! Don't you see how that would have changed everything? That last day at Dunkirk, you were slipping away in front of me. I felt I was seeing a ghost—' He gulped, desolation crawling over his face.

I held him close. 'Darling, I survived. I'm real. I'm here. I'll always be here.'

Zac had a vulnerable side he didn't let anyone else see. He'd spent far too much of his life having to be responsible, looking after others. Only now was he letting go of this and accepting that I could look after him too.

Later that night, he asked about the Sunday dinner. He'd recovered from his shock by then, and laughed at me. 'What will you serve – bread and butter?' Zac had learned to cook on a ranch in Canada and was quite a dab hand, while I could barely boil an egg. After some teasing, he said of course he would cook.

I added, 'Ruth can come too.'

'Are you up to something, Teddy?' I feigned innocence.

The next morning, I rang Ruth and told her to change

whatever plans she had for Sunday. She was coming to our place for dinner.

The meal was a great success. Ruth had assumed that Huw was Claude's new romance, but it soon became apparent his interest lay in another direction. When we were having coffee, Huw mentioned an exhibition at the National Gallery. I suggested, 'Why don't you two go off to see it?'

Before they left, Huw came into the kitchen and asked me, 'Are you having pain with your leg, Theo?' I looked at him, surprised, and admitted it. 'I'll arrange an appointment with an orthopaedic specialist. I think we can fix it.'

Afterwards, I couldn't help gloating about how well my plan had gone. I'd had an intuition Huw could be a good match for Ruth. I told Claude, 'Perhaps I can fix you up with someone nice?' But my joke fell flat. He made a chippy response and left soon after.

I said to Zac, crestfallen, 'Sometimes I seem to irritate Claude. I only want him to be happy.'

Zac shrugged. 'Don't you worry about Claude. He can be a touchy bugger sometimes. Come on, let's get out for a walk.'

We set off for Parliament Hill before dark. St Paul's and the ruins of London were barely visible through the fog. I told Zac what Huw had said about my leg, and casually mentioned that Monica's whippet was about to have puppies. Zac grinned and said, 'On one condition! The dog doesn't sleep on our bed.'

A few weeks later, we met Ruth in the pub. She chatted about her teacher training while a quiet radiance peeped through. When I asked, 'Have you seen Huw again?' she blushed. They'd seen each other several times and she liked him a lot.

'He's already passed my two most important tests. You both like him, and he's obviously relaxed in queer company.'

Then she looked at me closely. 'What's that look?'

I confessed, 'I planned the whole thing.'

Zac laughed. 'Let's just say, Theo had a feeling you two would get on.'

Ruth was amused. 'Theo, the matchmaker! Perhaps you should set up a lonely hearts agency?'

I had the hospital appointment soon after. The specialist said they'd improved their knowledge about my type of injury. A new operation would give me greater flexibility and length in the leg. The procedure was booked for early December.

I had an angry new scar on top of the others, but I'd long known my leg would not win any beauty contest. After I was discharged, we went to look at Monica's puppies. One came straight over and crawled onto my lap. Zac said, 'Well, that's our choice made.'

I gave her the name of my imaginary childhood friend. Pip was mostly grey, with a white blaze on her face carrying on down her neck and belly. What an intelligent and affectionate companion she became to us.

I'd bought Zac's Christmas present before I went into hospital, a beautifully bound notebook I'd found in Charing Cross Road. When he unwrapped it, I said, 'I thought it might be time for you to keep a journal again.'

'All my words, gone up in flames … I never really thought about writing again.'

'You tell wonderful stories, Zac. It would be a shame to stop that.'

29 December 1945

Theo. It seems only right to start with his name. It was the last word in my

82

old journals before they were turned to ash in the Blitz. He's lying on the sofa listening to the radio, Pip on his lap, as I write this.

How to describe him? I could write of his hair, golden like sunburned wheat or autumn leaves. Touching it is so sensual for me. Let me run barefoot through his hair. Or his chameleon eyes: fluxing shades of blue or sometimes green, depending on the light or his mood. His mouth – full and firm, soft, sweet. The most kissable lips. The best kisser. I could sing praises to the body I've traced with my hands, my mouth, my tongue. His swimmer's shoulders, tapering down to his luscious bum. His cock, the source of pleasure and delight. His left leg with tram tracks of scars running over wasted muscles, the source of pain and restriction. I could speak of his pale skin. When he's tired or in pain, it looks bruised (at Dunkirk, it was translucent). When he's happy or we're making love, it's flushed and rosy.

But what really makes him so beautiful is what's inside this body, these eyes, this skin. Yes, he's disorganised, messy. He's always a few minutes late for everything. Too dreamy, naive. He tends to sulk. And stubborn! But I'm never bored. He has a fine mind. He's optimistic, kind, funny. The sweetest thing I've ever known. So bloody sexy – everything I want in bed. His integrity stands out in everything he does. He has such strength and he can be fierce, in spite of his gentleness. This is the man I love. This is Theo.

After weeks of intensive physiotherapy, I went for a hospital check at the end of January. I could bend my leg halfway and slowly walk upstairs one step at a time. Best of all, the difference in length between my legs had been reduced. The specialist said I could use a lift inside an ordinary shoe to make my legs equal. No more of those ugly orthopaedic boots. I'd clumped around in them for more than five years and hated the bloody things. I'd always limp and need a cane, my leg would still ache if I did too much – but my lameness need no longer define me.

Theo and I went shopping for shoes in the West End today. Never thought one day I'd write those words. He's borne it bravely, but I know how much he suffered with his leg. After he paraded around at home in his new shoes, I asked what we should do with the orthopaedic ones. He said, I never want to see them again. I looked at him and he said, let's go to the Heath and bury them.

We set off with a spade and the shoes, and went under a copper beech overlooking the ponds. It was nearly dark and no one else was around. I dug a hole, Theo slung in the boots and we shovelled in the earth. Then he started prancing around, his eyes sparkling, saying it was the death dance. Oh, he was gorgeous. Little Pip was jumping around and I couldn't speak for laughing. On the way home he started a story about the boots being dug up in a hundred years and the police thinking it was a crime scene. The murder of the boots! he declared.

It's wonderful to see him so droll. He lost that after Dunkirk. He was tense, withdrawn, in terrible pain. I knew we were meant to be together, but he'd got himself into a state about things. Now I see the real Theo coming back. The adult version of that little boy, spinning around in his floral crown.

But I see a change in me as well. I'm having fun, in a way I haven't since I was a child. Life was too serious for me for quite a while. Even when I was wandering the world – I saw beautiful countries, I had affairs and adventures, but there was a sadness inside me. No longer. Sometimes, it scares me how happy I am. Going to bed with him every night, waking up with him every morning is the greatest gift possible.

On my return to work, I was moved to the Foreign Secretary's office. Ernest Bevin was a man of great vision and all the staff in his office were dedicated to "Uncle Ernie". I worked on the Dunkirk Plan and preparations for the Marshall Plan. This made a real difference in helping the reconstruction of countries after the war. People were desperate, starving. The economies of their countries were close to collapse.

I became friendly with my colleague Anna, a woman around my age. It started after the Private Secretary disparaged one of her ideas in a meeting. Anna just shrugged – she told me later she was used to being patronised by men – but I intervened, saying, 'I think Anna made a good suggestion.' I went on to support her idea. After a stunned silence, the PS grudgingly agreed.

Anna smiled her thanks at me and we started talking after that. She was petite, with a heart-shaped face and dark hair in a bob. Her parents were Italian but she'd grown up in Edinburgh. She had a direct manner along with a killing sense of humour. Any man trying to flirt with her found a feisty, confident woman who made her indifference very clear. Perhaps that was why she seemed to feel comfortable with me.

One day she stopped by my desk. 'Fancy going for a coffee?'

We talked at first about the war. She asked about my injury and told me of her WAAF work in anti-aircraft units. Then we started circling around our private lives. I picked up behaviour so familiar to me: a careful watchfulness, vague mention of a "friend". We looked at each other and I suddenly twigged. She said, 'I'm a lesbian, by the way,' and it all came out. She was in a relationship with Miriam, a nurse, and had wondered if I might also be queer.

'Am I that obvious?'

She laughed. 'Not at all, Theo, but you're the only man

not coming onto me. You treat me like a person, rather than a walking vagina, pardon the expression. Anyway, it takes one to know one.'

It made such a difference to have her as a friend and ally at work. Anna was the one who got me back to singing. She was in a choir in Whitehall and I went along with her one evening. Music has always given me something I need. When we're doing a choral piece – the orchestra and singers all combining, having a musical conversation – it feels almost spiritual.

Our first concert was in the summer. Zac sat in the audience with Miriam – a warm woman with a ready smile. The four of us went for a drink afterwards.

Soon after we sat down, I was surprised to hear Anna ask Zac, 'Do you like rugby?'

He wrinkled his nose. 'Good heavens, no. I can think of better reasons to be under a heap of sweaty men.' We all burst out laughing.

Anna became my closest friend, and the four of us formed a tight unit. Ruth and Huw were in the first flush of love and spent all their time together. We saw less of Claude that year. He'd become involved with a medical student, and socialised with Martin's friends.

Months later, when we were walking to rehearsal, Anna confessed, 'Do you know, Theo, I was nervous about meeting Zac.'

I stopped and looked at her. 'Why?'

'Well, you told me he'd gone to boarding school. Even his name sounded posh. I formed the opinion he was an arrogant, upper-class type. I was worried I wouldn't like him and it might affect my friendship with you.'

'Ah! Well, he went to a very minor school, and it got him

away from his parents.' I remembered then. 'You asked him if he liked rugby.'

'Yes, and Miriam kicked me under the table!'

We continued walking. 'So … what did you decide about Zac?'

She gave me an amused glance. 'I quickly realised I'd got it all wrong. After just a few minutes I thought to myself: yes, he'll do very nicely for Theo.'

28 September 1946

It's seven years today since I first saw Teddy. I'd been in the army a few weeks, commissioned – much to my surprise – on the basis I could handle a gun. There'd been an introduction for the new NCOs, and when I passed him afterwards, he gave me a delightful smile. Something about it touched me deeply. I studied him for weeks, feeling very drawn to him. He was a lovely man in every way – but I'd also picked up a sense of not quite fitting in, of being different, which chimed with me.

Sometimes a group of us went to swim at the end of the day. That was damned hard. He was next to me nearly naked, drops of water on his body drying off in the sun, golden hair slicked back. God, he was irresistible – but resist him, I must. When I saw him with Daniel, it confirmed what I'd hoped, and we became close. I looked forward all day to our talks. We'd sit by some oak trees, the sun casting long shadows, opening up to each other about our lives. A bunch of nuns could have sat with us and not been alarmed by our conversation. It was clear we were having a slow, sweet courtship – so different, in every way, from anything I'd embarked on before.

But I was his commanding officer. We were never alone. No one could guess we were queer, and we were about to go off to war. It was an impossible situation. So, I stopped myself. I've always been good at being in control, too good. On the surface, we were close friends, nothing more, but I knew I was deeply in love. I planned it all in my head: soon we'd get some furlough. I'd suggest we go away for a few days together, and I would tell him how I felt. But then we went over to France and into hell, and it was a case of just surviving.

9 October 1946

When we made love this morning, Teddy made a noise in his throat that took me back to our first night. I'd never felt like that before. All my affairs, my casual fucks – they were nothing. How he was as beautiful naked as I'd imagined. How I finally felt his lips against mine, his body move under my hands. How I could breathe in his smell, our bodies fitting so well together. Losing ourselves in each other. How I'd waited more than a year for this.

7 December 1946

We stopped off at the shops on the way home from work. I was frowning over the sausages when I looked over at him and suddenly thought – bloody hell, I'm doing the food shop with Theo Lawder. We'll go home and have dinner, go to bed. This is our life. I just stared at him, grinning stupidly, while the butcher asked for my order.

Now we're lying each end of the sofa, our legs entwined. Pip has squeezed in and is gently thumping her tail. I realised early on that he's a tactile Teddy. I'm more than happy to oblige, but what I didn't expect was how this physical closeness gives me a deep sense of peace and belonging.

Always I've been hard-headed, practical. None of that mushy stuff. But I'm incurably romantic when it comes to him. I could write an entire poem to his eyes, his hair, the curve of his bum. I've tried a few times, scribbled down some lines, but threw them in the bin as absurdly sentimental.

That winter was brutal. It snowed every day for weeks and we had frequent power cuts. We woke to find ice on the inside of our bedroom window. Zac would leap out of bed, light the gas fire then jump back in while we waited for the room to warm up, our arms and legs wrapped around each other.

Another Christmas passed with no word from my mother. Zac suggested I ring her, but I saw it as a point of principle. If she didn't want to accept my identity, that was her choice. I refused to sleepwalk through my days, taking the safe option – hiding behind a false front. I had grabbed my life with Zac by the throat and I wouldn't let go.

10

This was the time that Guy Burgess started to become a problem at work. He was in the Minister of State's office and often came into our room. You noticed him right away, because he wasn't the usual FO type. Burgess was flamboyant and good-looking, despite his scruffy clothes. He could be amusing, although less so in the afternoons, no doubt due to his lunchtime drinking. Sometimes he came out with outrageous statements and he didn't hide his homosexuality. In fact, he seemed to flaunt it.

He would come into our office and say, 'How's the beautiful boy today?' Once, he even said in a carrying voice, 'I'd like to grab that bum,' as I walked past. He would loudly flirt with me while I unlocked the cupboards. I had to concentrate on the combination lock – you needed to select several numbers, twisting it alternate ways – so I'd get into a muddle and have to start again. He seemed to find this hilarious. He often asked me out for a drink, but I always found an excuse.

One day, Zac and I were walking through St James's Park after lunch when he came up to us. 'So, this is the lucky boyfriend?' Zac glared at him and he walked off laughing.

Zac looked at me. 'Who's that joker?' I tried to make light of it.

I found him repellent and did my best to ignore him, but I was scared he could expose me. It was clear homosexuals were not welcome in the FO, or indeed anywhere else. Anna had told me that a senior diplomat had been forced to resign due to an affair with a local man. It was a mystery how Burgess seemed to be exempt. She warned me to be careful.

'He's a nasty piece of work, Theo. I really dislike him. Such a bloody snob, always going on about the Cambridge Apostles and wearing that mucky Old Etonian tie.'

'But I've seen him in meetings when he acts the model diplomat. He has a brilliant mind.'

'Don't be fooled by that. Burgess is dangerous. I'm worried he'll cause problems for you. Just try not to react.'

'It doesn't mean anything, Anna. It's just a game for him.'

'Mm, I'm not so sure. Once or twice, I've caught an expression on his face. I think he might have feelings for you.'

That startled me. 'What do you mean?'

'I've seen this look of ... wistfulness? Perhaps he sees in you the goodness he knows he'll never have? Oh, Theo, don't look like that. You know, you can be a bit soft with people. Don't feel sorry for him, for God's sake. The man's a complete wanker.'

We knew we had to hide our identities at work. In a way, our friendship provided unforeseen cover. People assumed we were a couple because we were often together. Anna told me someone had asked her outright, and she'd replied demurely that we were "just good friends". We laughed about that – but if Burgess kept up this behaviour it could be dangerous for me.

In the spring I had to apply for my overseas posting. All the other diplomats couldn't wait for their overseas tours, but I was torn, because three years away from Zac was unthinkable. I decided that, if we had to be separated, I would leave the FO. But Zac suggested we could try to get a posting to the same embassy. We spent a few evenings comparing FO and SIS options. Zac vetoed

Moscow and Warsaw, saying, 'The Soviets are bloody good at espionage, Teddy, and it's getting nasty with them. They have a way of finding out if you've got something to hide.' We agreed on the choices and put in our bids.

23 April 1947

Teddy and I plan to get posted overseas together, but it's causing me some problems at work. My boss called me in today and asked why I've limited myself to "less active" countries. I'm getting broad hints that I'm lacking in ambition and "wasting my talents". But I don't care. I know very well what my ambition is – to spend my life with Theo and safeguard what we have. Anything else comes a very distant second. I have no intention of playing spy games in some communist country away from him.

The situation with Burgess erupted one evening. Anna and I were locking up, due to go to the theatre with Zac and Miriam. He wandered in and sprawled on my desk, claiming he'd just seen the "Grey Lady", the FO ghost. His breath was the usual fetid mixture of alcohol, garlic and unbrushed teeth. We ignored him.

Anna got a phone call and said pointedly to me, 'I need to take down this submission, then we should go.'

As soon as she left, Burgess said, 'You don't fool me with this girlfriend business. I know you're queer and fucking your MI6 man.'

I turned my back without replying. Angry, shocked words piled up in my throat. I heard him get off the desk. Suddenly, he grabbed me from behind. 'Don't you know I have a huge cock? I'll make you scream with pleasure.' He started grinding himself against me.

Rage exploded bitterly into my mouth. I wanted to smash his face. I clenched my fists but, just in time, Anna returned and Burgess moved away. I turned to him and said, as coolly as I could, 'I'd rather fuck a dead cat.' That was an army expression I'd heard.

I saw anger in his eyes and some other emotion I couldn't identify. He said he had a party to get to, and walked out.

Anna asked, 'What the hell just happened?' After I explained she said, 'You've got to tell Zac about this.'

When I saw Zac waiting at the main entrance, I gripped his arm tightly. The feeling of coming home was overpowering. We started walking through the park in the fading light towards Haymarket and Anna said, 'I think you should know, Theo's having a problem with someone at work.'

I gave her a cross look but explained what happened. Zac heard me out without interrupting, although Anna couldn't resist saying, 'Poor cat!'

'Is that the man who came up to us in the park once?' Zac's eyes were narrowed but he spoke calmly. 'The name is familiar. Let me make some enquiries.'

16 May 1947

I finally got to sort out that shit Burgess today. When Teddy told me how he's been bothering him at work, I wanted to kick his teeth in. But I've made myself look at the situation dispassionately. Use your brains, not your caveman instincts, I've been telling myself. That's not going to help Teddy.

I've found out he used to work at my place and was forced out or sacked, depending on the version going around. I can't understand why the FO put up with him. I suspect he's got powerful backing somewhere – all the more reason to deal with this carefully.

I've been meeting Teddy after work and walking up Whitehall past the pubs where I heard he hangs out. When we crossed over today, he nudged me and said, that's Burgess. I saw a dark-haired man outside the pub with a group of people, picking up some papers he'd spilled on the ground. He looked more than half-cut. I walked up to him and said quietly, I'd like a word. I've been thinking about this all week. Being angry or righteous wouldn't work, and might even encourage him. I had to go in with a tactic he wouldn't expect.

We moved off to one side. Burgess was smirking, clearly expecting the outraged boyfriend routine. I said calmly "we" have been watching you for some time and know what you're up to. I decided to start off with that to confuse him, but I must have hit the spot because I saw his eyes widen and his face go white. By God, I thought, he looks frightened. I went on in the same tone: if you go near Theo again, I'll make sure you regret it. The whole exchange lasted perhaps half a minute. He didn't say a word. After we left, Teddy asked what did I say to Burgess, because he looked shocked? I laughed and told him. Let's see if it works.

19 May 1947

Waking up with Teddy is just the best thing. I still can't take it for granted after the years of separation during the war. If we were lucky, we'd get a few hours together each week. It left us anxious and tense.

I often lie and watch him in the morning. I still feel I have to pinch myself. How did this gorgeous man agree to be mine? He has such a peaceful expression. His spirit is so pure, it comes out when he's asleep. When he wakes up, I take him in my arms. He snuggles up and smiles from under his lashes. I love his smell – sweet and musky. It drives me crazy. I kiss his neck. I could eat him.

This morning, I finally dragged myself away and came down to make tea. I opened the door to the garden and found a fox staring at me, just yards away. A beautiful creature – why would you kill them for so-called sport? He didn't look scared, more curious. I felt this explosion of joy inside me. I feel – God, life is so good.

15 June 1947

I saw the fox again. He's sleeping in a hollow at the back of the garden. I like the idea of sharing our space with a wild animal.

I've been thinking a lot lately about happiness. For a long time, I believed: anyone who aims to be happy is a Panglossian fool. I used to think: we get through life as best we can. We have rare moments of happiness, periods of great despair and, if we're fortunate, most of the time we muddle along somewhere between the two. I would have said: the man who says he's happy is deluding himself.

Teddy has been teaching me how wrong I was, without saying a word – just by being himself.

He's clearly no fool. He's the most intelligent person I know – after Alan, of course – but he has a great gift of happiness. At first, I thought he was pretending. When he meets people, he expects to like them. He believes things will turn out well. He can be happy for the simplest things – a sunset, a beautiful view. If something bad happens, he's knocked off course for a while, but returns to his contented centre. He meets life with a smile.

I used to envy him. But increasingly, I get these flashes of deep happiness. I know I have my demons, things that hurt me, but they've faded to the background. I find myself whistling or humming a tune to myself. It just comes on me. I'm not consciously doing it. And it's not foolish. It's bloody wonderful.

Zac's tactic worked, because Burgess didn't come near me again. He moved to another department and was later posted to Washington. Meanwhile, I heard I would be going to Rome in

95

March 1948 as Second Secretary, and started language training.

I had several presents for my thirtieth birthday, the best one being Zac's news that he was also posted to Rome. He bought me a small upright piano that fitted into the corner of our sitting room. And I received a card from my mother. She wrote that she regretted her words. She loved me no matter what, and hoped I could forgive her. Zac said, 'Well, it took her two years, but good for her. She's seen sense.'

I rang her right away. We agreed to meet the following Saturday. This was a tremendous relief for me – her rejection had saddened me more than I'd admitted.

Zac drove me up to Oxfordshire. When I met my mother in the cafe she burst into tears, so the first few minutes involved looking for her hanky and ordering tea and cakes. She commented on the improvement in my leg, so I explained about the operation. I told her what a good life we had and that Zac was everything in the world to me.

My mother plucked at her hanky and asked, 'Will you forgive me for what I said?'

'Of course, mother. It's all in the past. I hope you can accept who I am, and grow to love Zac.'

She smiled nervously. 'I'll try ... But I'm afraid your stepfather refuses to meet you.' That was no hardship for me.

When we left the cafe, Zac was leaning against the car, with Pip on the lead. My mother looked puzzled. I wondered if, in her imagination, he'd been transformed into a screaming queen or some sort of diseased degenerate? And instead, she saw a smartly dressed man with impeccable manners, who would turn heads anywhere. They chatted for a few minutes and I could see her relaxing. She was positively beaming when she waved us off.

3 September 1947

Teddy's walking Alan to the tube. We got onto our philosophy of life over dinner, having quickly agreed the God business doesn't do it for us. Teddy mentioned his interest in humanism, and Alan explained his belief that the mind is embodied in matter, which came to him after his first love died suddenly. When he said that, I lost the thread of conversation for a while – yet again, I felt these ghostly fingers on my face. Knowing how close Theo came to death can still haunt me. Somewhere in another life is a Zac where Theo really did die. How is he? What is he doing? Is he in quiet despair – is he drinking himself to death?

Before Alan set off, he said: you two have something precious, you must guard it with your lives. He's always been Teddy's friend, but I've come to understand his idiosyncrasies and I'm fond of him. I do fear, however, he lacks a layer of skin. He's too trusting, unable to see through people's duplicity. In spite of his brilliance.

Our life settled into a rhythm. During the week, we were busy with long days. Not just work – I had choir and Zac started going to a fencing club. Other evenings, we'd meet our friends, or go to a play or concert. On the weekends we might go for trips to the cottage on the coast, or explore the countryside. If we stayed in London, we'd walk on the Heath, or swim at the men's pond in the summer. Anna and Miriam went to the ladies' pond and sometimes we met for a picnic under the copper beech.

Pip came on all our expeditions. She would curl up in the evenings, quiet and contented, just like us. Zac started working in the garden and discovered that he enjoyed growing things. It was good for his injured hand to do the digging and planting.

In a way, I knew from wartime what to expect, living with Zac. He did the cleaning and cooking, grumbling that I was a slob. I do have the philosophy that if I can't see dust, it doesn't need cleaning. But I hadn't realised what a difference it would make to share a home, as opposed to fugitive hours when we were living on our nerves. In public, we could never touch or stand too close, but at home we could relax. We would lie together on the sofa, listening to the radio, chatting or reading. Zac was interested in history but, really, he read anything – novels, biographies, even poetry.

I discovered new sides to him – a softness and sensitivity that had been repressed for too long. I witnessed his acts of kindness. He would help women with their bags of shopping, or chat to old men in the pub, showing interest in their stories. I noticed their eyes were always brighter afterwards and they held themselves straighter.

We had arguments, of course. I tend to flare up easily. When Zac got angry, he was quietly furious for some time. He found it hard to talk about his feelings and wore a cloak of iron control around himself. I was the only one he let inside, but not always. I'd say, 'Don't you trust me, Zac?' and he'd reply, 'I trust you more than I trust myself.' Sometimes he'd tell me he was happier than he deserved. I always replied that he deserved all the happiness in the world.

These were minor complaints compared to his occasional black moods, when he would retreat wordlessly inside himself. I missed him at those times – I felt there was an imposter in Zac's clothing, staring out dully from Zac's eyes. He always apologised afterwards. I would think: *thank God, Zac is back with me.* But I accepted this, because otherwise we were so happy. I was profoundly in love with him. I felt I could conquer the world, knowing I would always come home to him.

11

It was a foggy November evening when I met Daniel again. Bedraggled bunting from the Royal Wedding still adorned the streets, and a soupy mixture of roasted chestnuts, chimneys and exhaust fumes permeated the air. When we turned the corner by Charing Cross station, Daniel was coming towards us with a pregnant woman and a small boy. I recognised him instantly, but that was not to say he hadn't altered. He looked thin and drawn, with lines of tension on his face that hadn't been evident seven years earlier. His clerical collar glowed palely in the gloom.

I recovered from my shock. 'Hello, Daniel. This is Zac Bonneval. You may remember meeting him when I was in the army.'

Daniel faced us silently. The woman said she was Daniel's wife Eileen, and this was their son, Theodore. I started at the name.

Zac came to my rescue and said to Eileen, 'May I buy Theodore some chestnuts?' He went off with them and I was alone with Daniel.

His voice was quiet. 'You look very well, Theo.'

'Thank you.' Unable to say the same for him, I scratched around in my mind for some well-worn phrase.

Before I could resolve that dilemma, he said, 'Your leg seems much improved.'

I'd last seen him when I was in hospital after Dunkirk – tense, unhappy visits. I told him about the operation and mentioned that I worked in the FO. He said he was a vicar in a parish in Essex. I asked after his sister. I could no longer avoid the obvious topic.

'So ... you're married and a father.' I tried for a neutral tone.

He grimaced, but said only, 'I got married during the war.'

We stared at each other. There was so much to say, but the words perished in our mouths. After a pause he asked, 'Your friend ... is he the officer who came up to us in the pub that time?'

'Yes.' I took a breath. 'We live together and we're very happy.'

He inhaled sharply, then stammered, 'But – it – it's a sin.'

'No, it's not a sin, Daniel. It's just two people loving each other. There was a time when you and I had that. You decided it wasn't for you, and that's your right.'

His face contracted, but he remained silent. We stood unmoving while a river of humanity streamed around us: people in animated conversation, workers running for trains, newsboys calling. I waited, then said, 'Your little boy looks sweet. How old is he?'

He replied, 'Nearly three.' He continued to gaze at me, grief settling on his face like snow.

Eileen came back and said to Daniel, 'We must go. Theodore needs his supper.' She looked pale and pressed her hand into her back.

I smiled at the boy who was a miniature version of Daniel, looking gravely up at me. 'We should let you go. Take care, Daniel.' His unhappiness was clear. Then we went on our way.

When we got in, Zac built up a fire and came back with a couple of strong drinks. I realised I needed that. I related my conversation with Daniel, adding, 'I can see he's denying his own nature. It's obvious he's not happy. Well, he's still young. Perhaps, now, he'll start to accept himself.'

Zac frowned as he replied, 'But other people are involved. He has a wife, and soon two children. He's drawn them into his self-denial – they're affected by his lies. They did nothing to deserve it.'

I raised my eyebrows, startled by the impatience in his voice. He continued, 'Don't you know married men can be the worst? Who do you think most of my clients were, when I was on the streets? Men who went home to their wives and children. They were often the ones who liked it rough, and who most hate queers. They reject what's in their own nature. No one gains from that set-up. Everyone loses.'

I sighed. 'I know. I just feel so sad to see him like this. I wish I could help him.'

'Don't take responsibility for this, Teddy. You couldn't have been more forgiving when he treated you badly. If he can't accept who he is, then he's a coward and worse. You don't drag innocent women and children into your deceptions.'

26 November 1947

I met Daniel again last night. The man who had first claim on Teddy's heart. He looked at Teddy as if he were the promised land. He'd denied his nature to the extent he had a pregnant wife and child trailing in the wake of his confusion. The boy, by the most laughable homage, is named after my Theo. The wife seemed tired and beaten down by life. She didn't ask to fall in love with someone who can't give her what she wants. Another case of broken lives due to his refusal to accept he's queer.

From the first day, he was a shadow between us. He put Teddy through the wringer: I love you, it's a sin, I can't be with you, I can't be without you. All the time, I waited, hoping Teddy would realise that I was the man for him. I get the feeling that his resurgence into our lives isn't the last of it.

Zac had one of his black moods soon after we met Daniel. This one lasted longer than usual. I knew the drill by now. I didn't try to make him talk. The next morning, he was still terse, his eyes veiled with unspoken pain. I bit my lip and left him to it. When I got home from work, the stranger had gone.

27 December 1947

We were making love this morning when Teddy started speaking in Italian and bit my shoulder. He likes to bite me – I swear he was a cat once. Perhaps a tiger. After all these years he can still surprise me. Sexy beast. I've told him, you can talk Italian with me any time, darling. It will be interesting to see what three years in Italy will do. I might be a broken man by the end.

We were finishing our preparations for Italy. Zac was leaving in the middle of January, driving over with Pip, while I would follow in March. Our landlord had agreed that Ruth and Huw could move into the house while we were gone. Ruth came around one evening to tell us they would be getting married at the registry office in Camden.

'What took you so long, Ruthie? You're obviously crazy about each other.' Zac had opened a bottle of wine to celebrate and we were chatting by the fire, just like in the war days.

'God knows, I've been fed up with sneaking around his place. But women have to stop teaching when they get married, and I wasn't prepared to do that.'

'What made you change your mind?'

'When I knew you'd be away for some years, that decided me. I can't imagine getting married without you two around me. Huw said, "Just don't tell the school you got married".'

Ruth was radiant as she came into the registry room on Zac's arm. Claude sat next to me, looking pensive. His relationship had fallen apart just before Christmas. He'd gone home one day to find Martin with the barman from their local pub – who, incidentally, was married with three children. Claude threw him out and reappeared in our lives. 'Here I am again, Claude On His Own,' he announced dramatically when I gave him a hug.

8 January 1948

I knew bloody Daniel couldn't leave us alone. He rang Teddy tonight saying he wants to meet him. I'm not in the phone book because of my work, but Teddy's easy enough to find. I can guess what this is about.

It was a surprise to hear from Daniel, but I hoped it meant we could be friends. We agreed to meet the following day in a pub near Charing Cross station.

Daniel had chosen a quiet spot in the corner. As soon as I sat down next to him, his words burst out in tense, rapid sentences. He could no longer deny his identity. He'd tried to fight it for years, but seeing me again had made it undeniable. He couldn't stop thinking about me.

I interrupted his declarations to say, 'But, Daniel, you were the one who pushed me away!'

'Do you think I haven't regretted that a thousand times since?'

He continued in an unstoppable flood, describing his

years of conflict and loneliness. He'd signed up as an army chaplain, and became close to a soldier who wanted to love him. Daniel rejected him and prayed every day to be "released" from his nature. Eileen was an old friend, whose family had been killed in the Blitz.

'I felt sorry for her. We got on, and I thought it could be my chance to have a normal life. But I knew instantly it was a mistake. She wants to be loved, and I can't give her that. I can be her friend, but … I had sex with her out of duty.' His face twisted. 'As luck would have it, she got pregnant right away, so I had no choice. I'm trapped in the marriage. Seeing you again made me realise how unhappy I am. I still love you, Theo. I don't care if it's a sin. I want to be with you.' He waited for my answer.

This was not what I had expected. I responded carefully. 'My life is with Zac.'

Daniel started arguing with me, as if he could change my mind. 'I know you love me. Now we can be together—'

I broke in, my dismay growing. I knew I had to be honest, however much it might hurt him. 'No. I'm sorry, Daniel. I did love you once, but you didn't want me and my feelings changed. I'm concerned for you now as a friend, but I don't love you.'

He didn't seem to hear. 'I could get a ministry in a place where no one knows us. We can make a new life there.'

'That's not going to happen! Don't you hear what I'm saying? Zac is my love. I have the life I want.' He stared at me and I went on more gently, 'What about your family? You have a son, and Eileen is going to have another baby soon.'

'Maybe she will—' Daniel clamped his lips together with a look of horror on his face.

'Maybe she will what?' But he shook his head and would not reply.

Sudden understanding flashed through me. I needed to remind myself of the sensitive man I'd once loved. 'Daniel, you need to listen to your own heart and conscience. There's nothing wrong with us, no matter what society says. You must be true to yourself. But you need to think of your family as well. You said you and Eileen are friends. Why don't you talk to her? You could find a way to be yourself without hurting others, and one day you'll meet someone you can really love.'

'That's easy for you to say! Don't tell me what to do.' The bitterness of his words smeared the air. 'You've just rejected me – don't you think I feel humiliated enough?'

I said, 'Please, Daniel—' but he banged his glass down on the table and walked out, knocking over his chair. He didn't look back.

I decided to get steaming drunk. I had a few gins and worked myself up into a distressed state that quickly became maudlin.

9 January 1948

Theo went to meet Daniel after work. I had a brisk walk with Pip then settled with a book, although I couldn't concentrate. The phone rang about 9pm and it was a slurry Teddy on the line, wanting to tell me how much he loves me. He was in a phone box near Charing Cross. I said, come home darling. I walked up to the tube and had the pleasure of seeing him trip over coming through the barrier. The woman behind fell on top of him, so I had to hide my laughter and disentangle them. Fortunately, she was understanding. He'd lost one of his gloves and when I asked where his scarf was, he looked blank before pulling it out of his pocket. I wrapped it round him and got him home, steadying him on the way. He decided to sing me our song. He kept in tune in spite of being blind drunk, but I had to shush him a few times.

When we got in, I started out to make coffee when I realised it was the bathroom he needed. I got him to the loo just in time for him to chuck up the contents of his stomach, mostly liquid. He's in bed now, with a bowl by his side and snoring, which he never does. He's going to be one sick Teddy tomorrow. Thank God he's home with me.

I don't remember much about getting home that night. I just know it was the drunkest I'd been in my life. The next morning, Zac brought me tea in bed and sat reading the paper while the room dipped and dived around me. Pip watched me as though to say, what's up with you? Around midday I started to feel human again. I ran a bath and Zac cooked me fried eggs. I looked at them doubtfully, my stomach did a backflip, but to my surprise I felt better after.

It was one of those dank winter days where it never gets above a half-light – constant drizzle and mist, and the street lights coming on early. I lay in Zac's arms on the sofa and told him everything. He asked if I had regrets and my answer was emphatic. I was wretched that Daniel was so unhappy, but Zac told me, 'Believe me, Teddy, queers can get a nasty introduction to our nature – it's not easy in this bloody society. You were his first love. He couldn't have asked for more. It was his decision to reject all that.'

He was quiet for a while, stroking my hair, then said, 'I hate to think of all this suffering, all this unhappiness, simply because we happen to be queer. It's so wrong. We just want to get on with our lives and find someone to love.' He saw my face. 'What is it?'

'I could have ended up like Daniel. I was also at the stage

of thinking I would lead a celibate life, that I'd never fit in anywhere. If you hadn't come along—'

But he said I had it all wrong. 'You're too brave. You faced up to that all on your own, with no one supporting you. You'd never take the coward's way out. Don't be unhappy, darling. I know Daniel's in a bad place now, but he can find the life he wants some day.'

Zac held me quietly. He knew I was troubled. After a while, a log shifted on the fire, the sparks flew up and I came out of my thoughts back to the present. We started recalling our fear and loneliness when we realised our identity. Zac voiced my own thoughts when he said, 'If someone had told me, when I was a scared schoolboy, that one day I'd be happy and living with the man I adore – well, I'd have bitten their arm off to get that.'

We went to the Heath before darkness descended. The copper beech was naked and shivering in the London fog. Pip bounded off, and we were standing quietly when a kestrel swooped down a few yards in front of us. I recalled the kestrel we'd seen on VE day, talking about our future life together. I saw Zac was remembering this too. We clasped hands and smiled at each other. Then we called Pip and went home. We didn't see anyone that weekend. A few days later, he loaded up the car and set off for Italy.

Zac's letters entertained me with lively stories about Rome, such as the time a tram was delayed because the driver insisted on finishing his coffee, or when the two men he thought were having an argument turned out to be amicably discussing football. I visited Alan, who'd returned to Cambridge University after becoming frustrated when his ideas for an electronic brain weren't taken forward by his work. I saw Ruth and Huw, and regularly went on the town with Anna and Claude, who called us the "three musketeers". We visited several queer pubs, with one, the Salisbury, becoming a favourite. We would have serious conversations, then be shrieking with laughter. I told them about Daniel, who slammed down the phone when he heard my voice.

Anna was sympathetic. 'How many more men and women have to suffer because of society's stupid prejudice? When will they realise this is a public scandal? We're not sick. We're not evil. We just love our own sex.'

I looked at her thoughtfully. 'There should be a way to help young people who realise they're queer.'

Claude snorted. 'Dream on, Theo.'

12

7 February 1948

Things are working out well. The housing manager said he had a small flat I could move into now. There's a better one in the same building but it isn't available yet and they're thinking of putting Theodore Lawder in there. I said brightly, I'm happy to take the smaller flat. It's absolutely fine – when I think of some of the dumps I've lived in! Theo's flat is two floors below, with two bedrooms and a decent balcony. The accommodation could not be better – no one to see us coming and going.

Rome is fascinating and chaotic. I've been walking the streets with Pip. There's some bomb damage, nothing like London or Bristol, but it doesn't look very different from the Roman ruins. You walk along a street and suddenly you're in a derelict amphitheatre or temple.

5 March 1948

The high point of any day is when I get a letter from Teddy. God, I miss him. After being my lover, he's my best friend. I miss our conversations, the way we can talk everything through. I miss our closeness, making love. Waking up with him – everything, really.

Work keeps me busy. The Americans are splashing money around, all gung-ho about stopping the communists. The coup in Czechoslovakia has created a few shockwaves. Italy is on its knees, financially and in every way. Well, in the end they were being hammered by the Allies and the Germans.

Pip still looks around for Teddy. This evening she put her paw on my lap while I was having a smoke on the balcony. She seemed to be asking, where's Theo? I said to her, not long now. Twenty more days till he comes. Not that I'm counting.

25 March 1948

I came out of our section to find Teddy with the deputy ambassador. Thankfully, my reflexes kicked in. We did the friendly handshake and chat expected of two friends. All the time my heart was pounding and I felt almost shy. It was agreed I'd take him back to his new flat later this afternoon. Don't really know how I got through the day. I couldn't concentrate. I was in a meeting with some Italian dignitaries when I got a strange look, and realised I'd been whistling under my breath.

Finally – I loaded his bags into the car and we set off. As soon as we were away from the villa we gripped each other's hand and said phew, but I had to keep my attention on the road – Italian traffic is crazy. We got his things inside, slammed the door and I grabbed him tight into my arms. Then I showed him round the flat.

He's sleeping now. I took him out for dinner, Pip trotting along proudly. We walked around the streets but really, we just wanted to get back here and make up for lost time. To have his skin next to mine, to breathe in his smell – what can be better than this?

28 March 1948

Oh, Teddy. You amazing, delectable piece of work.

My first thoughts and impressions when I got to Rome were all of Zac. We didn't come up for air too often in the first days. When that settled down, I started to get an idea of the place.

My office was like a palace and it often made me smile. Zionist bombs had destroyed the British embassy eighteen months earlier, so we were based in the Villa Wolkonsky. The building was saturated with marble, gilt and chandeliers – it

110

even boasted a mirrored ballroom. The huge garden had an aqueduct and ancient statues, pomegranate and persimmon trees. Zac worked in a separate building in the grounds, which was probably for the best. We had to pretend we were army friends and I worried I might do something to betray us. Once, I brushed some fluff off his jacket at a function and saw the security officer eyeing us suspiciously.

It was an eventful time to be in Italy. Newly established as a republic after abolishing the monarchy, the country was desperately poor. The CIA were crawling all over in the hope that Italy might provide stability in the wider region. We loved the vibrancy of the people and culture, and agreed that the food put our bland nursery diet to shame. Zac said with a glint, 'If I never see bloody spam again in my life, it'll be too soon.' I found Italians a complex, proud people. We would sit in outdoor cafes and watch them parading around in the evening. We loved their clothes and sense of style. Zac found a good tailor who made us suits and shirts, a luxury when clothes were still rationed in Britain.

19 April 1948

General relief with the election results. I can't wait to finish work. I keep my stuff upstairs, but we spend all our time in Teddy's flat. There's a real warmth in the sun now, the days are longer and so much to see and do.

1 September 1948

Quite often the locals look at us, Teddy with his leg and me with my burns, and ask, la guerra? It's a good way to share experiences – we were on different sides, but we all suffered.

I do find that Italian men can be unpleasant in the way they treat women. They whistle at them, make obscene suggestions, grab them.

111

I don't understand why so many "normal" men don't seem to want to spend time with women. They like to fuck them – so why not talk to them? I find it strange you would sleep with, let alone marry, someone whom intrinsically you don't like. I find most women are much nicer human beings than most men, although no one is nicer than my Teddy. If he were a woman, he'd be my best friend. But he's not, thank God – so I have the best of both worlds.

3 October 1948

The world balance is shifting quite radically. The Soviet Union is blockading Berlin. China's falling to the communists. Italy seems stable for now. I think there's more of a danger from organised crime – ingrained corruption reaching right to the top.

26 June 1949

We're in Positano to celebrate Teddy's birthday. When we got back this afternoon from a trip along the coast, I watched him make it through the traffic to join me at the cafe. With his sunglasses and blue linen shirt – he's bloody gorgeous. I can't believe the traffic didn't stop dead, the sun didn't bow down in the sky in admiration. Even after all these years, I look at him in amazed gratitude. My God, he's mine.

His hair has bleached in the sun so it reminds me of the young man I fell in love with. And now he's 32. Where did the years go? I want to stop time, drag back the ticking hand. I want us to stay forever where we are now, who we are. Life is perfect. I sometimes have a stab of fear it can't last.

On weekends or holidays, we'd load up the car and go as far as possible. Pip was a hit with everyone and my Italian improved rapidly. We went to Florence, Milan, up to the lakes, down to Naples and the Amalfi coast. We explored Pompeii and strolled through olive groves. Our work was demanding, and I had to do evening receptions, but it was something we got through so we could resume our Italian adventure. Zac said, 'It's as if we're on holiday as soon as we finish work.' We started going wider in the region: to Sicily, Sardinia, Malta. There was nothing we loved better than being on an open road with Pip, a map and no commitments.

We never consciously decided to stay away from England – it just worked out that way. The first Christmas we wanted to explore Italy; the second Christmas I was on duty cover at the embassy. And we couldn't always get our leave together. We had to play the charade that we were just friends, so why would we need the same time off for holidays? But our friends came to visit, so we didn't miss the most important thing at home.

Zac's mother had recently died from a stroke, and when Ruth came with Huw to visit, she told us how their father seemed much diminished and looked to Ruth for support. She felt resentful, and who could blame her – where was he as a father when they had needed him? He died of a heart attack the following year. The money from the house, which sold for a good price, was split between Zac and Ruth. Zac said, 'Consider it compensation for the hard time they gave us.'

Anna and Miriam came out twice, as did Claude. On Claude's first visit, I picked up something different about him. We were at dinner when he told us he was in love, declaring, 'Just when I'd accepted my life would be one of work, friendship and casual affairs – he came and found me.'

'Stop teasing, Claude! Tell us everything,' I demanded, smiling with delight.

'I met Jordi when he came with his sister and nephew for a consultation. I was doing my professional doctor bit with the boy so didn't notice him too much, apart from thinking he had a charming accent and seemed nice. Some days later, I was in the hospital cafe when he asked to join me. I assumed he'd want medical advice, because people are always asking me about their earache or bunions. But no, we just chatted. When I had to leave, he asked if he could see me again. That was the first time it occurred to me it might be something more.'

'Good God, that's not like you! You must be losing your grip,' said Zac with a grin.

'Indeed! Well, it went on from there. A drink in the pub, then I asked him round to dinner at my place. He ate my food and stayed the night. I thought, let's have fun while it lasts. But I soon realised he was someone special. Finally, at the ripe age of thirty-five, I've found someone to spend my life with.'

I put my hand on his. 'I'm so pleased for you, my dear.'

Zac was impatient. 'Come on, Claude. What's he like?'

Claude became quite lyrical. 'He's so kind, warm and funny. He has beautiful eyes. I always did have a weakness for – oh, just coffee for me,' as the waiter came over. He added, 'Jordi told me he knew right away that I was the one for him. Lucky me.'

'Where's he from?'

'Barcelona. He left when he was fourteen. His father was murdered in front of him during the civil war, and Jordi barely escaped with his life. He made it to England with his mother and sister. He says he won't return to Catalonia until Franco's dictatorship has ended.'

I noticed that Claude's occasional prickliness, the way he used sarcasm to keep people at a distance, had softened. He visited again the following year with Jordi. He said it was time we all met because we were the three most important people in his life.

5 March 1950

We took Pip for a walk in the Villa Borghese gardens. Some boys were hanging around, far too young and clearly on the rent scene. That was barely three weeks in my life, but it still fills me with shame and – well yes, I'd say panic. It was a scary, lonely time and I felt sickened afterwards.

I said nothing, but Teddy noticed. He's always so observant. He got me to talk about this as we walked around. I know he's right – I do find it hard to open up about my feelings. We gave the boys some money, saying get yourselves a meal and a place to sleep tonight. I hope they'll be safe.

28 May 1950

This is a year of special anniversaries. It's ten years since I first kissed Theo on the beach at Dunkirk.

I made sure I was near him whenever we were in battle. Men around us died, but we seemed to have luck. And then, waiting for rescue in the horror of Dunkirk, I saw him go down. His leg was shattered and blood poured from a wound above his hip. He was fading fast, turning into a ghost in front of me. There was nothing I could do. I wanted to scream and howl. I wanted to take him in my arms, tell him how much I loved him, make him better again.

That last dawn, I was watching over him, everyone around us asleep. He opened his eyes and for a beat in time we were the only two people in the world. The light was crystalline and I could see every detail of his dead-white skin, the dark circles under his eyes, the bloodstains on his uniform. It was clear he was near death. I kissed him and he smiled. His lips were so soft and somehow, in spite of being filthy and with a wound starting to smell, his breath so sweet. Just one chaste kiss – but for all the affairs I'd had, no other kiss came close to matching it. Until we kissed again. Hours later, he was on a boat back to England and I was in the burning water with men dying around me.

It seemed an eternity before I found him again. I got myself into a state, convinced he was dead. Then some angel nurse answered the phone one day and said, yes, we have a Sergeant Lawder here.

I was in despair for many weeks after Dunkirk, but it all started from there. At the time it felt like the end of everything – but actually it was the beginning.

Zac and I celebrated our tenth anniversary in Florence. We talked about getting wedding rings for the occasion, but knew we had to be realistic. Our rings would be noticed in the worst possible way – we would get stares and questions. I had decided I would not deny my sexuality, or my love for Zac, if someone asked me directly. It felt wrong to lie about something so fundamentally true.

But he said I was too idealistic. If society fought dirty, we needed to do the same, including lying as necessary. Otherwise, we would lose our jobs – we'd go to prison. Or worse. 'People have died because they're queer. This isn't some philosophical debate, Teddy – it's our lives.'

It had become second nature by then. Don't talk about my private life too much; don't say "we"; deflect questions about girlfriends or marriage; behave in public as though we are just friends. Be constantly watchful and on guard. Control my feelings, how we look at each other. Always pretend, pretend, pretend. I often felt exhausted when we got home, depleted by the need to maintain the masquerade. We could only be ourselves when we were together or with our closest friends.

It got harder as time went by, not easier. In the first few years, our love was new and exciting. The outside world could go to hell. But as our relationship became the central core to our lives – the essence and catalyst for all we did and felt – the disconnect between my private and public life, the denial of the most important thing in the world, became so huge it felt unbridgeable. And it took a toll on us.

We reluctantly decided to get individual rings and placed them on our right ring fingers. We toasted each other with such joy and pride about what we had achieved, against all the odds.

8 October 1950

Autumn is my favourite season. That's something I miss about England. I think nowhere are the seasons more beautiful than there. Many people prefer spring. But autumn will always be associated for me with the beginning of a new life, hopefulness and deep happiness.

24 November 1950

Ten years with Teddy. What a gift. Words I never once dreamed I would write. I thought in the beginning I could not love him more, but, bloody hell, I was wrong. Finding each other was a life-changing moment. Anything good I've done since then, anything worthwhile about me, has come from him. I still can't quite believe I deserve this happiness. I don't know what will happen in the future. But this much I know – no one can take this away from me. The best years of my life.

Just before our last Christmas in Rome, Ruth wrote to say she was pregnant. That confirmed it was the right time to go home. Our double life had become harder to maintain. I was aware of questioning glances from people at work whenever Zac and I were together. When I walked into a room, the conversation would stop abruptly. Perhaps I was imagining it. Occasionally, we bumped into colleagues when we were out. They'd look at us together and I would see their thoughts as clearly as if they were fiery letters written across the sky. We'd hear about a work social event we hadn't been invited to, that sort of thing.

One day, the ambassador called me in and began to interrogate me. Did I have a girlfriend, because most men my age had settled down by now? I was rigid with anger – *that's none of your bloody business* – but did my best to hide it. I trotted out the tired line about being close friends with Anna, but my heart wasn't in it. In London, I left work and went home to my private life. Overseas, it was too much of a fishbowl.

'You appear to be great friends with Bonneval,' observed the ambassador with a sour face.

I responded snappily, 'Yes. I've known him since the army and he saved my life. Is something wrong here?' He looked surprised, no doubt unaccustomed to an insignificant Second Secretary talking back to him, and dismissed me.

When I told Zac that evening, his face tightened. 'Be careful, Teddy. I don't want your career to be affected.'

'Screw the lot of them. You're more important than any job.'

We were more careful after that. As much as I detested the furtiveness, and the accompanying sense of shame, I would not allow anything to threaten my relationship with Zac. But it seemed our charmed life had been shattered. We were walking home one evening when a group of boys followed us, shouting out. One of them threw a stone that landed on my back. Zac glared and asked what they were saying.

'They're calling us "fags".'

'Well, we're not going to be hounded on the street by snotty-nosed brats,' he declared.

We walked towards them. There was a certain bleak comedy in watching the skirmish between group swagger and fear on their faces. Their braggadocio turned and fled, and so did they.

When we got home, one of Zac's dark moods descended. I had come to loathe the way he froze me out and looked at me with dead eyes. He changed into another person completely. He went up to his flat and wouldn't answer when I knocked on his door. *Damn him and his bloody moods.* He crept into my bed in the middle of the night, Zac again.

I said to him the next morning, 'You mustn't let this thing rule you, Zac. Why can't you talk to me?'

'Oh, Teddy. I feel such despair and I hate myself. I know it affects you. I just can't seem to control it.' He agreed he'd talk to me the next time it happened.

Zac was waiting for me at Dover when I got back just before Easter. It was good to be home. Meat rationing was still in force, and the food compared poorly to Italy. But London looked more prosperous and there was a greater selection of goods in the shops. We found some Italian restaurants and coffee bars in Soho (Italy had ruined for us the brown liquid that passed for coffee in England). I caught up with my friends and my mother. Ruth and Huw had bought a small house in Richmond, and it was lovely to see her pregnant and happy.

Our relationship was solid. I thought we would survive anything life threw at us, because of our love. I thought nothing in the outside world could break us. I was too smug.

1951–1956: I'm terrified their hatred will destroy our love

13

On my return to London, Zac told me there was a Russian spy in the FO. SIS suspicions were focused on one man, but his name, Donald Maclean, meant nothing to me. While it was shocking to think one of my colleagues could betray us, it seemed fantastically unreal, like something out of a low-budget movie. I couldn't resist making enquiries when I saw a friend who worked in American Department. I bought him a coffee and asked what Maclean was like. Michael told me he was the typical FO high-flier: charming, Oxbridge educated. But lately, his behaviour had changed. He lost his temper easily and Michael noticed his hands would often shake. He thought Maclean had some sort of illness – 'Either that,' Michael said with a laugh, 'or he's a raging alcoholic.'

When I told Zac that evening, he narrowed his eyes at me. 'You bloody idiot, Theo. You're blundering around like an amateur. Do you think this is some sort of a game?'

'I just asked a few questions, Zac. I didn't see the harm—'

'And when it's confirmed Maclean's a traitor, and they find out you were asking about him? They'll know I talked to you about it!'

That hadn't occurred to me and I apologised. I knew from experience he took a while to calm down when he lost his temper, so I left him alone. He came to me after some hours and said with a rueful smile, 'I'm sorry I called you an idiot, darling. You're nothing of the sort.' We hugged and all was well.

I had moved on promotion to United Nations Department and started grappling with the intricacies of UN law. Anna brought me up to date on work gossip and we fondly remembered Ernest Bevin, who had recently died. One day, she had a satisfied expression when we met for lunch. 'Guess what, Theo? Burgess has been sent home from Washington in disgrace.'

'About time! What did he do?'

'There are stories going around about his drunken behaviour and the various Americans he insulted. They say he picked up multiple speeding fines, even that he attacked a traffic warden. Surely, now he's had it. What more does he need to do for the FO to sack him?'

When I told Zac that evening, he was quiet for a while. 'There's something going on here I don't like. Promise me you won't go anywhere near Maclean or Burgess.'

I laughed and replied, 'Obviously, I want nothing to do with that man.'

'Teddy, this is no joke.' His voice was grim. I looked at him, surprised. 'Don't you know those two are great friends from Cambridge?' That was when it stopped feeling like a game.

15 May 1951

I've got a bad feeling about work. I keep saying we should bring the interview forward. Don't they realise he might have been warned? But they just say they need to prepare the evidence. I'm starting to wonder if this goes a lot wider. Perhaps I'm overreacting – I bloody hope so. I don't want to think I'm somehow in a nest of vipers. At least, in the war, it was a case of people shooting at you or bombing you. That way you knew where you were.

I did see Burgess once. Anna and I came down Cockpit Steps after lunch and spotted him walking past on Birdcage Walk. He didn't look well – his face was puffy and his eyes bloodshot. He threw us a poisonous glance and pointedly turned his head away. His companion, a handsome fair-haired man, didn't seem to notice.

Anna muttered, 'Bastard!'

I gave her arm a squeeze, asking, 'Who's the man with him?'

'That's Maclean, the head of American Department.' I changed the subject, but felt a jolt of apprehension. I knew Zac was in the team planning to interview Maclean.

The following weekend, we went to our cottage on the south coast, which we now rented full-time. We spoke to one of the other weekend sailors about buying his boat, a small yacht with wooden trimming. After some friendly haggling, we shook hands on a good deal. We decided to call the boat *Argo*, the name Zac had given his boyhood dinghy. He said, with a reminiscent smile, 'That was the time I started reading about Ancient Greece.'

On the drive back to London we planned future sailing trips. The phone rang when we got home and I found Zac afterwards standing in the garden in the dissolving light, lost in thought. I put my hand on his shoulder, asking, 'What is it?'

He stared at me soberly. 'Maclean and Burgess have both left England. No one knows where they are. They're probably already in Russia.'

I didn't know what to say. The whole thing seemed unreal.

Never, in my wildest speculation, had I thought something like this could happen. Zac was frowning. 'This means they've been tipped off by someone in my work. And Burgess has reason to hate us both.'

11 June 1951

I feel I've been caught up in a game of double-cross. We're all studying each other covertly, trying to work out who can't be trusted. On one level, it's an interesting conundrum; on another level, I just want out. I've had my doubts about this job all along. The newspapers are full of the story and the boss is on the rampage. All thanks to those treacherous little shits.

The press ran sensational stories for weeks about the "missing diplomats". They became obsessed with the fact Burgess was queer and the "danger" of homosexuals and spies. They were like a pack of ravening dogs on the scent, and we were the prey. It was bewildering how suddenly the atmosphere at the FO altered. I'd taken for granted we were all dedicated and worked there for the same reason. Few checks were done – we'd been taken on trust. Anna said gloomily, 'I feel we're all watching each other now.'

It still seemed a minor issue that summer. The major event was Ruth becoming a mother. We made it to the hospital soon after she gave birth to Sian. I felt so moved, holding this new human being. I handed her over to Zac and saw emotions passing like clouds over his face: a sort of astonishment, then a look of love and hope.

1 July 1951

Ruth's baby came into the world yesterday and all is well. It affects me more than I'd expected. I wasn't keen when Teddy handed Sian over to me – babies have never been my thing. But I was amazed by a deep surge of love. She was screwing up her face and looking around. I had a sense of how little and vulnerable she is and that I'd do anything to protect her. My little sister – a mother. And me, an uncle – bloody hell. It feels good.

I visited Alan who was working in the university at Manchester and had bought a house. 'All I need now,' he said with a shy smile, 'is someone to share it with.' But our weekends were mostly divided between sailing *Argo* and helping with Sian. We often took her out so Ruth could have a break and catch up on sleep. One afternoon, we were pushing her pram by the river when a man cycled past and snarled, 'Dirty faggots.' A weariness dragged at my spirit. Why couldn't we live in peace?

But not much disturbed our happiness then. We all agreed Sian was the most beautiful baby in the world. I proudly agreed to be her godfather.

28 July 1951

For me, all babies are basically a blank sheet of paper, a smelly bundle of piss and poo, but Teddy loves to spend time with Sian. I've been wondering if he misses not having his own children. He often watches children with a soft look on his face. He can't have this. He can't be a father. Well, he could have taken Daniel's option and gone for a sham marriage, I suppose.

He asked me tonight what's up. Come on Zac, I know you're brooding about something. I can't hide anything from him. He said straight away he's never wanted to be a father. He likes to observe how children experience the world; he loves their innocence and natural happiness, that's all. He added, and I'm not a daddy to Pip either –

she's a clever dog who chooses to live with us. I had to laugh. He was referring to a guy we met in a pub who said his dogs were his babies. I must have had a nauseated look without realising it. Teddy was in fits afterwards.

I can see he means it, so that's set my mind at ease. I'd hate to think he's yearning for something I can't give him.

5 August 1951

It's all kicking off at work. Kim Philby's been forced to resign after it became clear he tipped off Maclean and Burgess. We all thought Philby was headed for the top. It's bizarre to think of those three as Russian spies. They're from such privileged backgrounds, for God's sake. The common thread seems to be Cambridge – there must have been a hell of a recruitment operation. I can't help thinking: who's next? The papers are hysterical. At least they can't say he was queer too.

Given I have this huge secret to hide, should I just cut my losses and run? Teddy says we can live on his salary and our savings. But I can't see myself doing nothing. I want to work. What else would I do? It's a bit bloody late for me – I'm 37 now and I've hardly had a brilliant career to date.

6 November 1951

Philby's still proclaiming his innocence. They're interviewing everyone. I had no problem answering questions about Philby. Then they got onto Burgess. Why was I asking about him in '47? I'd expected that and said I'd heard he was a loose cannon, so made a few enquiries, no more than that. They asked for FO names but didn't seem aware of Teddy, thank God.

I can't help feeling this isn't the end of it. I'm a queer working in a place where it's seen as a major liability. They're introducing full vetting and the message is clear – queers are not suitable material for the service. Apparently we're unstable, defective. Do I jump now, or wait until I'm pushed? But I fear Teddy will be in a similar situation in the FO. I think I need to hang on for now.

In February, everything I was reading in the papers, or hearing from our friends, coalesced in a sickening way when Alan was charged with gross indecency.

When I told Zac, the colour drained from his face and he immediately said, 'He won't survive prison. It will kill him.' Of course, those were my own thoughts. When Zac saw my distress, he pulled me into his arms and kissed me consolingly. 'Maybe he'll be let off with a caution.'

We drove up to Manchester over Easter. Alan had pleaded guilty on the recommendation of his solicitor. He was bitter about the fact he'd lost his security clearance and couldn't continue his government work, but said defiantly, 'I've done nothing wrong. Loving another man doesn't make me a criminal, whatever the law says.'

Unfortunately, he'd chosen a nasty creep to sleep with, whose friend ended up robbing him. Alan reported the crime to the police. Zac gave an involuntary shake of his head at that, and I knew what he was thinking – that Alan and I were hopelessly naive, believing we had a right to the same laws as anyone else. The court had given Alan two options: a prison sentence, or injections of female hormones to "reduce sexual urges". What a choice: how would you like us to destroy your life, Mr Turing?

Alan had chosen the injections. I couldn't stop myself blurting, 'Oh, no!'

He was philosophical. 'I have to take them for a year, but the effect will be temporary. Then I can get on with my life. Don't look so upset, Theo. It'll be a good opportunity to dedicate myself to work. Perhaps, now, I'll learn not to waste my energies on young men who don't deserve it.' I couldn't disagree with this last sentiment, but an uneasy foreboding gripped me.

In the car going home, Zac scowled at the road and crunched the gears. Sitting silently by him, distraught and heartsick, my soul shivered in sudden understanding. *This is how it's going to be for the rest of our lives. Always living in the shadows, ashamed of who we are. Thank God I have Zac and our happy life.*

13 June 1952

Things are ticking over at work, but I'm holding my breath. I'm on my guard, more aware of the need to protect myself and Teddy against the world. This business with Alan has sickened us.

The papers are coming out with vicious crap. Section 11: gross indecency – we're getting very familiar with it. One of the police tricks is to hang around public toilets waiting for men who are cottaging. Although, from what I hear, a lot of the arrests are entrapment operations and they've done nothing. Well, we're guilty of being queer, whether or not we actually do anything. I've warned Teddy we must stay out of public toilets. Another ploy is to go through the address book of men they've arrested and pull in everyone for questioning. Or they look for love letters. Maybe this journal isn't safe?

I do worry that Teddy's too trusting. His sweetness gets under my skin in a way no other man could, but I fear he won't sense when he's in danger. Always he approaches life expecting to find nice people – there are those who would take advantage of that. But then I tell myself, he also has a steel and strength about him. He's no pushover.

I don't want to feel like this – constantly on the alert, looking over my shoulder, feeling paranoid. We're not in some bloody war, for God's sake. We're not the enemy. It's just our lives.

127

14

We all noticed a change in public attitudes at that time. Homosexuals had never been accepted, but we could mostly survive, sidling around the margins of life, as long as we were careful and didn't draw attention to ourselves. But now we felt under siege, like exiles in our own country. We were called "evil" and treated as a pernicious influence on society. One newspaper spoke of finding a "final solution" to the problems we posed. The papers were fixated with queers and spies, particularly if the two aspects coincided.

When we were on the street, I sometimes saw hatred jumping off the faces of people passing us. A few would come up to inform us what repulsive blots on humanity we were, usually in graphic language. I was always shaken after these incidents, but I'd laugh it off for Zac's sake. It was second nature for us to be watchful, but now we took this to new lengths. We mostly met our friends in our homes, or in the safe queer pubs. We learned which places tended to be raided by the police and which areas were dangerous. Public toilets were to be avoided as much as possible.

It became the main topic of conversation whenever we met our friends. One evening, over at Claude's for dinner, Jordi's usual warm manner was strained. He'd been harassed by the police in Soho that day and said, 'There seems to be a programme to hunt us down, as if we are rats. It reminds me of the fascists in Spain.'

Claude drawled, 'Let's face it, we've never been flavour of the month. But it isn't a crime in some countries. We could all move to France – or what about Switzerland? We could take up yodelling as a hobby. We might be bored, but at least we'll be legal. What do you think, Zac? After all, before Theo, you spent most of your time anywhere but England.'

'We nearly died to protect this country. This is our home. Why should we be forced out?' Zac's response was emphatic and I was relieved. I'd loved our time in Italy and hoped to have more postings abroad, but the thought of being permanently exiled from England left me hollow with gloom.

Each time I visited Alan, my distress increased. The hormones were ravaging his body. He was a long-distance runner and had always been so healthy. Now, he was bloated, his body changing shape. One day in the winter, he was in despair. 'Look, Theo. I have breasts, for God's sake.' He pulled up his jumper to show me. 'I don't have any sexual desire and I hate it. Sex is an essential part of how we express ourselves. I have less creativity without it.'

I wished I could offer some solution, but it seemed he was trapped on this nightmare journey with no exit sign. All I could do was listen and offer my undying friendship.

17 December 1952

I collected Teddy from the station after another visit to Alan. It's been one of those days with a thick fog you can barely see through. It all just seems to add to the misery. Today, he was almost in tears. He told me of the effect of the hormones on Alan, went over and over what options he had, how hopeless the whole mess is.

When I see him with such pain in his eyes and I can't do anything to make it better – it kills me. He has such an expressive face; he shows his emotions so clearly. More than anything I love his happy smile. It lights up the sky. But there's too much sadness right now.

These are nasty times. The other day, someone spat at us in the street. I cleaned it off our shoes with a hanky, threw it in the bin and we went on our way. The newspapers are whipping up a storm. Every week there are reports of arrests and court cases. We're starting to hear of suicides.

I often find myself panicking. What if it happens to Teddy? He's so sensitive – it could destroy him. If I think of him in prison, I feel physically sick. These images come into my head and I can't stop them. I'd do anything to protect him, but far too much is outside my control. I'd like to surround him with a magic shield so he's never hurt, never in danger. I know he can look after himself. But it causes me a lot of anxiety.

We all heard about friends and acquaintances being attacked on the streets. Occasionally a group of toughs would storm into a pub and throw a few chairs and punches about. Zac and I had a close call once, when we were surrounded by men who started with the usual name calling. We stood shoulder to shoulder, getting ready for the attack, when someone shouted, 'Police!' and they scattered. We didn't wait; we got out quickly ourselves. I used to think the police were there to protect the public, but now I knew better. Some citizens had more rights than others.

That was the time I changed my attitude towards effeminate men. I had always resisted being put in a box marked "queer", and believed they stunted themselves by making their nature the sum total of who they were. But I started appreciating why you might huddle with others of the same kind for protection; why you might exaggerate your identity in a defiant response to the hatred. They suffered the bulk of harassment and beatings. I began to understand the courage they showed by being openly camp.

One evening, I was in the Salisbury waiting for Zac when an effeminate man sat down next to me. He was around fifty, with make-up and a lavender rinse in his hair, wearing an exquisite scarf and jewellery. I would once have politely frozen him out – but I saw a keen intelligence in his eyes. We started talking and Francis described his difficulty in holding down a job due to his appearance.

'Why don't you compromise if it causes you so many problems?'

Francis responded, 'I will, when society does the same to me.' He added, 'I'm not ashamed of who I am. I'm not a criminal. I've never involved minors or unwilling partners. I'm not going to hide away.'

Just then, Zac arrived and looked around for me. Francis gave me a warm smile. 'Ah, you have your own Prince Charming! No more than you deserve.' I made introductions and, as I turned to go, Francis put his hand on my arm. 'You two, look after each other. You have something special.' It reminded me of the day Alan had said that to us.

I looked out for Francis after that. I discovered that he loved reading and the theatre. I was glad to count him as a friend. We all started talking more readily to each other in the queer pubs. We would watch out for each other on the streets as well. There was a sense of us against the world.

Not everything was grim. Alan finished the injections and took himself off to Corfu for a holiday that summer, returning tanned and seemingly tranquil. Sian was the most delightful child. And my mother had become increasingly close to Zac. We would take her out for the day, to a restaurant or to the theatre. She attended all my choir concerts. I'd look over and see her sitting with Zac, her grey head bent towards his dark one as they chatted, and think with relief how far we had come.

But Zac's bleak moods visited him more frequently. I'd often see him with a frown or a tense expression. When I asked what was wrong, he'd say, 'Nothing,' and change the subject. He would snap at me, although he always apologised afterwards. I could not doubt his love – he made this very clear to me, if sometimes in a rather desperate way. I just knew that, increasingly, he was in a dark place.

31 December 1953

We've just come back from a party at Claude and Jordi's flat. Very sedate compared to the old days. Now we sit around and talk, drink but not too much, and go home with the same person. But I did manage to get some sexy slow dancing with my Teddy. He has the same effect on me as ever.

I'm not sorry to see this year finish. It's been an unpleasant one for us queers. Here's hoping '54 will be better.

I said to Zac early on, 'This is going to be a good year, you'll see.'

Ruth's second child, a boy named David Zachary, arrived in the spring. Ruth again asked me to be his godfather. Being part of these children's lives was important for us. To have this core of loving family and friends was the best antidote to the public hate.

Not long after, we went to the theatre with Huw and Ruth. It was her first night out, away from the children, in a long time. We chatted afterwards on the street while Huw fetched the car. I noticed a couple of men glaring at us and tried to ignore them. Then they walked past and said loudly, 'Fucking perverts.'

Ruth was enraged and shouted, 'You pathetic bastards!' Zac had to grab her arm to stop her going after them. But she seemed more shocked by our reaction. We winced, but I suppose she saw a resigned acceptance on our faces. She asked, 'This has happened to you before, hasn't it?'

Zac said quietly, 'Best to leave it alone, Ruthie.'

She nodded, looking at us sadly. She told me later she often wrote to the newspapers saying the persecution of homosexuals was disgraceful, but her letters were never published.

At Easter we drove up to see Alan. The effects of the injections had finally subsided, and his mood was optimistic. As ever, his focus was his work. We took him out to lunch and he tried to explain quantum mechanics, with limited success. He spoke of his determination not to let the ongoing police surveillance affect him. We discussed a recent high-profile trial of several men for gross indecency, and the increasing venom against us. Alan retorted, 'Every homosexual they send to prison is a political prisoner. I accept who I am. I refuse to hide it. The law won't stop me.'

But when we were due to leave in the late afternoon, his mood seemed to dip. He hugged us both tightly. 'You two, promise me you'll always look after each other.' The urgency in his voice startled me.

Zac said, 'We promise you, Alan.'

I kissed him on the cheek. 'Don't forget I'm always here, my dear. I'll always be your friend. Ring me any time you want to talk, or come and stay with us. You know you have an open invitation.'

His smile seemed wistful. I reminded him he'd agreed to come to London for a joint birthday celebration in June, and he said, 'I won't forget, my dear Theo.'

When I looked back at him, he was waving to us from his front door cheerfully enough.

30 April 1954

Now I'm 40. I'm middle-aged. We've had a quiet celebration at home. Teddy gave me a beautiful writing desk, one I'd been hankering after in a second-hand shop. I've been up and down recently, but I feel mellow today, thank God. I hate my bloody moods and I know he suffers with them.

When I look at my life, I have nothing to complain about and much to be thankful for. Work hasn't turned out the way I hoped, but I've accepted it's the part of my life where I'm never going to achieve much. Getting thrown out of home, and not finishing my education, completely bitched up my options. I've fallen into work opportunities ever since, some of them better than others.

Everything else, however, is an absolute miracle. And it all comes from Teddy and the life I have with him. God bless Theo. Sometimes I think he's an angel who's come down to live with me on earth. My own fair-haired sexy angel. I'll have much more of the same, thank you.

We spent the June bank holiday weekend on the south coast. We ate fish and chips with our legs dangling on the pier. Zac visibly relaxed. We made love with the sun pouring into our bedroom. I can still see him laughing up at me, his naked body luminous in the pool of light. On the Monday, the weather turned cool and choppy out on the water, but we sailed along the coast for hours, peaceful and absorbed, unaware of the approaching onslaught.

15

9 June 1954

I overheard at work this afternoon that Alan has been found dead at home. My colleagues thought it was hilarious, joking that at least one queer had the sense to kill himself. I went out to find an early edition of the paper. Sure enough, a small paragraph said Alan Turing was found dead in Manchester yesterday by his housekeeper. I rang Teddy immediately but he was in a meeting all afternoon. I couldn't concentrate, so came home. I don't care what my work thinks. Screw them.

I was in a state, pacing up and down, when I heard his key in the door. He came in with his happy face. Then he saw my expression and froze. But he didn't guess – he said, is it my mother? I had to tell him. All he said at first was: no, no, no. No.

He's sleeping now. He was inconsolable, although I did my best. I held him and we wept together. He's heartbroken to think of his friend being in such pain that he would kill himself. Why didn't he ring me? he kept asking. I didn't remind him we were out sailing all day Monday. We'll never know if Alan tried to call.

For now, all I care about is that Teddy's crying his eyes out for a decent man who didn't deserve to die. And I care about Alan, very much. When I think what he did during the war, the work he's been doing – we need men like him on this earth. Perhaps he was too good to survive in this rotten world.

10 June 1954

We didn't go to work today. We went for a long walk on the Heath and

135

sat under the copper beech talking about Alan. Pip usually races around, but today she sat next to Teddy, putting her head on his knee. He's calmer, but still desolate. At one point, he looked at me and asked, why do they hate us so much, Zac? What have we done to them? And I couldn't reply.

We've had a few phone calls with Alan's friends. They're all distraught – no one saw this coming. It seems he killed himself by taking poison, probably cyanide; he made a comment once about cyanide being quick. He didn't leave a note.

12 June 1954

Alan's body was cremated today in Woking. His mother is apparently saying it was an experiment gone wrong. If that gives her consolation, who are we to say differently? We spent the day remembering Alan – his funny eccentricities, his brilliant mind, his goodness. We want to remember this, remember the good times. Teddy can't understand why Alan did this when he'd seemed more cheerful lately. I suppose we'll never know. Perhaps something happened to suddenly bring him down, and it felt worse after he'd been happy. Perhaps he just lost all hope his life would get better. I know the way the police kept on watching him was a form of torture.

I need to be strong for Teddy, but I can't control what's in the outside world. The thought that he might go through a similar ordeal fills me with horror.

26 June 1954

Teddy's 37th birthday today, but it's not a day for celebration. He'd planned to have a joint party here with Alan, and all he's been able to think of today is that Alan is dead. I gave him Bach's Well-Tempered Clavier, something I know he wanted. He thanked me with a kiss, but he has such sadness in his eyes.

Alan's death devastated me. The thought of my gentle friend feeling so desperate, and the terrible injustice he suffered, tormented me for a long time. I don't know what I would have done without Zac when it first happened. He supported me, let me cry and talk it over repeatedly.

And yet – that was the time when we started to slowly drift apart.

Up to then, we'd always dealt with problems together. I'd taken for granted just how easy and right it felt living with Zac. But this time, we weren't united as we'd always been before. I was aware that Zac had closed down, but I was too wrapped up in my grief to make him talk. We both had worries and fears we kept from each other. And once you begin, it's easy to go on like that – not communicating, keeping things back.

It was imperceptible at first, but by the winter I realised that Zac had changed – a lot. His black moods took up lodging in our home. He stopped going to his fencing club and didn't want to see our friends. He'd always been a restless sleeper, troubled by the occasional nightmare – but now this was happening most nights. He would often be irritable and suspicious, or fret over things. It was so unlike him. Always his generosity of spirit, his loving kindness, had been fundamental to his character.

Sometimes he'd be the same Zac as ever. We'd have good weeks; then we'd have good days. When his mood lifted, I was overjoyed. We'd talk and make love, and all would be well. I became his shadow, basking in the light of the Zac I loved, before the tenebrosity reclaimed him. But increasingly he was morose, his eyes as bare as a blasted landscape.

6 January 1955

I was half expecting this. I got home to find a hand-delivered letter with my name and address on it. The note is short. 'WE KNOW YOU ARE SICK FAGOTS. YOU NEED TO PAY UP OR YOU WILL GET A VISIT FROM THE POLISE.' Then giving details how I should pay £200.

There's no point upsetting Theo with this. I have no intention of giving into blackmail. But where does it go from here? Why do I feel the spelling mistakes are intentional, and that it's someone at my work? Or is that me being paranoid? Yet again I'm assailed with thoughts of Theo arrested, in prison being attacked and raped, his career in ruins – and it lacerates me.

I don't know why these images keep coming into my brain – I can't seem to stop them. Much of the time I have this sense of looming disaster. I wake up with my heart pounding, gasping for air. I don't want to feel like this, but I can't control it. I know I'm offhand with Theo. I know I'm terse and irritable. I love him more than ever. He's all I ever want. But I can't seem to show it. I know I'm being a miserable sod. What the fuck is wrong with me?

At the end of January, I found a handwritten envelope addressed to Zac. I was so worried about him by then, I decided to open it. To my horror, I saw that it was a crude blackmail attempt, describing the consequences if he didn't pay up. When Zac got home, I showed it to him. He silently went to his desk and took out another letter. I read it dolefully.

'Why didn't you tell me when it first arrived?' He didn't answer. I lost my patience and yelled at him, 'For God's sake, talk to me, Zac! What's going on?'

He shook his head, not looking at me. I shouted some more and slammed up to the spare room. I could hear Zac going into our bedroom. I was wretched. What had happened to our happy life? It was fast retreating in the rear-view mirror.

Just then, I could hear Alan's voice, saying: promise me

you'll always look after each other. *What am I doing? This is my beloved man. He needs my support.* I went into our bedroom to find Zac sitting on the bed, staring expressionlessly at the wall. 'Darling, I'm sorry I shouted at you. Can we discuss this?'

He made an effort to talk, his voice creaky and dragging. We agreed we wouldn't pay up. The idea was obscene. When the next letter arrived, we threw it on the fire.

I didn't want to worry Ruth, who had her hands full with the children, and I didn't talk to Claude because he was Zac's friend first. Anna's support kept me going. She wasted no time in getting to the point, after a dinner at our place. 'My God, Theo, what's going on? You both look miserable, and Zac seems so changed. Please tell me you're not splitting up?'

I shook my head violently. Gradually, it all came out – how Zac had altered over the last months so he seemed almost a different person; the blackmail letters; my fear I might lose him. I knew after that I could always talk to her. She was concerned, she tried to advise me, but I couldn't see any way out other than just hanging on and loving him.

I'd expected to hear more from the blackmailers, so it was not a surprise when we arrived home one evening to find the glass pane in our front door had been smashed. Monica came out to tell us she'd heard a noise and Pip barking madly. She'd yelled at a man trying to get into our front door, who ran off. She added that she hadn't called the police, and looked at us enquiringly. I said, 'Thank you for being such a good neighbour. I don't think they need to be called.' She nodded. I was pretty sure she understood why that was. We found a brick lying on the hallway floor along with the broken glass, and cleared it up in silence.

The following evening, two policemen came to our house, asking, 'Does Zachary Bonneval live here?'

It was one of the rare days when Zac was his old self. I watched from the kitchen door as he put on his best army officer act. 'What seems to be the matter, constable?'

They'd received a report of a burglary and wanted to investigate. Fortunately, we'd already replaced the glass. Zac replied calmly, 'Of course we haven't been burgled. Wouldn't we know if that had happened? We haven't reported any crime.'

There was a stand-off at the door. The police tried to push past Zac, who stood, immovable. 'It's not convenient for you to come in. I'm sorry someone has sent you on a wild goose chase. I'm sure you have much better things to do with your time.'

This went on for several minutes. One policeman stared at me and asked, 'What's the name of your friend?'

'Look, you're overstepping the mark. We've had no burglary. There's been no crime. You don't have the right to come onto my premises without my permission.'

I held my breath. *Don't lose your temper, Zac. They'll arrest you if they don't like your tone.* The gods must have been watching over us, because the police gave up and left.

Zac closed the door and looked at me grimly. 'If they'd come in, we'd have had it. They would have seen we share a bedroom and we'd be done for gross indecency.' We knew that was how it had started with Alan and a lot of other cases.

That was when Zac decided he would leave his job. He told me he thought it was someone at work sending the blackmail letters. I couldn't see it – I thought it was part of his burgeoning paranoia. Perhaps it was a coincidence, but we didn't get further letters or visits from the police. In that, at least, we had luck.

3 March 1955

I handed in my notice today. I'm due to be vetted next month. What with that and the blackmail letters, my time's obviously up. So, here I am. An unemployed failure soon to turn 41. And on the point of driving away the man I adore because of my bloody moods. Which I can't seem to control.

When will this stop? Is it just going to go on and on? Sometimes I'm paralysed with guilt. I was so determined to make Theo mine, and now I've put him in this situation where he's hounded and persecuted. Perhaps he had the right idea after all – live a celibate life, under the radar. At least then he wouldn't have this viciousness seeping into every part of our lives. I'm terrified their hatred will destroy our love – that it will poison everything good and decent we have.

But the thought of not having him in my life is unbearable. I'm too selfish to let him go. I can't give up on him. He'll have to give up on me.

16

I'd hoped that Zac's decision to leave the SIS would improve his mental state. In fact, that was when the accelerating momentum of his decline turned into an avalanche. He would spend hours not speaking. He lost interest in food and drank too much. One day, I realised we hadn't had sex for weeks. Making love had always come easily for us, a treasured connection – but not now. I started noticing other disturbing changes. Previously so fastidious with his appearance, he would wear the same clothes for days. He'd forget to comb his hair.

I wasn't in great shape myself. I went through the days in a state of dread. I feared he would leave me, or harm himself. I longed for the old Zac, the real Zac. But I could still mostly see love in his eyes, along with a silent scream of despair.

One evening, after he'd spent several hours unspeaking, unmoving, he said suddenly, 'Don't leave me, Theo.'

I held him close. 'I'll never leave you, darling. You're my man. I'm with you until death.' I just wanted us to get through this. But I didn't understand. I still thought he could snap out of this thing that held him prisoner.

A new play in the West End was all the rage, and I bought tickets. Zac shrugged listlessly and came with me. The play was disappointing – tired jokes about who slept in whose bed. He sat through it without raising a smile. I was determined to continue with my plan to shake him out of his misery, so made him come to our queer pub afterwards. Always, Zac had been the more sociable one. I was shyer, but he could start up a conversation with just about anyone. He'd always been interested in people and their stories. But not now. He silently downed two gins and looked around blankly. The whole evening had been a failure.

I swallowed my disappointment. 'Let's go home, Zac.'

We took our usual shortcut through a nearby lane. Suddenly I heard pounding feet and shouts behind us. 'Oy, here are the queers!'

I turned to see three men upon us. Before I could react, Zac threw himself in front of me. He fell on the ground, with two of them punching and kicking him, while the third man came towards me. I swung my cane hard at his head. There was a loud crack and he collapsed. I could hear the fists and boots of the others connecting with Zac's body. My terror must have given me strength, God knows how. I pulled one man off Zac and brought my cane down on him. He shrieked and took off at a run.

I turned to the last one and started kicking him with my good leg. He was trying to get away but I couldn't stop. I punched his face again and again. I kicked his back, his head. I felt bones in his face shatter and kept on kicking. I was possessed – the Furies were upon me. I wanted to murder the bastard. I don't know what would have happened if Zac hadn't groaned, 'Theo, stop.'

It brought me to my senses. I'd never felt like that before, not even in the war when the Nazis were trying to kill me. I would have done anything to protect Zac – yes, even if that meant killing the man who attacked him. I'm not proud of it, but I'm not ashamed either. That's just the way it was.

I helped Zac to his feet and retrieved my cane. One man was unconscious, one was moaning and the third one had disappeared. Zac was bloodied and grunting with pain, but said only, 'We need to get out of here.'

We made it down the end of the lane, leaning onto each other, and came out on the main street. People were strolling along, oblivious to what had just happened a few feet away. The whole situation was dreamlike. Moments before we had been in a fight for survival and now we were mingling with women in fur coats.

I hailed a black cab and asked for the Royal Free Hospital. I knew Claude was working late that evening. All I could think was to get to him. Zac slumped against me in the cab, half-conscious. The cabbie was observing us in the rear-view mirror so I tried to give a casual laugh, even though I was trembling violently. 'Too much to drink, I'm afraid.'

Claude came down quickly at the hospital. The next part was a blur. I was vaguely aware of Claude talking to the doctor in casualty, and Zac being admitted. I was sore and bruised, my hand swollen, not that it mattered. Claude told me Zac had several broken ribs and they needed to x-ray his head injury. He came out with me to wait for a cab. I was still gripped by uncontrollable tremors.

'I wanted us to have a nice evening. I thought it might bring him out of himself. Oh Christ,' I uttered, 'what have I done?'

Claude gripped my arm. 'Don't worry, Theo. I've called in some favours. I told the registrar he fell down a staircase. Obviously, stairs don't reach out and give you two black eyes and a broken nose, but the important thing is to avoid the police getting involved.'

I hadn't thought of that. 'We can't let them know—' I was frantic.

'I'll make sure the police aren't informed. It makes no difference that you were victims of an unprovoked attack. We all know you're guilty of walking along the street while queer, or should I say breathing while queer.'

I couldn't respond. I was at my lowest ebb.

'Go home, my dear. Get yourself a strong whisky.' He gave me a hug and saw me into the cab, anxiety in his dark eyes.

I couldn't sleep. My leg was aching and the attack replayed endlessly in my head, as if on a loop. I could still hear the sickening sounds of them attacking Zac. I was in a state verging on hysteria.

I went back early the next morning. They wouldn't let me see Zac because only family were allowed in, and who was I, just a friend? I had to wait outside and wanted to scream. I found a sympathetic nurse who told me he had a broken nose, three broken ribs and concussion. Claude turned up, sorted out the paperwork and came home with us in a cab.

'Really, with these injuries, he should stay in for another night. But a couple of toughs were brought in overnight from Soho. I had to get Zac discharged before the police started asking questions. One of them has a broken jaw, you know.' I could feel his gaze on me. 'They told the police they were attacked by five men. I suppose they're too humiliated to admit they were beaten up by one poof.' That made me laugh bitterly.

We got Zac up to bed. His ribs were strapped up, and Claude told me his nose would heal up without help. The concern was his head injury: I should call an ambulance if he lost consciousness. Before he left for work, Claude gave me painkillers and instructions for keeping Zac comfortable.

The house was enveloped in a troubled hush after he went. I sat with Zac who slept or stared with empty eyes at the wall. He looked terrible. Bruises swarmed across the swollen landscape of his face. But the worst thing was his silence. I gently caressed him, pleading, 'Talk to me, darling.' When he slept, I kept on checking if he was unconscious. I had never known such terror, not even when I was lying half-dead on the beach at Dunkirk.

Anna rang me in the afternoon, having realised I wasn't at work. I told her briefly what had happened. She said, 'I'll be there soon. Hold on, sweetie.'

I must have fallen asleep. I woke to the sound of the doorbell, the house in darkness. Anna and Miriam were at the door with concerned faces. I took them straight up to see Zac. Anna held his hand, saying, 'You poor darling,' and Miriam asked him some questions, but still he did not speak. They were clearly shocked to see him like that.

I hadn't eaten all day and the house was freezing. They made tea and toast while I started the fire in the sitting room. Anna put a comforting arm around my shoulders. 'Is he talking at all?'

I groaned, 'No,' and dropped my head into my hands. They listened in silence, their faces pinched in anger, while I told them everything.

When I finished, Miriam said, 'Theo, you need to know. Zac has clinical depression.'

I was slow on the uptake. 'Yes, it's obvious he's very low.'

'That's not what I mean, my dear. People use the word "depression" if someone is moody or a bit sad. This is different. It can be a serious illness.'

I was shocked, but also aghast at my stupidity. I'd studied psychology. How could I have not worked this out? I stammered, 'But what – will he recover? What can I do to help? I'll do anything to get him better. I'll pay for any treatment.'

Miriam's face was kind. 'Most people get better, although it can take time – many weeks, if not months. Antidepressants can help, but it would mean Zac seeing a doctor, and it's possible he would be sectioned—'

I said instantly, 'No! They'll focus on him being queer. That will be the problem needing a "cure". They'll give him some ghastly treatment. I won't let that happen.' We'd all heard about the lobotomies and chemical torments being inflicted on men and women in the name of therapy.

Miriam nodded, unsurprised. 'All right. I think I can get hold of antidepressants from a doctor at work without any questions. That's a start. And, of course, the other main treatment is seeing a psychiatrist …'

We looked at each other. I asked, 'Do you know of any psychiatrist who wouldn't see Zac's sexuality as the problem?' They could only shake their heads.

I stared into the fire, my despair hardening to a steely resolve. 'I'll act as his psychiatrist. I'll do a talking cure with him.' We spent the rest of the evening working it through.

When I walked them to the door, I said impulsively, 'I don't know what I'd do without your friendship.'

Anna gave me a warm hug. 'I never expected to have a man as my best friend. I think it's been a surprise for us both. But it just works, doesn't it?' I was smiling faintly when I waved them off.

It was a relief to get a diagnosis for Zac. Understanding was the first step to finding a solution. The following morning, I went to Camden library and borrowed every book I could find on psychiatry or depression. I told my work I had a stomach bug. Then I rang Zac's boss and said he would be off work. When he asked who I was, I said, 'A friend,' and hung up. Zac had already handed in his resignation. I didn't think there was much they could do to him.

I spent the next days sitting with Zac and going through the books. I'd prepare portions of food – a sausage, an apple cut into pieces – and spoon bits into his mouth, feeding him as though he were a baby. I helped him to the loo and back to bed. And I talked to him. I had a strong feeling he needed to hear my words of love and reassurance. Pip lay on the bed close to Zac, seeming to know he wouldn't tell her off.

The books suggested that people become depressed due to either a chemical problem in the brain, a reaction to a specific event, or unresolved issues. While the attack was obviously a trigger, I knew there were things in Zac's past he hadn't dealt with. The way he tried to control things, his black moods – they all made sense now. My plan was to get him speaking about all this, but not as his lover. He needed to be free to talk without worrying about my reaction. I had to be a neutral sounding board.

I phoned my manager and said I needed leave due to a family emergency. He grudgingly assented. I explained to our friends how they could help and they agreed without hesitation. I knew they would. Miriam brought over the antidepressants and I started Zac on those the same day.

For the next two weeks, I spent every second with him. Anna or Claude dropped by with food to keep us going, although neither of us had any appetite. My first objective was to get Zac out of bed. It took some persuading, but by the end of the first week he was having a bath and getting dressed with my help. He'd come downstairs, shuffling along like an old man, and I'd settle him in the chair by the fire. I talked to him or asked questions. I continued that every evening and weekend once I was back at work. Ruth had put Sian into a nursery so she could spend the day with Zac, David toddling around behind her. I'd explained to her what she needed to do.

'Try to be calm and objective. Ask him open questions. Don't say things like "poor you, oh how awful". We need to give him the space to talk and work out how things affected him.' Ruth nodded, serious and concentrated.

Every evening I would study Zac's face, so beloved yet so altered, and wonder: *where are you, my darling?* He had gone deep inside himself, in thrall to some twilight, alternate world. When we went to bed, I wrapped my arms around him and spoke of my love. His body stiffly unmoving, he did not respond.

I was continually on the verge of panic. I would weep in the bath with the taps running to drown out my melisma of woe. Zac had vanished, to be replaced by this silent interloper. I missed him with a desperation that tunnelled inside my gut. But my feelings were unimportant. I never for a moment thought of giving up. I was in this for life. I'd do whatever was necessary to help him. And if the worst happened and Zac didn't get better – then I would cherish and look after him always.

17

I started off asking questions about Zac's childhood. It was a complete failure at first. I was often tormented by doubts on my course of action. Physically, he was recovering, but he remained trapped in a labyrinth so impenetrable, I didn't know if I could reach him. My words became my search party. When not questioning him, I would work through the Bach pieces on the piano, hoping it might give him some of the solace it provided me.

There was a breakthrough in the middle of April. I'd asked a question about his parents, to the usual silence. Then he said, in a voice so small I had to strain to hear, 'Nothing I did was ever right for my parents.'

Relief surged through me, but I made my voice neutral. 'Tell me more.'

Slowly, painfully, from that point he started speaking about his childhood. There were still days when he was mute. And if he did talk, he could erupt in anger. 'Why are you asking these stupid questions? Just shut the fuck up!' At least he was communicating.

By May, two months after the attack, Zac had improved enough to leave the house. I was thrilled the first time he came out to the Heath. It took an hour to do a walk he used to do in fifteen minutes, but it felt like a major achievement. I made sure he went out walking every day after that. If I was at work, Ruth, David and Pip would go with him to his favourite tree and sit overlooking the ponds.

I'd asked Ruth to concentrate on their family life. One day, she met me at the front door when I got home from work, her words bubbling out excitedly. 'He talked a lot today about the time he was sent to boarding school. Theo, he showed proper emotion! It's the most he's talked so far.'

'What did he say?'

'My father gave him a terrible beating because Isaac was killed by a train when we were out together. I have only a vague memory of that day, and my parents would never discuss it. Zac said he'd thought he was a murderer who deserved to be sent away. I remembered your advice and stayed calm, even though I was raging at my bloody parents in my head. I said, "What do you think now?" He was silent for so long I'd almost given up, then he said, "I was just a child myself. They gave me too much responsibility. I'm sorry he died, but I have no reason to feel guilty". Oh, Theo – maybe this really is working?'

I held my breath, hope putting out tentative tendrils.

Zac was now talking about his childhood. We had to push at first, but then the words would flood out. He spoke about the lack of love and warmth, his guilty belief that he'd done something to cause his parents' coldness. He started losing his frozen look and developed more of an appetite. One morning he came into the kitchen when I was trying to cook fried eggs, and took over from me. These signs of improvement meant everything to me.

I moved onto asking about his life at school. He talked about this readily enough, because in many ways it was his happiest time as a child. He described how the wife of his housemaster had comforted him when he'd arrived, scared and lonely. She'd tucked him into bed on his first night and sat for a long time, holding his hand and chatting to him. I got the impression she and her husband took on a parental role, but with far more warmth and kindness than his own parents.

Claude spent Tuesday evenings with Zac so I could go to choir. Everything else in my life was put on hold. I left work every day at five, and my boss informed me in portentous tones of his disappointment at my "lack of commitment". One of my colleagues was frequently absent due to a sick wife, and received sympathetic understanding. I knew that was an impossibility for me. Although I still loved working at the FO, I'd developed a certain fatalism. They had started vetting staff and I knew they would get around to me. An envelope had also arrived from the SIS with Zac's last salary payment enclosed; but work felt supremely unimportant.

The summer passed us by, a distant train glimpsed fitfully on another track. No swimming or picnics, no trips to the coast to sail our yacht. At least we were seeing definite, if slow, progress. Zac was still mostly monosyllabic, but now he responded to people. The vacant look in his eyes had disappeared. Miriam told me, 'You must be a natural at this sort of thing.'

Anna often urged me to come out with her. 'I'm worried you'll make yourself ill, Theo. You look exhausted. You're giving everything for Zac and getting nothing back.'

I just shook my head. My only focus was on getting him well. The alternative was unthinkable.

The anniversary of Alan's death came around. I couldn't help reflecting that had been our last happy day, the year before. When I got home from work, I suggested, 'Come to the Heath with me.' Zac nodded and we set off silently with Pip. We ended up at the men's pond and I was surprised to hear him say, 'Why don't you have a swim?'

The fact he'd actually thought about me lifted my spirits enormously. Zac sat on the meadow with Pip while I borrowed swimming trunks from the lifeguard and dived in. A dragonfly hovered before me, shockingly beautiful, and the corners of my mouth creaked upwards. It was the first time in months I felt a relaxation of the sick tension that had become my faithful companion.

My birthday arrived. Zac seemed unaware but I didn't care – it wasn't a reason for celebration. I'd moved on to the time he was on the streets as a rent boy. That evening, I asked what had happened to make him leave London.

He responded with the usual irritability. 'For Christ's sake, what does it matter? Why do you keep asking these stupid questions?'

I'd learned he reacted that way when I was close to a painful memory, so I repeated my query. Zac hunched his shoulders and glared in my direction, but his eyes were cloudy, turned inward. Then he responded, his words halting, his voice hoarse.

'If you must know … I agreed to go to a punter's car to give him a blow job … He said he wanted to fuck me. I said no, that's not the deal … I started to open the car door.'

Zac stopped, his breath harshly punching in and out. I made myself remain still. 'It happened so quickly. He banged my head on the door. I was dizzy. Had this ringing in my ears … Before I could react, he forced me down onto the seat … He pulled my trousers down and raped me.'

I had to dig my fingernails into my palms. *He mustn't see I'm upset.* But it didn't matter, because Zac was viscerally reliving the memory. I could hear the terror and shock in his voice. He described the taste of the leather seat when his face was forced into it. How he realised, halfway through, there was a child's toy on the floor. The pain of the attack. How the man opened the car door and pushed him out when he'd finished.

'How did that make you feel?'

Zac stared angrily at me. 'What do you think? Humiliated, ashamed. Dirty. Like a worthless piece of shit.' The revulsion was clear on his face as he spoke. It was miraculous after the way he'd seemed devoid of emotion.

He seemed to direct a lot of his rage at me. 'Are you satisfied, Theo? You pushed and pushed. You needed to know, didn't you? Zac Bonneval, lying on the street with his trousers around his ankles!'

'Who are you really angry at?'

He muttered, 'Bloody fool question,' but it gave him pause. 'I'm angry with that bastard.' He hung his head and I realised he was trying not to cry.

I could no longer sit apart, play-acting the role of a psychiatrist. I went over and held him. I told him how much I loved him. I kissed his hair, his face. He wept for a long time. When we went up to bed, I took him in my arms again. After a few minutes, he sighed and relaxed against me. I lay sleepless for many hours. He'd been only seventeen: thrown out of home for being queer, alone in a hostile world. In every way, Zac had shown such courage.

That was the day Zac slowly started coming back. He still had days when he was absent, grey-faced, but I saw an improvement from that time.

We talked about the rape many more times. It was like peeling an onion. With each layer we uncovered some new truth and got closer to healing. I'd been shocked to find he somehow believed he'd brought the rape on himself. 'How do you think you were to blame, Zac?' With each answer he came up with, I questioned him further. 'How could you have seen the signs he'd be violent? How could you have given the impression you'd go along with it? How could you have physically stopped the rape when he was bigger and heavier?' Each time I asked these questions Zac would lose his temper, but he started to examine his own assumptions about that night. Eventually, he could talk about it with perspective.

We went out of the house more in July and August. My mother arrived back from a cruise to New Zealand with my stepfather, and we took her out for lunch. Zac said just enough for her not to notice how he'd changed. I didn't want her to know what we'd been going through – it would have distressed her for no reason.

Ironically, she said to me during the lunch, 'You don't look well, darling. Have you been sick?' I gave some response and changed the subject. Zac eyed me wordlessly.

The first time we went down to our cottage, we walked by the harbour and sat on the boat. The next time, I suggested, 'How about we take *Argo* out?' We didn't go far, but I rejoiced at a certain tranquillity on his face.

The worst of the depression appeared to have lifted, but Zac wasn't much fun to be around. He was simmering with rage, a pot ready to boil over at any moment. It was mostly directed at me, usually when I encouraged him to talk. He would explode, 'Why can't you leave me in peace? Why don't you just shut up?' I kept telling myself it meant I had touched on something that was controlling him. But it wasn't pleasant. I still felt lonely. I missed his warm and loving nature. I told myself, *he's coming back. Just be patient.*

18

12 August 1955

I've been unwell. I felt bad for a long time. A black mood that went on and on. I lost myself. But I think I'm getting better.

We spent most weekends with Ruth and the children. Zac could hold a basic conversation and occasionally showed interest in seeing our friends. Once or twice he even gave a sound approximating a laugh when Claude made one of his jokes, although I noticed the smile didn't connect with his eyes. In August, I decided to stop the talking cure and antidepressants. I didn't have to rush home from work every day to be with him. In fact, I preferred to stay at work to be out of his way.

If Claude was around, he would protest when Zac snapped at me. 'You're a rude bastard, Zac. Why are you so damned crabby with Theo? He's done so much for you!'

Zac would mutter, 'Sorry.'

Claude used to ring me regularly. 'Theo, I don't know how you can put up with his bad moods. You've done everything for him. You single-handedly pulled him out of the swamp.'

'I suppose it's part of the process. I can take it.'

'But at what cost to you? You're too pale and thin. You seem so sad, my dear. I worry about you. This can't go on.'

I kept my voice offhand, unwilling to acknowledge how much it affected me. 'It will go on as long as it needs to.'

We resumed some aspects of our former life. But he

uttered no words of love. I was deeply grieved by the absence of tactile contact between us. Always, before the depression, we loved our physical closeness. When we woke, we would go into each other's arms, and that was often a special time to make love. But not now. I'd turn to him when I woke, and he would get out of bed. And he never called me "Teddy". That was my private name, and the way he'd said it had felt like an endearment. I missed that, like I missed many aspects of the Zac I'd known and loved.

Had I killed his love by making him talk about his buried memories? Or would this have happened anyway – perhaps he felt our relationship had reached the end of the road? My soul shrivelled at the thought that his love had curdled into a polite indifference. I pushed those fears away. I didn't want to go there. All I knew was that I wouldn't give up on him. I would never go unless he told me to go.

23 August 1955

I've lost months out of my life. As if I've been dead and come back to the living. Here I am, 41, unemployed. Where do I go from here? I need to feel I'm contributing to society. I feel useless. A failure.

I don't know how much longer this would have continued. But we were on the south coast one weekend when Mark, a neighbour we'd become friendly with, came over to us in the pub. He was in his fifties and mad for sailing. When he said he hadn't seen us around lately, Zac was vague. 'Oh, we've been busy.'

Mark asked, 'Do you know anyone who'd like the opportunity to sail with me to Brazil? I've had someone pull out on me.'

Zac looked at him, his eyes suddenly bright. 'Tell me more.'

Mark explained that a wealthy Brazilian man had bought a yacht while on holiday, which needed to be taken from Portsmouth to Rio de Janeiro. There was no pay, but expenses were covered including the air fare home. The boat had to be delivered by January.

Zac hadn't looked this alive, this interested, in a long time. He said instantly, 'I can do it.'

We spent the rest of the evening talking it through. They would need to leave by the middle of October. Mark had planned the route: down to the Canary Islands, over to the Caribbean for another stop before heading down the coast of South America. When we got back to the cottage, Zac couldn't stop talking about the trip. The change in him was striking. He'd been given a purpose and I realised this was just what he needed. He was well enough to go back to work by then, but of course the problem was – what work would he do? This opportunity came along at the perfect moment.

5 September 1955

I've been given a lifeline. I'm going to sail a 50-footer called *Salsa* to Brazil with Mark. To be out on the water again, doing something worthwhile – it's just what I need. We're leaving in six weeks. I can't wait. This is the first time I've felt slightly alive in bloody months.

Zac was now occupied with arrangements for the trip. He met Mark for planning sessions, bought equipment and provisions, and spent hours poring over maps. His face was animated and he joined in conversations with our friends. He was less impatient with me, his bad temper mostly gone. In many ways he was a facsimile of Zac, with the essence of the man who had once loved me only glimpsed in flashes. There were other differences: his brain still worked sluggishly and his emotions seemed blunted. I could only hope these were all transitory leftovers from the profound depression he'd passed through.

The polite distance between us continued. We maintained a friendly communication with none of the small rituals and signs of lovers. When I tried to talk about why we weren't having sex, he clammed up or changed the subject. I started once to make love to him and he wordlessly pushed me away. I gulped down that bitter lesson and didn't try again.

Another opportunity came up for him. A former SIS colleague contacted him to say *The Observer* needed a piece on the history of espionage. It had just been publicly confirmed that Burgess and Maclean had been spying for Russia, and the papers were full of it. Zac went to the British Library and put together an article that was published the following Sunday.

I suggested, 'Perhaps you could become a journalist, Zac?'

He said, 'Hmm,' sceptically, but I could see it was good for his self-esteem.

11 October 1955

We leave in a few days. The last weeks have been busy, full of purpose. It's made all the difference for me. Theo's being very understanding. As always. At least I'm less of a moody bastard with him. I've felt so guilty over that.

And I was paid to write an article for The Observer. The editor asked if I'd be available to do more articles. I can't think that far ahead. I still feel like I have a fog in my brain.

On Zac's last night, he finished packing his bag after dinner. We sat down in front of the fire. He had been chatting about the trip, but now became pensive. I was quiet, choked by my unvoiced fears. After a while, he stirred and said awkwardly, 'Theo, I've never thanked you. I know you did a hell of a lot to bring me out of that depression. You gave me so much.'

The words came out of my mouth before I could stop them. 'Do you still love me, Zac?' The minute I said it, I cursed myself for a bloody fool.

Zac gave an involuntary sigh. 'Oh, Theo.' He said nothing more.

All the air seemed to go out of me. I thought I would faint. *Oh, Christ. This is where he tells me it's over. He's stopped loving me.* I'd feared this moment – and now it was here, I reacted in a panic. I got up and walked blindly out of the room. I couldn't hear those words, not now. Zac called me, but I didn't turn back. I opened the front door. I had to get out. He was behind me, saying my name. I shook my head and started out onto the front path.

He grabbed me from behind. 'Don't go, Theo. Please stay.' I sagged, and he held me tighter. 'Turn around. Look at me.' I refused. I shook my head, unable to speak.

Zac put his head next to mine and spoke into my ear. 'How can you doubt my feelings?' I could feel the warmth of his body next to mine. 'I know everything you've done for me. You've been magnificent. So strong. I've been a miserable bastard. But can't you see? I've lost my self-respect. I need to feel I can be an equal in this relationship. I've got to go away for a while, to get myself back. Please understand.'

His breath on my cheek was as soft as a butterfly wing. He said, 'Come inside.'

I turned and went back into the house. He shut the door and we had a long embrace. How I'd missed this bodily contact with him. I was angry with myself – I'd been determined not to make a scene. I was aware he had not actually said he loved me. But I also felt some reassurance.

Zac said, 'I think we need a whisky.'

He sat close to me, as of old. We didn't speak further about our relationship. We kept to safe, impersonal topics. I think we both felt raw and exposed, aware we only had a few hours left. We didn't make love, but he held me close in bed and told me what a special man I was. After the months of his emotional and physical distance, that would have to do.

He was quiet the next morning. I only woke when he shook my shoulder. I opened my eyes to see him bending down to me, the light on in the hallway. It was still dark outside.

'The car's here. I need to go.' He gave me a brief, dry kiss. 'Take care, Theo. I'll be back in the new year.'

I was half-asleep. 'I hope you find what you're looking for.'

Then he was gone. I listened to the car driving away. *I love you so much. Take care. Come home soon. Come back to me.*

19

25 October 1955

We've settled into a routine. We do 4-hour shifts and I've got the one I wanted – midnight to 4am. This morning dolphins were swimming alongside, jumping out every so often, then falling back into the group at the stern. They looked at me with curious eyes, as if they were sizing me up. I could watch them for hours.

29 October 1955

Knowing we're just a tiny speck in a large ocean helps to put things into perspective. The stars fill the night sky, so bright and beautiful. Last night I saw shooting stars. And the sunsets, the moon rise – I take pleasure from simple things like this. Surely, a positive sign I'm getting better?

I'm busy every waking hour. It keeps me occupied and that's just how I want it. Mark and I have a chess game each day. My mind's starting to work after months feeling so dull and stupid. He's a decent man, not talkative or demonstrative, which suits me fine. We should be in Las Palmas in a few days.

Of the emotions I felt when Zac first went, relief was predominant. I put aside my fears about our relationship and went out drinking with Claude and Anna. Claude called it "the return of the three musketeers". I visited Richmond most weekends. Sian was a bright child, full of curiosity. David sat in my lap and babbled away. Sometimes, I felt I was seeing Zac as a toddler, and dread would jolt through me. Ruth asked no questions, but I flinched at the sadness on her face.

The autumn was mild and I spent a lot of time out of doors. I was propositioned once or twice when I walked Pip on the Heath. I did miss sex, but a quickie up against a tree with a stranger didn't interest me. I wanted only to have Zac's body against mine. He was always in my thoughts. I wrote letters with chatty news and sent them to the post office in Las Palmas. I didn't mention that Philby had been officially cleared in the House of Commons as a spy.

4 November 1955

We've arrived in Las Palmas. It's a short walk into town, which has a pleasant old part and a market.

8 November 1955

We've stocked up with fresh food and fruit. I had two letters from Theo, quite cheerful. That was a nice surprise – I thought he might be full of reproaches. God knows, he has a right.

Just think, this is where Columbus stopped off 450 years ago. And now me, setting off on the next leg of my adventure and hopefully getting back to myself – getting answers to some questions.

13 November 1955

We're heading SSW to pick up the trade winds and head over on the rhumb line. I found myself whistling today while I was checking the rigging.

18 November 1955

We're in the doldrums. Becalmed. Not a breath of air. Mark says it could go on for weeks. I don't mind. We're in the middle of the Atlantic and

163

that's enough. But with little to do, I can no longer stop my mind. It's not an albatross around my neck – it's thoughts of Theo that are choking me.

I feel a deep grief about him. That last evening, when he asked if I still loved him – oh, God. I know his motto is "it's good to talk". Even in the worst of my depression I was aware what he was doing. He was implacable, but it seemed to do the trick. I told him things I'd never told anyone else. And he was right – unspoken, they were controlling me. I always knew I had a thing about guilt and humiliation. Now I understand why. And yet – guilt is what I feel most of all now.

Theo showed himself to be far stronger than me – he gave all he had to save me. Impossible to find a better person on this earth, or one with a bigger heart. So why, these past months, have I looked at this beautiful man, who's been everything to me – and I feel nothing? Who wants to make love and I haven't a quiver of sexual desire? Why is my cock this piece of useless flesh?

The thought I may have stopped loving Theo devastates me. I can't see my life without him. But right now, my feelings for him seem to be non-existent. Claude said it's all part of the depression. It deadens everything – physically, mentally, emotionally. It takes time to come back. It's true I have more energy in my body now. I'm sleeping better. I have an appetite. My mind is starting to work properly. I hope it's just a case of being patient. But –

19 November 1955
Still no wind.

I had to stop yesterday. It was too painful. But I want to work it out. So – what if it isn't a case of the depression still lifting, my emotions being deadened?

I've imagined worst case scenarios over the years, but always they were about Theo leaving me. I feared he'd stop loving me, or someone else would take him from me. When we first got together, quite a few on the scene said I'd move on soon – that was what I did. I didn't stay in relationships long. I held a part of me in reserve. I suppose no one could have imagined that, 15 years on, he would still be everything for me.

What the hell is happening? Did he play the part of a psychiatrist too well? Did it somehow change our relationship so I no longer see him as a lover? If that's the case, what a bloody irony. He saved me from my depression, but in the process we lost our love. Or rather, I did. I know he feels the same about me. I know he's suffering.

I feel terrified, guilty. Confused and desperately sad. And I don't understand – if I can feel so heartbroken about the thought I no longer love Theo, if I feel the pain so much – why can't I feel the love?

27 November 1955

I couldn't write before. We had three days of gale force winds and storms, and waves of 20 feet or more coming at us broadside. It was a real reminder of what insignificant beings we are. I don't mind admitting I was scared. We finally managed to get back on course two days ago, but the rudder has taken a bashing.

We're about ten days behind schedule, but we're alive. In the storm I realised: I don't want to die. I want to live. I feel exhilarated now. Life is good.

Today I beat Mark at chess for the first time. Something heavy is lifting from me.

My stepfather retired in November and moved with my mother to Hampshire. The tenants in my family house asked if I'd be interested in selling it. The timing was right – I knew I'd never live there again. We agreed a price, and the house was sold by Christmas. If Zac didn't find a job, we'd have enough savings

165

to keep us going for some years. That is, if he came back to me.

I had a bad day on our anniversary. I left the scarf Zac had given me on the bus, and took it badly as some sort of omen. I lost all perspective and spent hours tearfully berating myself. Otherwise, I kept busy and cheerful enough.

It was my mother's birthday a week later, and I took her to tea at the Ritz. She would ask politely about Zac's travels. But that day she said, 'I hope Zac comes home soon. I miss him, and I'm sure you must too.' I looked at her, surprised, and she patted my hand. 'You know I find this difficult to talk about, but I do think you two have a lovely relationship. I can see how well he looks after you. And I've become very fond of Zac.'

I smiled and squeezed her hand, wincing at the irony. Just when we might be breaking up, she accepted our relationship.

30 November 1955

We've caught more fish. I'm getting sick of bloody bananas. And cabbage.

I'm thinking of Theo a lot. In the first weeks I blotted him out of my mind, but now, even when I'm occupied with tasks, he's there in the background. When I wake up, I get out his picture. Even with my feelings so dulled, I know he's an exceptionally lovely man. It was our 15th anniversary when we were in the storm. I wonder what he did that day.

I still don't have answers, but I need to get my fears in the open so I can work through them. Pushing them down just makes things worse. Theo taught me that. But then, if I start listing everything he's given me – I wouldn't stop.

This afternoon, a whale come up to spout then dived down, its tail hanging in the air. Theo would have loved to see that. He takes great pleasure from nature. Well, from everything really. I wonder if I'll find letters from him when we get to St Lucia?

4 December 1955

We got into Rodney Bay yesterday. The rudder needs fixing, so I'll have time enough to explore.

The post office gave me letters this morning from Ruth and Claude. I was so disappointed I couldn't move for a minute, then insisted they look again. After bloody ages they found two letters from Theo. Claude's letter made me laugh in an angry way. He and Anna are out drinking a lot with Theo. He said it's hard work fighting off Theo's admirers, but someone has to do it. Theo did sound cheerful in his letters. He seems to have a busy social life. He said Pip sends her love and just signed his name. Good to hear they don't miss me. I wouldn't want to feel guilty about that.

One evening before Christmas, I was out with the musketeers and went over to greet Francis. He asked, 'Is that your new boyfriend?'

'What, who?' I looked around, confused.

'The dark man with you.'

'Heavens, no. That's just Claude, Zac's best friend.'

He shook his head with a smile. 'Where's Zac? I haven't seen you together for ages. Are you two bona?' I tried to shrug carelessly but it obviously didn't work, because he put his hand on mine. 'What's happening, my dear?'

'Oh, he's gone away for a few months.'

Francis raised a plucked eyebrow. 'And left you on your own? He's either crazy or careless.'

I was still determined to be positive about Zac's absence. I'd received a couple of letters from him that helped, even if he did say they were behind schedule. There was nothing personal, but he wrote vividly of his adventures and the old Zac came through on every line. He put in his last letter, before they left St Lucia, that he thought of me a lot. I read that often.

19 December 1955

The rudder's fixed and we head off tomorrow. We've done some exploring and I've enjoyed a quiet life on *Salsa* with a few beers, reading or playing chess. I feel peaceful. I really believe I've beaten this bloody depression.

Mark's a good man. He said to me today: you and Theo are a couple, aren't you? I looked at him and thought, oh God, here we go. But he said, it doesn't bother me at all. It turns out he had a queer uncle who died in the Blitz. Mark had been very fond of him and his lover. If only more straights could be like him! I do wish, though, I didn't feel surprised and grateful when I get treated decently, like a human being, in spite of who I am. There's something terribly wrong in society with all this.

I thought, damn it, I want to get drunk for the New Year. I started in an Italian bistro in Soho with Anna and Miriam, then we went on to the pub. I gave Francis a kiss and bought him a drink. Claude and Jordi turned up. We toasted the year to come and just about everything else. An Italian friend of Jordi's came over and started flirting with me. After the unremitting grimness of the last year, his attention sent a warmth zapping through my body. It was a reminder that I was still flesh and blood. Claude hovered around us like an overprotective father, asking, 'What are you two talking about?'

When we got ready to leave, Gino was blatant. 'Come home with me.' When I declined, he scribbled down his number and said, 'Call me any time,' before pulling me towards him and giving me a deep kiss. *Bloody hell, that's good.* I was hesitating, in two minds, when Claude hustled me out of the pub, saying we'd miss the last bus.

I snapped at Claude, who scowled back. Jordi smiled enigmatically at us, murmuring something I didn't catch. When I asked, he said, 'It's nothing, my dear Theo. Just a Catalan proverb.' He threw his arm around my shoulder and chatted amiably.

The first day of January was spent brooding on the Heath with a hangover, while Pip raced around. I found Gino's phone number in my pocket and threw it in a bin. In the dark heart of winter, I longed for Zac's return but also dreaded the truth it might bring. The slate sky reached down to envelop me in gloom.

5 January 1956

It's been slow progress. We're hugging the coast to avoid bad weather.

For a while I couldn't call up Theo's face, but now I see it clearly. Last night, I dreamed I was playing chess with him on a raft in the middle of the ocean. He told me: you need to choose what you want. It's your move. I woke up with the sound of his voice in my ears, as if he'd been here talking to me.

19 January 1956

We arrived in Rio last night and did a big clean-up. The owner came on board this morning. He's a fat man with bad skin and a cigar, obviously a Mr Big, or Semi-Big, in the local criminal fraternity. He seemed satisfied with what he saw and we're invited to drinks at his place tomorrow. We move our things to a hotel later today. Mark plans to fly home soon but I want to stay and have a look around. Rio is the most beautiful city I've seen. Who knows if I'll ever be in this part of the world again?

20 January 1956

We've just come back from Mr Semi-Big's place. Good drink, boring conversation, hideous furnishings. We were waiting for the plane tickets so we could go. He was surrounded by young women more than half his age, all acceptably nubile I suppose. No doubt there's a downtrodden wife in the background. One or two women cosied up to me and I thought, don't waste your time dears. I might as well fly to the moon.

23 January 1956

I saw Mark off this morning. We said take care, see you on the south coast. Then he said, don't be away from Theo too long.

I've moved to a cheaper room in the same hotel on Copacabana beach. Rio's a fascinating place. I'm not bored – but I didn't expect to feel lonely. I used to enjoy exploring places on my own, so something's changed. I can't help thinking that Theo would love it here. I tried to ring him this evening, but he must have been out.

25 January 1956

I got talking to a couple of Brits in the hotel bar yesterday, here on a Royal Geographical Society expedition. Bob said they leave in a couple of weeks for the region north of Pico da Bandeira, doing botanical and geological surveys. They need another man – am I interested? It's hard work and long days, basic pay. We've agreed to meet again tonight to discuss it. I didn't give a firm answer but I'd be mad to turn down the chance. Perhaps this could be my new line of work? I need to think this through. And I need to talk to Theo.

20

Zac should have been home weeks earlier, and I'd become fearful at the lack of news. He phoned one evening at the end of January.

When I realised it was him, my heart started drilling a hole in my chest. It was the first time I'd heard his voice in nearly four months. He sounded strong and confident, just like the pre-depression Zac. He told me about their delay, some of their adventures and how he was enjoying Rio. When I asked if he was exploring the city with Mark, there was a momentary pause.

'Ah, well, Mark flew home a few days ago.'

Apprehension darted through me. I made my voice casual. 'So, when might I expect you?'

That was when he started explaining he was planning to go on a geological survey in Brazil for a couple of months. 'It's a great opportunity for me, Theo.'

I didn't say anything while Zac talked on. I couldn't, because I was standing in the hallway – the kettle starting to whistle and Pip looking up at me – stricken by the truth I could no longer deny. He wasn't coming back. He no longer loved me. This was his way of letting me know. I should stop the pretence he'd gone off to recover from the depression. He'd left to get away from me. A slab of grief pressed down on me. I realised he'd stopped speaking and told myself: *don't make a scene. Show some pride.*

'Zac, you must do whatever you want. You don't need

to explain. I understand. Have a good life.' I could hear him speaking as I put down the phone, but it didn't matter. Nothing mattered any more.

The kettle was screaming its summons. I went into the kitchen and stopped it. I sat down and laid my head on the kitchen table. Moans crawled out of my belly, scratching at my throat. The phone was ringing, Pip was anxiously whining, but I couldn't move from the chair.

All this time, I had a running commentary in my brain. *Stop snivelling, Theo. Don't be so pathetic.* I dried my face and decided to drink myself into oblivion among strangers. No one who knew me to laugh at my humiliation. That the love of my life no longer wanted me. That our perfect relationship had crashed and burned.

I took the tube to a queer bar in Lambeth I'd once visited. I rarely crossed the river, but I didn't want to be on my home patch. I threw down some alcohol and got into conversation with a group of men sitting near me. All this time, I stopped myself from thinking. I just wanted numbness. I hadn't eaten, and the drinks achieved their effect. One of the men, older with a kind face, started talking to me more directly and I didn't discourage him. When he asked if I'd like to go back to his place, I said yes. It was that easy.

That was how it started. I thought I wanted company to help me forget. But really, what I wanted was the sex. Having someone hold and touch me helped to get me through those first hours. Simulacrum of closeness though it was, for a few seconds in the dark I could pretend it was Zac's arms around me.

I got a cab home in the morning, changed my clothes and went to work. On the way, I stopped off at a cafe for breakfast. My act of catharsis had been an attempt to purge my grief. And, for a few short hours, it worked. My mind wasn't just fixated on the fact Zac had left me. I was also remembering I'd had sex with someone who told me I was desirable. I'd discovered a new side to myself. No more "sweet" Theo. No more being nice. From now on, I was going to think only about myself.

My veneer of bravado soon faded, but nascent anger bubbled over the next few days into molasses of rage – a fury that gripped me by the throat and left me shaking, my temples pounding. He'd promised he would love me always, and he'd abandoned me. The bastard. How dare he?

26 January 1956

Bloody awful phone call with Theo yesterday. Hearing his voice affected me more than I'd expected. It took me back to the days when I'd ring him in the hospital and hang on his every word, trying to interpret how he felt about me.

It seemed to be going OK, but when I told him about the expedition, he basically told me to piss off and put the phone down on me. I rang back a few times but he didn't answer. I was desperate to find out what he meant. But it's obvious. He's finally had enough of me. He's given me the shove. Who can blame him? I've been a selfish, miserable shit. I would have tried the patience of a saint this last year.

I saw Bob after the phone call and got more details about the expedition. Then I walked the streets, trying to think it through. If Theo no longer wants to be my lover, why should I hurry back? Then I thought – I must go back to salvage our relationship. But what do I really want? I'm a wreck after the phone call, but my feelings are still so unknowable.

I ended up in a queer bar. I had a few drinks, got chatting to someone. We went out the back and he sucked me off. It was soulless and functional, about as sexy as having a wank. But that's the point – my body functioned. For the first time in months, my cock came to life.

173

I'm not just some impotent loser. I'm still a sexual being. At least that's one less worry. Christ knows, I have enough left.

My head is telling me the expedition is a good opportunity. And my heart's telling me – go home to him, you idiot. Go home and save the most precious thing you've ever had. But what if he tells me to go?

Anna looked at me oddly during rehearsal, and sat me down with a strong drink in the pub afterwards. 'Come on, Theo, what's happened?'

I tried to sound casual. 'I heard from Zac last night. He's decided to go on an expedition in Brazil. Nothing about coming home. It's obvious he's left me. Our relationship is over.' Anna stared, visibly shocked.

'Oh, Theo, that isn't so. He's still trying to find himself after his depression …'

I shook my head. 'No. I can't pretend any longer. The writing was on the wall a year ago. I just refused to see it.' She put her hand on mine, but I said quickly, 'Don't be nice to me. I can't take it right now.'

'If that's the case, he really is a stupid bastard—'

I flared up at her. 'He's nothing of the sort. He's a wonderful man who went through a depression. He didn't deliberately set out to stop loving me.'

'OK, OK. Just let me know if I can do anything. I'll always be here for you, my dear.' I didn't respond. I couldn't, really.

After a silence, she asked, 'What will you do now? Will you find somewhere else to live?'

I was surprised. 'Hell, no. He's the one who left me. He has to have the guts to come back and tell me it's over. Why should I move? It's my home.'

Anna said, 'But—' then stopped herself and looked at me mournfully.

6 February 1956

I caught sight of myself in a mirror last night in some dive and had to look away. I didn't like what I saw. I don't like the man I am right now.

I've been spreading my favours around the queer community here. For some reason I seem to be popular, but even so, I haven't been fussy. I get drunk and pick up someone quickly. My cock works fine, for what it's worth. I have a second's spurt of faint pleasure, followed by 24 hours of self-hatred. When I think what I had with Theo, I want to weep and frequently do. How did I manage to throw away that life? At least I don't need to worry about the way I was so numb. There's nothing numb about me now.

8 February 1956

Spent today with the group, trying out the wagons ahead of the trip next week. I found it tedious – hacking through undergrowth, being bitten to death by mosquitoes, leeches on my ankles. I bloody hate leeches. Give me a boat and the open sea any day. It hadn't occurred to me I might not actually enjoy a geographical expedition.

I ring Theo every day. He either refuses to pick up the phone, or he's never there. It's clear he's given up on me.

I didn't intend to repeat my Lambeth escapade. I saw it as a one-off act of defiance to help me get through that first night. But a few days later, I had a crying fit and told myself – *stop this right now*. This time, I went to my usual pub for a drink. Gino came over immediately and we ended up at his place. He was a passionate lover and wanted to see me again. I didn't analyse my behaviour, because it helped to anaesthetise the pain. But when

175

I spent a second night with Gino, it felt wrong. He was becoming attached, and I didn't want that. I knew my relationship was over, but until Zac looked me in the eyes and said he no longer wanted me, I wasn't free. I told Gino I couldn't see him again. His dramatic response only confirmed my decision.

My adventures with other men had boosted my confidence – and I needed that affirmation. I decided to set myself some rules. I would only do one-night stands. I'd go to places where no one knew me. I wouldn't bring anyone to our home.

I was growing a tough carapace around me, but it had too many cracks. I veered between devastation and rage, my emotions skidding around like an out-of-control spinning top. I preferred the anger – at least it gave me a sort of energy. The grief just tore me apart. There were too many memories in our bed, so I moved into the spare bedroom. I walked past the ringing telephone, not wanting to hear Zac's polite concern for his rejected lover. I did answer the phone after some days, but it was only Claude. I told him it was clear Zac had left me. Claude didn't seem to know what to say – I don't think he'd come across this side of me before. I was implacable.

My behaviour became more reckless. I went out to pick up men several times a week. It became a ritual: put Pip in the garden and go off on the prowl. I'd look around to see who took my fancy, go over and start talking. I had stepped out of my skin and adopted a completely different persona – that of a sexually confident man who drank too much and got what he wanted. Once, I didn't even make it into the bar – I noticed a man outside, we gave each other a look, and that was it.

The sex was mostly good, although it never came close to what I'd had with Zac. I met decent men. Many wanted to see me again, but I quickly knocked that on the head. After we had sex, we talked. They seemed to want to tell me their life story and I was glad to listen. They varied in age from their twenties to their fifties, and their jobs ranged from cab driver to judge. With all of them I could see the hurt, and struggle with self-esteem, caused by society's rejection. I recognised this in myself as well. What we wanted was simple: love and companionship; a refuge from the hatred on the streets; acceptance for who we were. I learned a lot about myself. Sometimes, I would be abused on the streets as "queer" or "faggot" and I'd think: *yes, I fuck men. So what?*

For a day or so after a pick-up, my thoughts were occupied with that. Then Zac's absence came crashing down on me. I would lie in bed weeping and kissing his photo, an emotional shambles.

I never for a moment stopped loving or wanting him. I kept myself busy. I worked long hours. I went out every night and drank too much or picked up men. I worked through the Bach pieces. I read trashy novels. I saw Ruth and the children nearly every weekend. Then I would realise: *soon I'll lose all this, because they're Zac's family.* And I was flung back onto my spinning torments. What had happened to the self-sufficient Theo – the one who was content with his own company and kept others at a distance? Zac had spoiled that by showing me what it's like to share your life with the person you love. Where had that life gone?

Anna would watch me drink too much and flirt with other men. She'd say sadly, 'You're in a strange place, Theo.'

Claude once asked abruptly, 'You're on the town, aren't you?' I didn't reply.

I refused to discuss Zac. But I did talk to Anna about the FO vetting regime. A committee had decided homosexuality was grounds for refusing security clearance. We started hearing about queers who'd been dismissed from the FO, even that one man had killed himself. It was causing devastation for men who'd spent their lives hiding their identity. We often discussed what we'd do when it came to our turn.

I was angry. 'Why should I lie about myself? I'm not ashamed.'

Anna was more conflicted. 'Ironically, it helps that women are forced to resign when they get married. We're all single, so I don't stand out. Of course, they're mostly "normal" women who've made work their priority. They've sacrificed their personal lives. I suppose they have a cat to love instead.' That made me laugh morosely. 'It's easier for me to get away with a deception than for men.'

'But – if you're asked directly?'

Anna looked at me proudly. 'That's different. I'll never lie about that. I wouldn't change myself for a second.'

9 February 1956

It's 2am and a blindfold has been lifted from my eyes. Suddenly – I see everything so clearly.

I was so disgusted with my cheap tart act, I vowed never again. But after another failed call to Theo and pacing around in my usual state, I went to the queer bar. They were having a dance competition, something to do with their carnival. Men danced around in colourful costumes, often dressed as women. Everyone clicked their fingers if they liked the routine. It was all a bit weird, but nice. One guy was dancing and smiling over at me. That's when it happened – like a thunderbolt from the sky.

He was dark-skinned, with black hair and eyes, but in every other respect he had an uncanny similarity to Theo. The same mouth

178

and dimples, identical shape of his face and body. The same sweet, gentle energy. No wonder I couldn't take my eyes off him. When this came to me, the words crashed into my head – of course I'm still in love with Theo! He's the only man for me. How could I have doubted it? I laughed out loud and felt quite joyous at the truth standing before me.

I don't understand why I had the ridiculous idea I had no feelings for him, or why they came back in such a rush now. I only know I must get back as quickly as possible and save our relationship. I'm grinning like an idiot while I write this. It's mad really – he's given me the push, I'm on the other side of the world. But now I know what I want. And I'll do whatever it takes to get him back.

10 February 1956

I've been busy. I told Bob yesterday I'm not going on the expedition. He said I'd messed them about and I wouldn't get this chance again. I don't care. Then I went to the airport to book my flight home. After endless negotiations, I'm on a reserve list for a flight to New York next week. All flights are full because of the carnival. I'll ring every day to check if a seat becomes available.

I feel a bit like Odysseus, tramping around the world trying to get back to his love. Only, I don't see Teddy in the role of Penelope, patiently waiting and unravelling his weaving each evening.

After another failed phone call, I've written him a long letter, trying to explain everything and asking him to please give me another chance. The hotel said they'd post it. I have a bloody awful headache so I've come back to my room.

Isaac just turned up. How did that happen? He looks so young. I said, you're dead, what are you doing here? He said, why did I let go of your hand? It was all my fault

I'd heard nothing since that one phone call in January. Zac had

179

seemingly fallen off the face of the earth. He could be dead. The depression could have come back and he might have killed himself – the secret fear in the back of my mind. He could have been attacked by robbers, or become sick in the middle of the jungle. A wild terror was added to the crescendo of emotions assailing me. Sometimes I needed to concentrate on just breathing in and out.

21

I've been in hospital. Can't remember much. Think I wrote that yesterday, a bit lost on days. I'm sitting up now.

24 February 1956

I'm clearer now. I was delirious with dengue fever. Someone took me to hospital. They had to put ice on my body. I'm back in the hotel now. The doctor says I'm over the worst but still aching, headache. I lost quite a few days.

29 February 1956

I managed to sit downstairs for an hour today. That's progress, although I'm still so weak. The headache comes and goes. The rash on my body is fading. Everyone at the hotel is being so kind. I wonder if Teddy is thinking about me – if he's worried? I'm writing him a letter.

4 March 1956

No fever for a week now, headache and rash mostly gone. Slowly getting stronger. I can get dressed and sit in the lounge for a few hours. I look out the window at people passing by. I've started making up a story in my head about a young man going to sea. Not sure where that came from – too much time on my hands, I suppose.

The thought of Teddy is always with me. I love and miss him so desperately. Sometimes I'm terrified I've lost him. But mostly I try to keep positive. We've often said that, as long as we're both alive, there can never be anyone else for us.

7 March 1956

I made it to the bank and the airline office today. After a lot of phone calls and discussion – they do talk everything to death – I'm on a flight on 17 March. Ten more days! Then I went to the post office and rang Teddy. No reply again. Maybe the phone is broken? Maybe he moved house? I'm trying not to panic. I must concentrate on getting my strength back.

8 March 1956

Today was a very bad day. I miss him, I miss him. I feel lost. Can't see my life without him. I touch his ring and tell myself we can get through this.

I got a letter at work saying I would soon be put through vetting. My colleagues grumbled about it in the canteen, but I didn't join in. For them it was a nuisance – for me it meant the end of my FO career. It just added to my sense that everything in my life was falling apart. On an impulse, I checked the overseas postings and applied for a temporary duty in Rabat. At least I could get away for a few months and put off the inevitable outcome. I soon heard that I would go out in May for six months. I couldn't help wondering if I'd hear from Zac before then. Or did he plan never to contact me again?

When I went for a drink with Anna and Miriam, they told me they were planning to go on holiday to Corfu the week before Easter. 'Corfu!' I couldn't help remembering Alan had gone there, the year before he died.

They looked at each other and nodded. Miriam said, 'We'd love you to come with us. You deserve a break.'

Anna gave me an encouraging smile. 'Come on, Theo, it'll be great fun. Sun and warmth. Good company. A break from grey London.'

It was all decided by the time we parted. Monica agreed to take Pip. She carefully didn't ask after Zac.

14 March 1956

Feeling much better now. I have an appetite and go out walking every day. I notice how people here hug and kiss. They show a warmth I never had from my parents. I know that things from my past affected me. Talking about it helped. I know Teddy did all this for me.

I still don't understand how my feelings for him were so dulled. I suppose it was the last bit of the depression to lift. To think there was ever a time when I couldn't feel love for Teddy – what madness! I can't wait to explain all this to him. I've tried to ring him and Claude again, still no answer. Where are they? I miss them all so much. From this distance I see that my life was paradise. I want it back.

18 March 1956

I'm in a hotel in New York, waiting for the connecting flight tomorrow. This really does feel like the bloody Odyssey. Perhaps it would be quicker to walk home.

The cold is a shock. I'd forgotten about winter. New York is not really my sort of place – too many scrapers, not enough sky. I just want to get home. This whole trip has shown me that nothing in life is more important than being with Teddy. I've written him another letter saying all this. Perhaps he'll read it when we're together?

Two nights before we were due to leave, I was at home packing my case, when panic started ripping at me. Going on holiday meant I'd accepted Zac wasn't coming back. This was my life now. A life without Zac. I didn't know how I could get past this. I grabbed my coat and went out to a bar, in an effort to push away the misery. Recently, I'd been enjoying my adventures less. They were no longer cathartic; I felt empty afterwards. I'd thought about stopping – but that night I needed comfort.

20 March 1956

I'm home. I got in last night to an empty house and Pip in the garden. She was delighted to see me. Perhaps she's the only one? Teddy seems to be sleeping in the spare bedroom and he's packed a suitcase.

I rang around. Ruth burst into tears when she heard my voice and said how worried she's been. Anna and Miriam didn't answer. Claude did – and he's furious with me. I'm a selfish, inconsiderate bastard. Don't I realise how much Theo's been suffering? He thinks I've left him. I was letting Claude have his say but interrupted to ask, what about my letters? What letters? he said. It seems the ones from Brazil haven't arrived. And when I asked where Teddy is, he told me – probably out with some man. He's been spreading his favours around, you know. I didn't give too many explanations. There'll be time enough for that.

It's dawn now. I slept for a while in the armchair, hoping he'd come home. Where is he? I can see he must have been through hell. He thinks I don't want him. He didn't get my letters. And he's fucking other men – but I'm not letting myself think about that right now. The priority is to get him to forgive me. What God-awful mess have I created?

I had a dream about Zac. He was in a group of people on the street, everyone in strange costumes. I went up to him, saying, darling, didn't you see me? He looked at me so coldly. He said, of course I got bored with you. Did you think it was forever? Then he walked away. I woke myself up moaning. My face was wet and I realised I'd been crying in my sleep. My companion was snoring next to me. *What am I doing here? Why am I having sex with strangers?* It was that ghostly hour before dawn and I felt so low I could die. I dressed quickly and went out into the night.

184

There were no cabs, no buses, no people on the streets. I turned towards the river and started walking home. Memories of London during the war came back to me. The sound of the bombing, the fire engines, the burning buildings. The death and destruction. Anything but thinking about Zac. This kept me going as I walked over Waterloo Bridge, the river dark and silent beneath me, and up through Covent Garden, past street sweepers cleaning the rubbish and workers setting up their market stalls. Two flower girls eyed me curiously, one calling out, 'Who's been on the razzle, then?'

I continued walking, through Soho and Euston and towards Camden, while rosy streaks started painting the sky. The dawn chorus started, the beauty of the birdsong contrasting with my desolation. My leg started aching on the final stretch and I jumped on a bus. I had reached my nadir. I walked drearily to the front door and stepped inside.

Zac was standing in the hallway, facing me.

I stared, speechless. Pip was jumping around, but I was conscious only of my automatic response – *this is my man.* A second or so later, my rational mind kicked in. *Yes, the man who abandoned me.*

He appeared equally shocked. Then he said, 'Hello, Teddy,' and it broke the spell.

I took off my coat and scarf, and stated, 'So, you're back.'

I saw his eyes flick to my neck then back to my face. He appeared wary. 'I got back last night. It's been a bloody nightmare getting home.'

I faced him silently, my anger coming to the boil. *This is the bastard who swanned off to have adventures, who didn't bother to write, who had me terrified he was dead. Selfish, arrogant man.*

'Where have you been, Teddy?'

Who the hell did he think he was to demand this? 'Out.'

His mouth twitched. 'Well, I'd worked that out.'

I felt very much on the back foot. I'd had little sleep and I was mortified that Zac could guess I'd been with someone. I couldn't help noticing he looked damned good: tanned and wiry, confident and in charge. The contrast from the depressed man of the previous year was staggering.

I said curtly, 'Look, I have to get to work. I don't have time for this. You can't expect me to stand around and throw a welcome home party.' I went up the stairs to the bathroom, ran the bath and sat on the side, trembling.

When I was dressing, I saw in the mirror I had a love bite on my neck. That must have been what he was looking at before. My defiance was queasy. *Why should I hide what I've been doing?* As I was buttoning up my shirt, he knocked and came in with a cup of tea and some toast.

His tone was still mild. 'You should have some breakfast before you go to work.' I hesitated, then thanked him and took the tea. He perched on the chest of drawers, watching me.

'Teddy, we've got a lot of talking to do. But I want you to know, never for a moment did I think I was leaving you. I'd never do that. I love you. I'm with you for life.'

I retorted, 'Do you think you can turn up after all this time and expect everything to be all right? Am I your little poodle, to come running when you call?'

I thought he might be angry, but he just looked at me. 'Claude tells me you didn't receive my letters from Brazil. Is that true?' I had a mouthful of toast and nodded. 'I tried to ring you but you never answered the phone. Please forgive me, Teddy. I can see I've made you very unhappy.'

186

I turned my back on him. I said nothing because I could not.

He went on, 'I know I have a lot of explaining to do. When you get back from work—'

I broke in angrily, 'Well, you chose a good time to finally show up. I'll be back late tonight, and tomorrow I'm going to Corfu. You can have a few weeks to think about what you want.'

I was struggling with my tie and it wasn't going well. 'Let me, Teddy.' I stood immobilised while he knotted my tie, standing inches away from me. Unable to meet his eyes and determined not to give in to his charms, I focused on the kink in his nose, memento of that nightmare evening.

Zac put his hands on my shoulders for a moment. 'I don't need to think. I know what I want. I want you. And I'll wait as long as it takes.' He left the room.

I deflated onto the bed. Within the last hour I'd gone from thinking I might never see him again, to having him say he'd wait for me always. Part of my anger was at myself. After all these months – was I going to fall swooning at his feet? I lectured myself. *Get a grip. Don't give him all the power.*

When I went downstairs, he came out of the sitting room and asked what time I'd be home. 'May I have a hug before you go?'

'No.' I thumped out of the house. I was halfway to work when I realised I'd left my music behind. I spent the day flummoxed, good for nothing.

20 March 1956

Well, I've seen him. It was about as bad as I'd feared. I could tell he'd had sex in the last few hours. He's thinner, pale, and with a bloody great love bite on his neck. He's furious with me and he's hurting. His eyes were cyan marbles, glaring icily at me. But my instant reaction was – how could I have left this glorious man for so long? I was mesmerised, unable to speak at first.

I tried to tell him I loved him, that I hadn't left him. I don't know if the message got through, because by God, he was in a rage. He was quite intimidating. But along with the anger, I saw something on his face that showed he does care. And he still wears my ring. He refused to give me a hug, he left in a huff, but I'm telling myself – if he were indifferent, he wouldn't act like this.

I finally slept around lunchtime. I ate something, had a bath. I've spoken to Miriam. She's a good friend. She told me where they're going and promised she won't say anything. Tomorrow, if Teddy doesn't cancel the holiday, I'll make arrangements to follow him. I'm just waiting for him to come home.

As I walked with Anna to choir, I told her Zac had turned up and was saying he still loved me.

She asked, 'Why on earth are you here, Theo? Why aren't you with him?'

I couldn't even explain it to myself. 'He left me for months with barely a word. We can't just pick up where we left off. Why should I change my plans for him? I want to go on holiday. He can work out what he wants.'

I was distracted at rehearsal and made a lot of mistakes. It didn't help having to read the music over someone's shoulder. The conductor got increasingly irritated. When I came in too early on an entry, he exclaimed, 'What's wrong with you tonight, Lawder?' All I could think about was Zac, waiting at home. As soon as we finished, I grabbed my things and told Anna I'd see her in the morning.

Zac was in the sitting room with the fire going. Again, his

manner was calm. He got me a whisky. I sat down in the other armchair and Pip turned her head one to the other, obviously confused. She wasn't used to us sitting so far apart.

We talked for probably half an hour in a tired stalemate. He didn't go on the geological survey. He'd planned to come home, but got sick with a fever and ended up in hospital. As soon as he was better, he booked the flight. He tried to ring me many times. He wrote me several letters.

'I know you gave everything to get me out of my depression—'

I snapped, 'I don't want your fucking gratitude! I did it because I loved you. What a joke that it destroyed our relationship.'

'I know you have a lot to forgive, Teddy. I know you need time. But nothing has destroyed our love. If anything, I think our relationship can be stronger than ever.'

I looked at him stonily. *Speak for yourself.* I was fighting my response to him. The way we communicated on such a deep level – his energy and charisma – the memory of all this had dimmed, especially as the depression had so altered him. But I also knew that, however much I still loved him, this last year had affected me badly. *He's hurt me too much. We can't recover from this.*

He asked quietly, 'Teddy. Did you really think I'd left you?'

'Of course. You used the trip as an excuse to get away from me.'

He leaned forward. 'The last thing I wanted was to hurt you, darling. Just tell me one thing. Have you stopped loving me?'

I hesitated, then shook my head, looking away. How

could I ever stop loving him?

'So, why are we sitting so far apart?'

My anger flared. 'Sometimes, love isn't enough. A relationship can die because there's been too much hurt. Events can force two people apart. You've been away for months on your adventures, and I've been making my own life and – and sleeping with other men. A lot of men.'

He didn't seem surprised. 'That changes nothing for me. I love you, Teddy. I'll do anything to make things right between us.'

I heard a fox coughing in the distance. My mind dragged lethargically through lack of sleep. Zac must have realised because he said in a practical tone, 'You need to sleep. I suppose you're leaving early tomorrow?' I nodded.

He went on, 'Are you still determined to go?' I nodded again, beyond words. 'May I hold you before you go to bed?' I shook my head and left the room. I knew what was likely to happen if we embraced, and I still had too much hurt rusting my soul. I fell asleep within minutes.

In the morning, I woke to a concrete sky and bulky rain. I dressed quickly and grabbed my bag. Zac was hovering in the hallway. 'Shall I drive you to the station?'

'Thank you, that won't be necessary.' We looked at each other. 'I'll be back on the eighth. We can talk then, if you're still here. If you haven't changed your mind.'

He winced at that. I said goodbye. But I stood by the front gate, immobilised with regret. It took several minutes to get the strength to open the gate and walk away. I didn't look back.

21 March 1956

We started talking last night. I wanted to hold him tight and weep at all the pain I've caused him. He looks at me with such anger and hurt. I can't bear to think I did that to him. He thought I'd left him – or I was dead. I don't know what happened to my letters. Of course he would have come to that conclusion – who can blame him? I know my behaviour was strange before I left. We didn't get far because he was obviously out on his feet. He looks exhausted. This holiday will be good for him. Good for us, I hope. I asked again for a hug and he refused.

He left quickly this morning. I watched from the window. He stood at the front gate, in the rain, for several minutes. I said out loud: turn around darling. Come back to me. But after a while he dropped his head and went off. I've been to a travel agent and booked a flight to Corfu. I'm going through my savings but I don't care. It's only money.

When I discovered he'd survived Dunkirk, it seemed a miracle. How many chances do you get to be with someone like Theo? And here I was with a second chance. But he'd come back from the brink of death. He was in terrible pain and had built a wall around himself. I waited for him to give the sign he was ready. And when he came to me, he matched me passion for passion. He gave himself in every way. We made a vow freely, with an equal commitment and love. That was the foundation for our life together. Now, I must remember that lesson to bring him back to me again.

22

The journey to Corfu took nearly two days, by train to the south of Italy then a boat trip to the island. I questioned myself exhaustively. *Why didn't I stay with Zac to sort things out? Am I mad?* In the next breath, I would think our relationship was broken beyond repair. When we finally arrived, I fell into bed and slept for twelve hours.

We had rooms in a hotel in Corfu Town. On our first day, we went exploring, the azure sky and warmth a benediction. We wandered around the narrow streets and ate ice creams in front of the sea. I felt more hopeful, and decided I'd write Zac a long letter. But when we went to dinner, lights shining on the water, my mood plummeted and I again tormented myself with regrets.

As we were leaving the taverna I heard my name. There was Zac, sitting at a table in front of me. I halted, mouth agape. Was I hallucinating – had I somehow conjured up a chimera through my longing for him? For a moment, I was back in the Blitz of 1940, glimpsing him through clouds of smoke.

I stammered, 'You – what are you doing here?'

Zac was speaking, but I couldn't take in his words. I turned and my feet took me a few yards along the street with no idea where I was going. Then I stopped. *He came after me. He's here.* I walked back and looked long and hard on his face: so beloved, so deeply missed.

He smiled tentatively. 'May I buy you a drink?'

Anna and Miriam had disappeared. I nodded and sat down, saying, 'I think you owe me an explanation.'

For the next two hours, Zac told me everything. I questioned him mercilessly and he never once flinched from replying.

'I still can't really understand it, Teddy. I knew intellectually I loved you, but somehow I just couldn't feel it.' He explained he'd also feared he was impotent. 'Can you understand why I didn't ring you? I didn't know what to say. I was so confused. I felt as if all the certainty had fallen out of my world.'

He told of his misery when I hung up on him. He thought I'd had enough of him. He kept ringing me after that. I admitted, 'I thought there was no point. I didn't want to hear your explanations about why you'd left me.'

'So, all those times I rang, you were there refusing to answer?'

'Sometimes.'

When he said his sexual encounters in Rio confirmed he wasn't impotent, he stopped to check my reaction, but I said only, 'Go on.'

He explained how his love for me came flooding back. 'It's the strangest thing, Teddy, but it's the truth. It was like a lightning strike – all these feelings just came jumping out at me. Do you believe me?'

And I had to say, 'I do.'

'But then I got sick …'

The waiter came up and told us the restaurant was closing. We'd been too immersed in our conversation to notice we were the last customers.

Zac asked, 'Would you like to come back to my room for a drink?'

'No, I'll go back to my hotel. We can continue this in the morning.'

'May I walk with you?' I agreed. He kept looking over at me.

When we got to my hotel, the lane was quiet and dark, just a lantern at the front. I said goodnight and turned to go. His voice was urgent. 'Let me hold you.' I shook my head mutely. 'It's been so long. I've missed you so much.'

I stood with my back to him, irresolute. 'Oh, Teddy … I feel so scared and lost.' I turned and saw the vulnerability on his face.

At first I was stiff, hugging him the way I might a friend – keeping my body back, the unhappiness of the last year a barrier between us. Then I started to let go. I relaxed into his embrace and hugged him back. Then we were holding each other tightly. *I love him, I love him. I just love him.*

He said in my ear, 'Please forgive me. It was never my intention to hurt you.'

A motorbike came roaring into the street and we jumped apart, laughing nervously. I suggested, 'Shall we meet for breakfast?' He nodded slowly, and I went into the hotel.

I hardly slept that night. Myriad thoughts and emotions wheeled through my mind, but hope kept pushing through.

23 March 1956

I arrived this afternoon after a flight to Athens, then a small plane to Corfu. From the air it's green and mountainous. I hope we'll explore it together at some point. I booked into a hotel in the old town. I hope to have happy memories of this room. But not yet.

I found them in a seafront taverna, as planned with Miriam. She spotted me, but I got a table at the front. Anna chatted away while Theo stared into space. The way I feel about him, it doesn't matter how he looks – but what a bonus that I find him so desirable. That part of me has completely woken up.

When they walked past my table, I said hello. He stared as though he'd seen a ghost, the colour draining from his face. He turned abruptly and walked away. After a while he turned around and looked at me. Then he came back.

We stayed until the restaurant closed. I told him everything. He challenged me, but he listened. He started to let go of his anger. I walked him back to his hotel and asked again for a hug. This time he agreed. To have him in my arms – I thought I might cry. Oh, my Teddy. We looked at each other, then a bloody noisy bike went past. He sprang away and said goodnight. I waited outside for ages, hoping he might change his mind, but no. I'm anxious, but hopeful. I'll wait as long as he needs.

I tapped on Anna and Miriam's door the next morning and said we'd be meeting Zac for breakfast. As we walked there, Anna couldn't stop grinning at me. 'Theo, you look the best I've seen you in ages.'

Miriam linked her arm through mine. 'I suppose you know I told Zac where to find us. Do you mind?' I shook my head. How could I object to my friends showing such care and concern?

We found Zac waiting at the taverna with a coffee. He told us stories about his trip. Anna said, 'Oh, Zac, it's lovely to have you back. We missed you.' He kept smiling over at me and I smiled back. The glacier of sorrow I'd carried around for the last year was melting away.

As soon as we finished breakfast, the others got up to leave. Miriam announced, 'We're going shopping. I'm sure you two can keep yourselves entertained.' It was only some hours later that I remembered they hated shopping.

Zac and I walked by the water and went for a swim. I had my things with me but Zac needed to go back to his hotel room to get his trunks. I waited in the doorway. I didn't want to go inside. Not yet. The turquoise water was clear and cool. Then we lay on our towels on the sand, the sun warm on our bodies.

The words fell out of me. My loneliness when he was lost in his depression. The rejection I felt when he pushed me away. How I believed he no longer wanted to be my lover. My anger and devastation at being abandoned. And, some weeks after that, my terror that he was dead. How I'd sought solace through casual sex with other men. I could see silent tears dotted on his face, but he listened without interruption. He let me talk out my anger and hurt. I saw in his eyes all I needed to know.

We wandered off and had a late lunch, but I couldn't stop yawning. I told Zac I'd pick him up at his hotel for dinner. I went back to my hotel, lay on the bed and instantly sank into a dreamless sleep.

Around two hours later, I came wide awake, knowing so clearly how I felt. *What am I doing alone in my hotel room, when Zac is nearby?* I scribbled a note saying "all is well", slipped it under Anna and Miriam's door and left.

Outside, the light glowed copper and chestnut in the last hour before sunset. I used to find this a melancholy time, but that day I exulted in its mellow beauty. The shadows were lengthening, rendering everything larger than life. Swifts careened through the air and geraniums shouted at me with a vibrant crimson. The honeysuckle dripped its sweet smell. I could see and hear acutely. All my senses were fizzing. I felt intensely alive, intensely joyful. Part of me wanted to linger, to savour the anticipation of going to Zac, but I could not bear to waste any more time away from him.

There was no one in reception. I went straight up to his room and knocked on the door. He opened it, in his shorts with no top, and I realised I'd woken him. He'd partly drawn the curtains, with the sun streaming through a gap. I was so consumed by my feelings, so focused on what I wanted, that I stared at him without speaking. I saw his fear.

He said, 'Give me a moment,' and walked to the bathroom at the back. I heard what sounded like a sob. Had he misunderstood my intention?

I went to the bathroom and found him standing in front of the sink, his head bowed. I put my arms around him from behind. He said my name and I said, 'Shh.' I pressed myself against his back. I caressed his body and our eyes met in the mirror. He tried to turn around, but I wouldn't let him. I slipped my hand under his shorts. I wanted him so much my skin crawled, my bones ached. I started kissing his neck and back, stopping occasionally to watch his face in the mirror. His eyes were shut; his face echoed my desire. He was too strong and turned around.

All our longing for each other, all those months apart, came out in an explosive way. We would stop to rest for a while and talk, then we were off rotating again on cycles of passion. We didn't leave his room that night. Sometime around midnight we realised we were hungry. He found biscuits and a couple of apples and we ate them in bed, curled together. We were euphoric, possessed by the magic of having found each other again. We felt fresh, brand new – bounding on springy legs, peering trustfully at the world.

And I knew all the casual sex had amounted to nothing

– a mere physical release, a transient comfort when I thought I had lost him. Nothing could better this. Nothing could match the pleasure and commitment I felt when we made love.

25 March 1956

He's mine again. I'm the happiest man on this earth. He overwhelms my senses, my mind, my heart. I had forgotten his smell. I had forgotten the sweetness of his smile. I'm wild for him. Exultant.

We spent most of yesterday talking. He told me what a crap time he went through, thanks to me. I could see his resistance to me falling away. It took all my willpower not to touch him. When he said he was going back to his hotel for a sleep, I wanted to scream with frustration. I told myself – be patient. But when he knocked on my door and looked at me so fiercely, I was suddenly terrified he'd come to tell me it's over. For a moment I couldn't control my grief. Then he was there with his arms around me and I went from despair to joy.

I can see the sunrise from a gap in the curtains. We haven't left the room – we're in the grip of a monumental passion. We have a year to make up for, after all, and I have a strong need to obliterate any other man's touch on his body.

I'm looking at him now as I write this. He is unique, exquisite. How beautifully appropriate that we've found each other again on the island where Odysseus rested on his journey home to Penelope.

23

We barely left the hotel room for the next couple of days. We fell asleep entwined and woke up at the same time, smiling at each other in delight. It was the best way to tell our deepest fears and truths. We knew this intensity could not last but, as Zac said, 'Let's enjoy it while it's here.'

On some days, the four of us explored the island, sampling the secret coves and beaches. Other times, Zac and I took off on a scooter, my arms tight around his waist. If no one was around, we would scream out with the sheer joy of life. We spent hours swimming in the sea, naked if we found a deserted cove. The Mediterranean was dazzling – a fusion of every blue and green hue, including the colour of Zac's eyes. I would think with a smile how I'd always wanted to dive into his eyes.

We joined our friends every evening for long meals and conversations, until there came a point when Zac or I would yawn and say, 'I think it's time for bed.' Anna and Miriam teased us, but we couldn't wait to get back to our cocoon.

Zac gave up his hotel room to move in with me. The hotel management didn't question this – they were more agitated when they saw us coming out of Anna and Miriam's room. The manager lectured us, 'No men in the ladies' bedroom, no good.'

'Of course not,' we assured him solemnly.

We found countless reasons to touch hands or brush our bodies together. If no one was around, we held hands and stopped regularly to kiss. We couldn't keep our eyes off each other. We couldn't stop grinning. Zac said, 'Look at us, like two lovestruck teens.' We felt we held the world in our hands. Together, we were invincible with the strength of ten.

During this time, we continued working through the events of the last year and the causes of Zac's depression. He told me, 'You rescued me, Teddy. No other man would have done that. You healed me.'

I shook my head. 'It's mutual. You healed me, too. The strength and confidence I get from your love – it means everything.'

We were having coffee in the seafront taverna. I put my hand lovingly to his cheek as an elderly Greek woman walked past. She averted her face and crossed herself, muttering. I continued, 'Anyway, if you love someone, you don't just walk away when it stops being easy. You're with them through the good and the bad. I know you'd do the same for me. But Zac – you've changed! Before, you couldn't talk so openly about your feelings.' He nodded.

'Yes, I have. I think my moods over the years, the depression, all came out of things that controlled me. I couldn't talk about them. Now I can. You did all this, Teddy. You set me free. You really are the most exceptional person.' He added, 'You've changed too. You're tougher.'

One day, we drove past groves of cypresses and ancient olive trees to a hilltop monastery. I still had the postcard Alan had sent me after his visit there, writing that he'd left feeling peaceful and optimistic. Walking around, following his footsteps, brought me for the first time a sense of acceptance about his death. I spent a long time gazing down at the view. Zac found me there and stood close with an enquiring look. I smiled at him.

'I'm glad we came here. I feel I've got back my happy memories of Alan.'

29 March 1956

I'm the luckiest man in the world. I get to fall in love with Teddy twice in my life. The first time, we knew this was life-changing for us. We built the most beautiful life. Until my demons from the past, and the hatred we face, came close to destroying us. And now, we're tried and tested. We know our love and commitment. We know what we want. The hatred is still out there, but it can't break us. My one, my only love. Life has given me the most precious gift.

30 March 1956

The sun has real warmth in it now without burning my pale-skinned merman.

I have a fountain of optimism bubbling up in me. There's nothing I can't talk to him about. I'm like a child with a new toy. I often wanted to tell him my worries before, but it was such a habit to keep them locked away that the words stuck in my throat. Now, I say what I'm feeling and each time it gets easier. He listens to me carefully and treats my quaking little fears with respect – and it all seems more manageable. The feeling doesn't control me. Sounds simple – but it took me all my life to get here.

We've talked a few times about our sexual adventures when we were apart. Perhaps at some point I'll feel jealous. But it's too theoretical when we're on this enchanted island in our world of love. I do know he's more confident. Last night, the waiter was definitely flirting with him. Once, he wouldn't have noticed. But he flirted right back. He's going to keep me on my toes.

1 April 1956

They celebrate Easter here by throwing clay pots down from towers.

Smashing fun. We spend hours exploring, going to a cove to swim, or wandering in the hills. Teddy says this is our best holiday ever. I told him it's our second honeymoon.

In the last days of the holiday, we moved onto more pragmatic issues. I went through my options on the vetting I faced at work. I didn't want to lie and it was unlikely to work anyway – who knew what Burgess, or my Rome colleagues, might have reported about me?

Zac urged me to avoid the humiliation of being sacked. 'I know you've loved working at the Foreign Office, Teddy. It would be a rotten way to end your time there.'

Whatever I did, there was clearly no future for me in the FO. Our discussions confirmed my belief that I needed to have some control over the process. The only way to do this was to resign.

But what could I do next? I was thirty-eight, very late to think about a new career. I half-heartedly mentioned a few possibilities, but Zac commented, 'You're not really convinced, are you?' I agreed. 'What about psychology? Look how you helped me. People always talk to you about their problems. You have a gift.'

I protested, 'But I'd need to go back and do another degree. It would mean years with no money coming in.'

'We've got savings, don't forget. We'll get by.' We tossed the idea around for a while and he said, 'At least consider it as a possibility.'

'What about you, Zac?'

We agreed that he would come with me to Rabat, as I hoped to defer vetting until my return to London. But this was where Zac surprised me. He told me he'd had a story in his head for weeks and wanted to write it down.

I asked, 'Do you mean – write a book?'

'No, no,' he said quickly, 'I don't know what will happen. I can't call it that.' We were lying on the beach and he trickled sand through his fingers, glancing at me from under his eyelashes.

I was intrigued, but it seemed so obvious when I thought about it. I'd wondered if he could write for a living, but my thoughts had been more of journalism.

'What's it about?'

He was hesitant, almost bashful. 'Oh … someone going to sea to escape a wrongful arrest.'

'Zac, I think it's the most marvellous idea! You must do it.'

He grinned like a boy. We agreed he would at least write while I remained in the FO. We could live on my salary and his small SIS pension. He gave me his most charming smile. 'I'll be your kept man, Teddy.' I laughed. This was proof indeed of how much he had changed.

At the end of that day, I went off with Anna and Miriam to get presents for our family and friends. I bought necklaces for my mother and Ruth, toys for the children, bracelets for Claude and Jordi, and two blank notebooks for Zac.

I gave them to him in the evening. 'You can use one for writing and the other for putting down ideas.'

Zac kissed me. 'I don't know if this will work out. I may decide in a few days that it's rubbish.' The sweetly excited look on his face gave me a flash of the happy child he must have been, before his parents tried to crush that out of him.

'Look, Zac, all you can do is give it a try.'

6 April 1956

Dawn is coming. I can see a sliver of light next to the sea. Teddy's asleep, a faint smile on his lips. It's our last full day before we start the trek back. Part of me wants to freeze time, to keep us here always. But mostly I'm excited about our future adventures and journey together. Life is bona. So damned good.

Zac came back with us on the overland journey. We got home late on the Sunday evening and fell into bed. There was a pile of mail and no food in the house but Zac said, 'Don't worry, I'll take care of that.'

Getting up early the next morning and leaving him was a shock. I daydreamed through work, counting the hours till I could get home. When I did, I found food in the fridge, the house spotless, Pip dancing around – and Zac's letters from Brazil. I sat down and read them right away, then admitted, 'If these had arrived in time, you'd have had a different reception when you got home.'

Zac shrugged. 'It doesn't matter, Teddy. The important thing is how we are now. And we got to have the best holiday ever.'

When we went up to bed, I saw he had strung our Christmas fairy lights around the room as a reminder of our Corfu holiday.

We had six weeks before I was due to leave for Morocco. Monica agreed to take Pip. I contacted the British Psychological Society to get my degree accredited. My vetting form arrived and I threw it in the bin. Zac spent most of his days at the British Library, full of positive energy. I realised he was expressing a creative drive that had previously lacked an outlet, aside from his private journals.

He folded seamlessly back into our circle, although

I noticed Claude's initial coolness with him. Zac explained, 'He's angry with me for the way I hurt you, and who can blame him? I hope he'll forgive me.'

A few weeks later, Claude was teasing us again – 'Look at you two making eyes at each other. It's indecent!' – and I laughed in relief. I knew how important their friendship was.

My mother gave Zac a warm kiss on the cheek when we took her out to lunch. Commenting afterwards on her change in attitude, I said, 'We should never lose hope. It's always possible for things to change for the better.'

Zac replied, 'That's what I'm learning from you.'

Not long before our departure, a man I'd slept with during Zac's absence came up to me in the pub. I said hello and turned away, but he didn't get the message. Zac regarded him with flinty eyes while he suggested, 'How about more of the same? We can make it a threesome.'

Upon which, Zac stood up and calmly poured his beer over the man's head. I pulled Zac outside, ready for his reproaches – but instead he started laughing. After a stunned moment, I joined in. When he could speak, Zac said, 'Well, I think you got a better deal with me.' I just grinned at him. He suggested, 'While we're here, why don't we walk through that lane?'

This was the time to expunge those memories. When we got to the area where we were attacked, Zac stopped. 'I'll never forget what you did for me that night. You saved my life.'

'But you threw yourself in front of me – so you'd already done that.' We had a few quiet words, then went home.

12 May 1956

I haven't been writing here – too busy with my project (far too arrogant to call it a book). I'm doing as much research as possible before we leave for Morocco. My head's buzzing with ideas. I don't know what will come of this but I've decided, with Teddy's support, to just see what happens. That means he'll be the wage earner with me the kept man. Teddy's gigolo. He says I need to fulfil all parts of the role and I told him, absolutely no problem there, darling.

I have this deep sense of peace, of connectedness and family. To be home, back in my life – I'll never again take it for granted. It's a bloody wonderful life, with my family and good friends, Pip, and of course, Teddy at the centre.

He's so sweet, like honey. I could lap him up. But no – honey's too cloying and he's never that. Honey with a hint of chilli – a kickback at the end? Or, no, he's like dark chocolate.

I often stare at him, entranced. I'm like a boy struck dumb with calf love. I feel the same intensity of love and passion as I did when we first got together. But it's different in many ways – better. We know each other inside out – all our faults and flaws, our mistakes and hurt we've caused, although God knows it was mostly on my side. We've come through this crisis and we're even stronger.

I met one of his pick-ups the other night and got satisfaction from a childish gesture. Of course, I have no right to complain (in fact, his adventures have given him a confidence I find very sexy – although I hope he won't do that again). He's proved himself to be the best of men. I always knew it – and that I'm a better person for being with him. He's forgiven me everything. There's still hurt. We'll just keep on talking and getting through it.

But every now and then, in the midst of my joy, I get this shiver and think – God, I nearly lost him.

1956-1973: We are both lover and beloved

24

We drove to Morocco, stopping at Dunkirk on the way. I'd agreed as it seemed important to Zac – personally, I never wanted to see that place again. Blowsy clouds scudded across the sky on the day we arrived. We strolled down to the port and the beach beyond. I had only vague memories of the town, so couldn't tell how changed it was. But the beach was unrecognisable. Broad and sandy, with children building sandcastles and flying a kite – it bore no resemblance to the hell on earth I'd known. I sank onto a hillock and stared around in perplexity. Surely, we were in the wrong place?

Zac sat down next to me. 'That's where we were dug in after you got hit. That's where you were taken onto the fishing boat from the mole. And over there,' pointing to the left, 'that's where the rest of us got bombed.' A shudder rattled his body. 'I was the last to go. I wanted to make sure all my men got on the ship. What a joke! I thought I was keeping them safe. We were up to our waists in the water when they bombed us. The ship went up in front of me and ... Always before, I saw the sea as my friend, but not that day.'

His eyes were unseeing, turned inward to his memories, his voice hushed. 'The water was on fire, Teddy. I saw my arm burning. I dived down to get away from the flames. My lungs were bursting. When I came up, men were dying all around me.

Some of them were on fire—' He sucked in a breath. 'Oh, God! War is so cruel. What you see, what you do – it never really leaves you.'

I took his burnt hand in mine, unable to speak. 'And, all that time, I feared you were dead. Strange, because that was when I first kissed you, yet it was the worst day of my life.'

We stared out to sea, talking over our memories of Dunkirk, something we'd never really done in detail before. I started recognising landmarks on the beach.

'Let's go down to the water,' Zac suggested.

We took off our shoes and socks and rolled up our trousers. I found myself walking gingerly, as if to avoid stepping on the phantasm soldiers so vivid in my mind. And then, in one lucid heartbeat, I was right back there. I could see the soldiers who were no longer illusions. I heard the noise of the diving planes. As we passed one sandy tussock, the young soldier who'd been lying there in 1940 was again in front of me – his legs blown off, bleeding to death and screaming for his mother. I gasped and staggered, shot through with unbearable anguish.

Zac threw his arms around me. 'Steady on, darling.' Slowly, I came back to the present. Zac's eyes were fixed on me. 'I'm here,' he said.

The distant sound of children's laughter floated past on the wind. My breathing calmed and we went on to the sea.

Squatting down, Zac trailed his left hand in the water. He couldn't fully straighten the little and ring fingers, but the burns had faded and he had most of his grip back. 'Come here, Teddy,' he said and started to trickle water onto my scars. 'The water is healing us.' He smiled up at me and a flash of unexpected joy suffused me.

'Oh, Zac! We came so close to death that day. What

a miracle to be here now – to have our life together.'

He stood up and put his hands on my shoulders. 'Yes. Finding you, surviving that horror, changed my life completely.'

I didn't care who was around. I leaned forward and kissed him. 'Our second kiss on Dunkirk beach.' As we resumed the drive south, our Dunkirk experience now carried a peaceful sense of resolution.

The FO housed me in an apartment in the centre of Rabat, a quiet town with white-washed buildings. Morocco had achieved independence only weeks earlier, following years of rioting over an unpopular ruler imposed by France. The Sultan had just returned to the throne and I was involved in complex negotiations. I was also the consul, sorting out lost passports or British tourists needing medical care.

I worked as hard as ever, including the usual weekend cover and evening functions. But something inside me had shifted. Working for the FO had always been more than just a job, and my colleagues had felt almost like family. But now I knew that I was viewed as undesirable, my emotional ties had loosened. I was judged deficient in the right type of masculinity – my loyalty was suspect. Hurt by the rejection, I turned down social invitations from colleagues. I needed to cut off for my own protection.

Morocco was a completely different proposition, and one we embraced. When I wasn't working, we explored Rabat or swam in the sea. We'd eat a simple meal out, then sit on our balcony. We read, played chess or talked for hours, lying in each other's arms. Zac told me about his writing. He carefully refrained from calling it a book, but had thrown himself into it in his usual organised way. We spent hours wandering around the medina, drinking mint tea with shopkeepers while we haggled over the price of a trinket. We got rugs for our house and presents for our friends. I bought Zac a silver bracelet; I would have given him the sun and moon. We didn't socialise at all the first few weeks. We just wanted to be together. We wanted for nothing, no one.

It was the second anniversary of Alan's death soon after we arrived. There was sadness, but also acceptance. I said, 'Alan always told us to look after each other, so I don't want to feel guilty that we're so happy.'

'We don't need any more guilt in our lives, Teddy. I should know. It gets you nowhere. Alan would want the best for us. We'll always remember him.'

14 June 1956

We've been in Rabat for three weeks and most of the essentials are sorted. I've rented a room and keep a few things there. I need it in case we run into trouble in the future. I know the SIS guy at the embassy, so it's best to keep a low profile.

I've set up Teddy's second bedroom as a study of sorts, and I'm settling into a routine. I write all morning, stop for a late lunch then get out for a walk. That way I'm completely free when he finishes work. I don't know where this writing will go, but I'm loving it.

We haven't made it out of Rabat. For now, we're content with a quiet life. We bought each other djellabas in the medina. Never thought I'd find myself wearing a sort of dress, but it's damned comfortable. And, bloody hell, Teddy looks so delicious when he wears his. I watch him with a look of stupefied delight.

After a few weeks we started travelling on free weekends: to the nearby Rif Mountains, along the coast, visiting archaeological sites, or driving to the larger towns. We went most often to Tangier which had a small homosexual community, mainly Americans who all seemed to be writers or artists. They tended to be heavy drinkers or drug users and made liberal use of Moroccan boys, something we found distasteful. One American writer used to boast how he liked them young. I got into a furious argument, telling him it was the worst form of exploitation and he was no better than a slave owner. Zac had to pull me away. I refused to speak to the writer after that.

But, sometimes, it was a relief to let my guard down and just be myself. As Zac said, 'We need to treat the scene with caution. Take from it what's positive, but don't let it drag us down.'

After a day or so we had enough, and returned to our quiet life in Rabat. Then I'd go home after a stuffy embassy reception, fending off the usual questions about my private life – or after tearing up another vetting form – and say to Zac, 'What about a trip to Tangier?'

One encounter there helped me decide on my future career. I'd noticed a young man with sad eyes hovering uncertainly on the edges of the crowd. One day we invited him for coffee and he told us his story.

Brad came from a conservative family in the American South. After his parents found him kissing another boy, they made him attend a clinic for a "cure". He was shown pictures of naked men while a doctor administered electric shocks. When that failed, he was given drugs to make him sick and forced to sit for hours in his vomit and shit. That was when he tried to kill himself. Eventually, he realised the only solution was to pretend the treatment worked. Brad told us he was still queer, only he felt nauseous whenever he had sex. All the sorrows of the world were on his young face. 'My parents have told me I must go home. But I can't bear it! I can't keep pretending.'

I had to clamp my lips together to stop from shouting out my rage. How could this be done in the name of psychiatry? But I knew my anger was not what Brad needed. Instead, I asked what he achieved by suppressing his nature to please others and suggested various options, stating it was in his power to make a good and happy life. Brad listened intently. He asked about our lives. When I told him of my mother's acceptance, Ruth's loving support and our circle of friends, he began to look hopeful.

A few weeks later, Brad came up to us in Tangier, energised and determined. He'd written to tell his family he wasn't returning, and had the details of someone he could stay with in New York while he looked for work. We wished him the best.

Zac said to me afterwards, 'You have a real skill in the way you listen and draw people out. You should use it. Just think what good you could do.'

I started contacting universities in London.

30 July 1956

We got back last night from Tangier and the usual crowd – loud Americans overly pleased with themselves and their artistic brilliance. After a day I've had a bellyful of them, but in small doses it's tolerable. I don't know what they make of us – probably a boring married couple – and don't care. As long as I keep my tone polite, they don't seem to notice if I'm rude. I had an amusing conversation yesterday with a drunk guy who fancies himself a Great American Writer:

> GAW: Goddam it, that boyfriend of yours sure is cute!!
>
> Me: He's not my "boyfriend". He's my lover.
>
> GAW: Same difference, he's still cute!!

Me: No, he isn't.

GAW (jaw drops): You don't think your boyfriend is cute?

Me: "Cute" is patronising. "Cute" is twee. There's nothing twee about Theo. He's gorgeous, he's brave, he's strong, he's intelligent, and he has more integrity in his little finger than you could hope to have in your entire life.

GAW: Ha, ha! I know you Brits are big on irony!!

Teddy's feeling his way at the embassy. He has a detachment that's new. Always he was so dedicated – they bloody well got their money's worth with him. No longer. We need to make the most of this last overseas posting. He told me he's enquired about courses in clinical psychology. I just said good, but I'm delighted.

26 August 1956

We've been having an absorbing conversation on and off over the weekend. We went for a swim, wandered around the medina, made love, wrote letters – but kept coming back to it and teasing it through, like unravelling knots. It started when we were lounging on the balcony and Teddy said I get more handsome every year. I laughed and said I don't think so, but thank you for saying that. If he finds me easy on the eye, that's just fine by me. I adore feeling cherished by him.

That set onto something I've been mulling over since our crisis. I'd always feared he'd leave me one day, because I loved him more than he loved me. And when I followed that thought through, I could see we'd fallen into certain patterns in our relationship. I was the more experienced lover, and he was the younger, more innocent beloved. It certainly had some truth when we first met – helped by the hierarchical military business, my bossiness and his natural sweetness. But I suspect we got a bit fixed in those roles as the years went by.

When I explained this to Teddy he listened attentively (as he always does), and said he's been thinking about this as well. He

213

wondered whether our youthful fascination with Ancient Greece was to blame. That was like, boom, a light bulb crashing on in my head.

He said: let's face it, we don't have any blueprint for our relationship. All we see are heterosexual couples, so a lot of queers tend to parody that – one being more masculine and holding the power, the other more effeminate and submissive. Or we look to Ancient Greece, when same-sex love was tolerated if it fitted into a certain mould: an older man and a boy. The lover fucked and looked after the younger beloved, and it was viewed as masculine behaviour. The boy was sexually passive in the traditional female role. But when he grew up, the relationship was no longer acceptable – because to have two adult men as equal lovers was as shocking then as we queers are for society now. Teddy thinks he read too much Plato when he was working out his identity and it unconsciously influenced him.

He said, so where do we fit in? We're not acceptable now, but we would have been equally shocking in Ancient Greece. It's like we're freaks – but we just love our own sex. Where can we be at home? I told him: we make our own life, Teddy. We love and protect each other, we have our family and friends, and we squeeze out a small corner for ourselves in this world.

And here's the thing – he does love me equally. How he's proved that! He gave everything to save me from my depression, or those thugs in Soho. He says it's no more than I'd do for him. Of course, that's true. He's so strong – he's not the naive innocent when we first met. Now I'm letting go of my need for control, I realise I can (sometimes) let him look after me. Since my depression I can see we're more fluid in our relationship. Increasingly, I have this feeling of deep contentment.

We agree, we feel proud of who we are – two men in love with each other, equal in every way. Bugger what society thinks. We know what we have, and it's priceless. We are both lover and beloved. We want the same things. We agreed, we're just going to make it up as we

214

go along – and keep on talking. I really feel we're on a journey. It's all fantabulosa.

25

Just as in Rome, I started noticing an atmosphere at work. It started when we were sitting outside a cafe and the SIS man walked past, then stopped. 'Why, if it isn't Bonneval!' It was too polished. Zac trotted out a story about just visiting, old army friends and so on.

After he left, Zac muttered, 'This could be a problem for you, Teddy.' Our secret existence had been exposed, but I just shrugged. I knew my time was up in the FO.

A few days later, I was called into the ambassador's office and asked if I shared my official accommodation with a friend. I replied, truthfully, that he had his own place. When asked, 'Are you friends with this Bonneval chap?' I admitted it proudly. The ambassador's face screwed up in distaste as he contemplated the queer fish laid out on the slab in front of him. He stated, not meeting my eyes, 'Your temporary duty is finished, Lawder. You need to return to London for your vetting.'

Zac and I went for a long walk around the town that evening. My letter of resignation was already in the diplomatic bag to London. I'd been in correspondence with King's College about qualifying as a clinical psychologist, and could start in January. I didn't want Zac to stop his writing – but how would we survive for three years, with no income, while I did a PhD?

Zac was nonchalant. 'We'll be fine, Teddy. Our pensions should just about cover food and bills, and we've got savings. I've already contacted newspapers, and hopefully I'll get some journalism work.' He added with a cynical laugh, 'If Philby can get work as a full-time correspondent, there's no reason why I can't.'

As it turned out, *The Observer* asked him to write a piece on the political situation in Morocco. The money was not much but, as he said, it meant he got his foot in the door.

24 October 1956

We're packing to go back to London. This time last year I'd started on the trip to Brazil, just emerging from my depression – and in a crisis over Teddy. What a difference a year makes! Our visit to Dunkirk peeled away another layer of pain and control. I've been free ever since of that recurring nightmare – men screaming as the ship went down, mangled bodies, blood and flames in the water.

My life is uncertain in terms of work and money, but I couldn't care less. I have such certainty with everything else.

On our return to London, I finalised arrangements for my course and had meetings with FO personnel, who tried to persuade me not to leave. I was polite but did not offer explanations; nor did I tell my mother the reason I had resigned. She was fussing enough about the "risks" we were taking. I responded as brightly as I could, but in truth I was nervous myself. Zac continued with his book and picked up newspaper commissions to write about the intelligence background to the Suez Canal crisis. My mother proudly cut out the articles and kept them.

My final day at work came shortly before Christmas. All my colleagues had asked why I'd resigned. By then, I had such a repugnance about lying that I explained I was leaving before the FO could dismiss me for being homosexual. A few looked shocked and backed away, but others expressed their disagreement with the policy. It made no difference to the outcome, but their support provided a mild balm to the injustice that tore at me.

On my last afternoon, I walked around the FO building, which I'd come to love. I wandered through the fine rooms, up the grand staircase, along the corridors, past my favourite statues and paintings, silently saying goodbye.

31 December 1956

We've just come back from a party at Claude's to welcome in the New Year. This has been an "interesting" year – certainly a branching out for both of us. Not that life with Teddy can ever be routine, but it's particularly thought-provoking right now. It started with so much pain and confusion, the terror I'd lost him – it ends with our relationship, and me, in a better place than ever.

We've had a lot of ends and beginnings – an end to his time in the FO, which I know grieves him deeply. An end to my depression and nightmares and black moods. And new beginnings in terms of career or however our plans turn out.

I embarked on a journey with him in 1940, and it's full of surprises and twists and turns. Who knows where we're headed next? Just so long as I have him always by my side – my lover and my beloved.

I began the psychology course in January. We spent two days in lectures and research, and the rest of the time in supervised clinical placements. I needed to catch up quickly, as the others had started in September. I floundered at first and often came home despondent, fearing I'd made the wrong choice. It was strange to be a student again, not having the authority to make decisions. It didn't help that I was missing the FO. But, one day, I made an observation on the clinical placement that turned out to be valuable and realised: *I can do this*. I started letting go of the FO.

Zac got more commissions from newspapers. We scraped by on our small pensions and the money from his journalism, dipping into our savings when necessary. Our only holiday for many months was a return to Bristol in the spring. Zac needed to check some details for his novel, so we decided to make a weekend of it and revisit our old haunts.

He spent the afternoon following up some research, while I wandered around the town centre. Many of the streets held memories for me, and I recalled with astonishment my confusion about Zac at that time. After dinner, we walked to the port area. When we saw the pub we used to visit, Zac suggested, 'Let's go and have a drink for old time's sake.'

We took our glasses over to the table where we'd always sat. Absorbed in our reminiscing, we didn't notice the atmosphere at first. Then I heard someone loudly say, 'Fucking queers.' I looked over to discover the hostile stares of the other drinkers. We were only talking – was there a flashing sign over our heads?

Zac muttered, 'Bloody hell, this place has changed. We'd better drink up and go.' We did so, followed by shouted insults.

We soon heard feet running after us. *Oh God, not again.* Several men surrounded us. One thrust his face up close to mine, screaming invective and spittle, appearing maddened by my existence. We knew a beating was coming and placed our backs against each other. I managed to get in a few punches and whacks with my cane, and Zac floored one of them. Then I took a volley of blows. Zac grabbed me as I staggered.

Suddenly, we heard a whistle. A policeman appeared, demanding, 'What's all this?'

One of the men shouted that the poofs had made a pass at

him and he was defending himself. I exclaimed, 'That's a bloody lie,' already knowing with a sickening thud it was useless. Arrest and prison lay ahead. I sneaked a glance at Zac, grim-faced by my side.

To my surprise, the policeman peered at us and said, 'I know you.' He turned to the men and told them to clear out before he arrested them for disturbing the peace.

I was slow after the punches to my head, but Zac said immediately, 'You were a warden during the Blitz.'

'That's right, Lieutenant.'

I remembered then. 'You lost your youngest at Dunkirk.'

The memories washed over me – how we'd escaped death from the unexploded bomb, and later found Gordon had been killed. The warden, or sergeant now, was more grizzled but looked much the same. Suppressing a giggle at the surreal situation, I asked, 'How's your wife, Sergeant?'

'She's fine, thank you kindly for asking. My daughter's given her three grandchildren and they're the joy of her life. One of them's named after our Harry. I remember you two – brave boys who got injured protecting our country. Them young louts don't know they've been born.' He added, 'You don't live around here now, do you?'

When we said we lived in London, he nodded as if he expected that. 'This area's changed since the war. You want to be careful down here in the evenings. Well, you'd best be on your way.' As we started to leave, he said unexpectedly, 'I'm glad to see you're both all right. You take care.'

Zac said to him, 'Thank you.' But we still walked off briskly, in case he changed his mind.

After a few minutes, we stopped under a street lamp and checked each other over. We both had cuts and bloody knuckles;

I had a blossoming black eye – but we were in one piece. I said, 'Well, that was a piece of luck!'

'Christ, yes. Any other policeman would have arrested us on the spot.' An edge of hysteria tinged our eruption of laughter.

We'd had to book two rooms in the hotel, but Zac came straight into mine. We talked quietly with our heads close together, calm and philosophical: accustomed to these attacks by now, or perhaps the surprising outcome having restored some faith in humanity.

I murmured, 'Do you think his Harry was queer?'

'Mm, maybe. Or else the Bristol luck stayed with us. We always did have a charmed life here.'

'Do you really think so?'

Zac kissed me. 'God, yes. This is where we became lovers. This will always be the luckiest place in the world for me.' He was gently tugging my hair at the nape of my neck. It always made me shiver. He laughed soundlessly. 'My cat.' We had to be quiet, the walls were thin.

The following day, we walked to his bombed building, now an ugly block of flats, then around the corner to my old place where we lingered with happy memories. Our final destination was the cemetery, a tranquil green space, to put flowers on Gordon's grave. It looked well tended and I guessed his mother must visit regularly. A robin, perched in a nearby tree, cocked its head at us and trilled a series of arpeggios.

I'd been waiting for one of Zac's black moods after the attack. Now I thought about it, he hadn't had one since recovering from the depression. I certainly didn't miss them. I took his hand. 'Zac, would you go back to those days now if you could?'

His eyes crinkled as he examined his memories, but he

replied, 'No. It was an exciting time for us. We were discovering each other, body and mind. But I love where we are now, who we are.'

That incident decided something for me. As we drove back to London, I told Zac I wanted to give evidence to the Wolfenden Commission, which was reviewing the law on homosexuality. We'd discussed it with our friends – there'd been inevitable jokes about Lord Wolfenden's son providing expert evidence, and the usual cynicism that nothing would change. I'd had enough of being treated like a criminal. Why should I depend on luck, or one-off acts of decency, to keep us alive or out of prison? Instead of swallowing my anger, I wanted to turn it outwards into something positive.

I thought Zac might tell me it was a waste of time, but he responded, 'You always were a revolutionary in your quiet way, Teddy. And it's not like we have jobs to lose. Go for it!'

The following week, after they'd agreed I could give evidence anonymously, I went in front of the Wolfenden panel. I told them about the verbal abuse and physical attacks, the blackmail attempt, needing to leave our jobs, the constant subterfuge. When my time was up, the chairman asked if I had any final comments.

I chose my words carefully. 'I think we're either born this way, or it's fixed early in our development. It's an unchangeable part of us. We're not demanding special treatment – only to have the same rights as everyone else. Putting us in prison, or through aversion therapy, creates misery and ruins lives. How can you justify preventing us from achieving our potential and contributing to society? That decent people are killing themselves?'

The thought of Alan and all the wasted lives momentarily

pierced me. I steadied myself and concluded, 'Making it a crime doesn't stop homosexuality. How can this be the mark of a civilised society?' I left with a certain satisfaction that, at least, I'd made a stand.

Zac finished the book in early summer. I offered to type it up, having learned at Bletchley. I borrowed Ruth's typewriter and set to work. At first, he hung around self-consciously, but soon relaxed. It helped that I thought it was marvellous. I learned of Jack's story, caught up in the Blackshirts in the 1930s and escaping by signing onto a merchant ship at Avonmouth. The passages describing his experiences at sea were particularly powerful. By August it was a typed, completed novel with a title: *The Accidental Mariner*.

7 June 1957

The anniversary of Alan's death. Now we can remember the happy times – what a brilliant man he was. It seems cruel, but life does go on. And life is damned good. I'm sorry it wasn't like that for Alan.

Teddy does hours of typing each week. He's gentle with my mewling infant. He says he thinks it's very good. He's being kind, of course, but his opinion means everything.

26 June 1957

Theo's 40th birthday today. It doesn't seem quite real to write that – my shining man. We're at the cottage this weekend. Ruth, Huw and the children came down yesterday and we had a picnic on the beach. Breakfast in bed and champagne for later.

We're coming into our prime. We're as poor as church mice, but we couldn't be happier. I'm much more open to new ideas and experiences than before. I'm doing something completely different,

Teddy's loving his course and we're on a new path to somewhere.

16 September 1957

Just back after two weeks sailing on the south coast. I've come home to my first rejection. The note said I should put in more of a romance. Well, I'll just try again.

When the Wolfenden Report was released, I was elated to see they'd recommended decriminalisation for men over twenty-one. Claude commented, 'Don't hold your breath, my dear. The government won't support it.'

He was right, of course. But there was something else I considered equally important. The report stated that homosexuality was not a mental illness – it was compatible with full mental health. I thought of Brad in Tangier, and all the others who'd suffered torture at the hand of psychiatrists. *That is justice*, I thought.

26

The vetting regime in the FO roared on like a blast of wintry air. Queer men would check on each other discreetly – most were leaving or being dismissed. One evening in the autumn, Anna turned up at the pub, her usual vivacity crushed. A colleague had been found dead at home after receiving a letter of dismissal. He was not long off retirement, a gentle, clever man. The FO had been his whole life.

'They've broken my loyalty, Theo,' Anna told me tearfully. 'I can't work in a place that treats people so cruelly. The British Museum have offered me a job and I'm getting out. It'll have to do. Things are tight enough anyway, considering we earn less than men doing the same job.'

Around that time, our landlord died and his son came to look at the house. We had carefully set up the spare bedroom, but it was obvious he realised. He was curt and left quickly. We weren't surprised to get a letter the following day, giving us three months' notice. At least the timing was on our side. Zac was at a loose end, with just some newspaper commissions.

16 October 1957

I'm busy house-hunting. The minute I saw the landlord's son I knew our time here was up. The hostility was seeping out of him. He'll probably scrub the house with disinfectant once we're out. Ignorant piece of crap. We've decided to use our savings. No more money wasted on rent. No one to throw us out. I love the idea of buying our home – that's a proper commitment. Maybe I'll grow roses around the front door.

20 October 1957

I found something today, not far from here and closer to the Heath and our local. It's shabby and rundown, but that keeps the price low. We'll need to paint, change the electrics, but it's a jewel of a house. We can buy it outright with just enough left over to keep us going until Teddy finishes his course. But I'll have to make a decision soon about what I do if this writing business doesn't pay off. I've had another rejection, this time with just the editor's slip. Thank you and goodnight. I'm trying not to feel too knocked back.

Our new home hid shyly at the back of a grand square. Zac spent weeks working on it and I helped in the evenings. Jordi's professional carpenter skills came in handy – he built cupboards, and made a beautiful oak table for our kitchen. Some nights we were there until midnight, with occasional squabbling. Zac thought my plastering was "slapdash" and I thought he was too meticulous. My mother gave us brightly coloured cushions as a house-warming present. This was our refuge, our haven. No one could make us leave. I look forward each summer to the perfume and colour of Zac's roses. I could never live anywhere else.

At midnight on New Year's Eve, we raised a toast as usual. I said, 'Here's to being legal,' which everyone thought was hilariously optimistic.

24 January 1958

New year, new career – or a bloody failure? Yet more rejections. Poor Teddy, I've been snapping at him. Not the best of starts for our new home. He sat me down tonight and demanded to know what's going on. I feared I might be heading for another depression, but after talking I feel much better. He tells me I'm not a failure. Of course he's biased, but his support means everything. I've decided to try one more publisher. If this doesn't work, it's going in the drawer and I'll have to find a job.

The news came on a rainy Saturday morning. We were lazily propped up against the pillows, dropping crumbs and reading the papers. Zac went down to shush Pip, who always barked at the postman. He came back holding a letter, his smile lighting up the room. 'They want to publish my book!' We jumped around the bedroom, the tea going everywhere.

He had an appointment with the editor a few days later. I offered to go with him and he said right away, 'I'd love that, Teddy.' His excitement touched me deeply. I knew he'd always had a frustration about work and the limitations caused by his injury, although he never complained.

The office was on the third floor of a rickety building near Seven Dials. A tall woman with messy hair came to collect Zac. When they emerged an hour later, he proudly introduced her as Julia, his new editor. He was busy after that working on the final copy. *The Observer* also asked him to go onto their permanent staff, which meant guaranteed payment. This was the time Zac's career as a writer really took off.

24 April 1958

Everything seems to be working out. Mariner will be published in September and now I'm a proper journalist. Perhaps I've finally found my line of work? I can't stop grinning.

When Zac's book was published, I realised he'd put "To TPL" at the front. I told him it wasn't necessary, but he just said,

'I couldn't have done it without you, Teddy.' Sales were quiet at first. Then it got some decent reviews, saying "promising debut". It went into paperback, then a second edition. In the spring he told me, 'I have an idea for another book', and he was back in the routine of research and writing, fitting this in with his newspaper work.

I was in the last year of my course and worked often with Hannah, an impressive woman who'd escaped the Nazis in Vienna and settled in England. We got on well together and had similar ideas. I knew I wanted to work with queer men and women, helping them to accept their identity and deal with the hostility they faced, while Hannah's interest was in family and child therapy. We started discussing the idea of setting up our own practice.

I was flicking through the newspaper on the bus home one day, when my eye was caught by a heading: "Man, 41, killed by train". The short item said that the man who died at Clapham Junction the previous day had been identified as Daniel York, a vicar, married with two children. I had to get off at the next stop and nearly passed out on the street. People were kind to me, but I couldn't really talk. All I could think was to get home to Zac.

He comforted me as I wept for Daniel. My grief was compounded by guilt that I hadn't tried harder to help him. I calmed down after some hours and we were in the garden when the phone rang. Zac came back. 'There's a Diane on the phone asking for you.'

He looked at me questioningly and I said, 'Daniel's sister.' My legs were leaden as I trudged to the phone.

The call was short. As soon as she heard me, Diane said, 'You've heard the news.' Her own voice was muted, tearful. We agreed to meet the following day in Soho Square. I dreaded being faced with accusations of having failed Daniel as a friend, but it was no more than I deserved. I had a restless night with strange, unhappy dreams. A weeping Daniel was punting on the Cam in his clerical clothes, telling me, 'I'm lost. I can't find the way.' I woke up and curled into Zac's arms.

15 May 1959

Daniel has thrown himself in front of a train. I hate that Teddy's so unhappy. And I'm damned angry – for what Daniel went through – that another queer has ended up like this. Christ, sometimes I feel this society is cruel, just wrong. How many more people need to die like this?

When I got to the park, Diane was waiting on a bench. I hadn't seen her for twenty years, but the resemblance to Daniel brought me to a temporary halt. The recriminations I'd been expecting didn't materialise. She told me, in bare and simple words, Daniel's story.

She'd always suspected we were lovers, but Daniel had denied it. 'If only he'd talked to me then, Theo. I tried to let him know I loved him no matter what – but he changed. He wouldn't mention your name.' She fell quiet, watching a group of children playing around the old hut in the middle of the square.

I found my voice. 'He didn't want to accept he was homosexual. He pushed me away. He thought it was a sin.'

Her sigh was like a sob. 'He became so grim and stern. The only thing that seemed to bring him happiness was his children. But then, a few years ago, he turned up at my house saying he wanted to talk. That's when we became close again. He described his torment over his nature and said he couldn't

229

go on denying who he was. It was destroying him. He started meeting men for anonymous sex …'

She glanced at me questioningly and I nodded. The cottages and commons in London were full of married men who led double lives.

She went on, 'He looked happier and spoke of being true to himself. But … last Sunday Daniel rang me in a dreadful state. He'd been arrested in a public toilet and charged with gross indecency. He said he couldn't bear the shame. He couldn't live with the consequences …'

A guttural moan was forced out of her. She slumped back against the bench. 'Daniel was a good man, Theo. His children have lost their father. I've lost my darling brother.'

I closed my eyes, tormented by the thought of Daniel in such desperation. What must have gone through his head as he waited on the platform? Diane put her hand on mine.

'I wanted you to know the truth.'

I managed to reply, 'Yes, always I want the truth. I just wish he'd let me help him. I should have persisted … I regret so much—'

'Don't have regrets. Daniel often talked about you. He'd been unhappy, but that passed and he remembered you with love. He'd say to me, "Theo is proof that one day I can have a happy life". I think it gave him hope.'

Diane was quietly watching me with Daniel's grey eyes. 'Society's very wrong in the way it treats homosexuals. This must change.'

Going home on the tube, I felt emotionally battered, full of a cosmic sadness. Only the knowledge that Daniel hadn't been completely alone, that Diane had loved and supported him, gave me a scrap of comfort.

On the morning of the funeral, Zac brought a cup of tea and toast up to me in the bath. All the time we were talking, there was a voice in my head. *Lucky me. How did I get to have a wonderful life with this man? Why couldn't Daniel have found some peace?*

On the train to Essex, I sat looking out the window. People pottered around their gardens, enjoying the sun and warmth. Two little boys waved vigorously at the train and I watched them in a haze of indifference. As we were walking up to the church, my body suddenly closed down. *I'm going to Daniel's funeral.* I bent my head and concentrated on breathing. After a minute, I felt calmer and raised my head to find Zac looking at me tenderly.

'Ready to go on, darling?' I nodded.

19 May 1959

Daniel's funeral today. Teddy nearly lost it before we went in and I wanted so much to comfort him. Of course, we were in public so I couldn't touch him. I stood next to him, raging in my head at the restrictions we need to accept, at our hole-in-the-wall lives. That good men are dying.

26 June 1959

It's Teddy's birthday. He didn't want any celebration. I know he's having bad dreams. I hear him muttering in the night. He's playing the piano a lot, something he does when he's troubled. I just need to help him get through this.

Some good news in the midst of all this – he passed his course with flying colours, not far off the top result, which was gained by Hannah. They're looking for rooms for their new practice. They'll be the brainiest clinical psychologists in London. I'm so proud of him.

Daniel's funeral service provided succour in a way I hadn't expected. I saw that he was loved and valued. But I struggled with feelings of remorse. I couldn't have got through that time without Zac's unfailing support.

Hannah and I were busy fixing up rooms for our clinic in Highgate, not far from Zac's wartime flat. The clinic was due to open at the end of September, but my grief over Daniel had sapped my energy. Zac suggested we go to Crete for a break. The holiday finished off our savings but was worth every penny of it. We swam every day, visited the ruins of Knossos and wandered through wildflower meadows. We returned to London with renewed energy and optimism.

10 September 1959

If Teddy's not swimming, he can sit for ages gazing at the water. Always, I've believed the sea has curative powers. I certainly rejoice to observe his happy spirit creeping back.

Today, we swam along the coast, going into a series of little caves. The water was reflected on the roof of the cave so it became a rippling world of blue. We were peaceful, just smiling at each other.

19 September 1959

We found a deserted sandy beach today. I was stroking Teddy's hair and feeling amorous. Then we couldn't stop ourselves and we made love, right there on the beach, in the open. At first, we stopped to check we were alone, then we got caught up in it and – well, it was bloody beautiful. His lips were so sweet, his skin tasted of the Mediterranean. After all these years – my God, he still does it for me.

Afterwards, holding each other and murmuring sweet nothings, we came back to the outside world. A goat stood just a few feet away, staring at us. Teddy exclaimed, you randy goat! Then we ran into the

232

water. When we walked back to the hotel, the fading light was red and gold and purple. There were fireflies dancing around in a field. Teddy said look, Zac, they're putting on a show for us.

We're sitting on the balcony while I write this. Teddy's yawning over his book and giving me his happy smile. The crickets are chirping. The stars are bright silver spangles in the sky. This has been the perfect day. I want to remember it always.

My stepfather had always refused to meet me. After his death, our communication with my mother became increasingly close and honest. She visited us regularly and fussed over Zac, checking he wasn't reading in a bad light or that he was getting enough to eat. He'd wink at me but I knew he enjoyed it. She gave him the mother's love he'd never known.

I was recovering from my grief over Daniel, and Zac was brimming with creativity. King's College offered me work as a tutor one day a week, which at least gave me some guaranteed income. I was determined to focus on helping queers, but couldn't exactly publicise my services. Over the months, my practice slowly built up, mostly through word of mouth.

Our relationship had moved to a new level, with greater balance and openness. I'd grown in confidence and self-belief, while Zac could show his vulnerabilities and talk more easily about himself. His dark moods disappeared and I saw more of his gentleness, which had often been buried before. He was still Zac of course – he could still be impatient and bossy; he still tended to hang onto a grudge.

Anna teased me once, 'We all wonder if you've taken a magic potion that gives you eternal love?' I made a joking response. I only knew that Zac and I had come through our crisis stronger than ever. I would never take him for granted.

27

We'd all laughed bitterly when the Prime Minister said we'd "never had it so good". It may have been that way for some – queers, for a start, saw it differently. We were hounded and persecuted as if we were the enemy. The hostility on the streets, in the papers or on TV, was so visceral it felt like a second skin. Claude was unusually serious as we gathered to celebrate the end of the 1950s. 'We're unwelcome in our own country. It's getting worse, not better.'

'I know … But it hasn't been great for women either,' Ruth reminded us as Zac filled our glasses. 'After everything we contributed during the war – now we're "little women" who need to stay at home. We're told we're weak and fragile, a sort of sub-species. Women who don't spend every second nurturing their husbands and children are considered sick.' Huw smiled at her sympathetically. Ruth had faced a lot of disapproval for returning to teaching.

'And if you're not married or a mother – well, you're just unnatural or evil,' Miriam added.

'I've always thought women's fashions are a real mirror of the times,' said Anna. 'I bloody hate the "New Look". All those voluminous dresses and pointy bosoms, emphasising our femininity.' She shuddered theatrically. Anna would stubbornly get around in her tailored slacks and flat heels, and her sexuality had become harder to ignore. Some bastard in a pub had recently proclaimed she needed "a good slap and a fuck".

Jordi, going through our record collection, glanced over with a smile. 'Voluminous. What a lovely word,' he said.

I raised a glass. 'Here's to a change in the law, and to a new and better decade.' I knew the others thought I was too idealistic. We had many more years to wait for the first wish, but the 1960s soon sent a blast of change into our stifled society.

24 November 1960

It's 20 years since our bathtub vow and I'm so proud. It's not just the length of time – any fool can stick it out in a joyless marriage. It's because we keep on developing and finding new things about each other. God knows, we have our arguments, but I'm never bored, never anything other than fiercely in love with him.

We're down at the cottage. We spent the morning in bed. Sweet and hot, just like him. We had a sail on *Argo* but it's cold and stormy, so we came back and shared a hot soak. That made us think of our time in the bath with bombs falling around us. Now we're hunkered down on the sofa. Teddy's listening to the radio while I write, his lovely face in half shadow smiling over at me. There's so much to celebrate – our anniversary, the publication of my second book. Life.

Our new careers were taking off. Zac's second book did well, and he started receiving regular cheques.

'I remember him scribbling away in his journals,' Claude said. 'He'd give me sections to read about his adventures, although once he met Theo he'd hover, ready to snatch it back. No doubt he'd put his yearnings about you on the next page.' Zac smiled over at me. 'He always had his nose in a book, when he wasn't off being an action man somewhere. It makes sense for him to be a writer.' Zac tried to appear nonchalant, but I knew he was thrilled at the way it was working out.

I obtained great satisfaction from my counselling work. I often thought of Alan and Daniel, in a way seeing my work as a tribute to them. I had a few regular clients to provide an income and to subsidise the lower fees for my main focus: young men and women coming to terms with their sexuality, or older homosexuals who'd repressed their feelings for years. Some had been through aversion therapy – all had been attacked or abused. It was rewarding to see them gain self-belief and make positive changes in their life. Pip often accompanied me to the clinic, slower and stiffer now. Everyone fussed over her and she loved the attention.

Around this time, Francis became our practice receptionist. He'd come out of a spell in prison for "gross indecency" and told me he was seeking work, adding jauntily, 'As much as one would like to live for love, dear heart, one needs filthy lucre as well.' He'd looked beaten down by life, and behind his jocular tone I sensed his fear. Knowing he would refuse charity, I asked if he'd be interested in a receptionist job. It was the perfect solution. He brightened up the clinic with flowers and his bright clothes, and provided a warm and welcoming atmosphere.

Not long after Francis had started with us, I was minding the reception while he popped out to buy milk. I looked up to see two policemen entering. One asked, 'Is Theodore Lawder here?'

I made my tone casual. 'That's me. How may I help you?'

They'd received a complaint that I'd been "encouraging" a client to "believe he is a homosexual". This was a young man whose parents had forced him into aversion therapy. We'd been making good progress, but he'd missed his last appointment. When the police demanded to see the record of our therapy sessions, I replied that my notes were confidential. I reminded

236

them they were on private property.

They departed with a surly warning: 'We'll be back with a search warrant.'

Francis passed the police on their way out and raised an eyebrow, exclaiming, 'What's Lilly Law doing here?'

Hannah had emerged from her room and said, shocked, 'It reminds me of the Gestapo in Vienna.'

I was fearful the police could wreck my work. After all, I was openly counselling men who were considered criminals, as indeed I was. But Francis sorted everything in his efficient way. He rang the British Psychological Society, who provided details of a solicitor and confirmed that the police could not force me to hand over my notes. When they returned the next day, I started dialling the solicitor. After a tense discussion, the police left.

I heard afterwards my client had killed himself. Yet another human being, with so much to offer, had seen death as the only option. I told Zac in a rage, 'This killing must stop.'

7 September 1961

Pip died at dawn. She looked up at us with her soft eyes and thumped her tail, then slipped into unconsciousness. She was nearly 16, a grand old age for a dog. She had a good life and a good death.

It was a hundred years since they'd abolished the death penalty for buggery, which Claude claimed was a cause for celebration. 'At least they don't hang us now!' I joined the Homosexual Law Reform Society and we worked to get the Wolfenden recommendations passed, writing letters and lobbying MPs. Queer men were being arrested and hounded as much as ever.

Zac and I were lucky. We had the usual abuse in the street, of course, and there was one time, with a group of young louts in Soho, which could have turned nasty. Zac walked up to the ringleader, getting his Lieutenant Bonneval act out of storage. 'Just what is your problem, you little crap?' They scarpered.

I remember once smiling at a baby in a pram, only to have the mother spit out, 'Dirty homo.' The feeling of rejection and humiliation ripped through me. I still found it hard to think I could be so despised for just being me.

26 June 1962

Teddy turns 45 today. We're having a quiet weekend down at the cottage and, as usual, we got in champagne. Always I need to toast the day my beautiful man was born.

The cottage is up for sale and we're buying it jointly with Ruth and Huw. I'm earning decent money from writing and Theo's practice is going strong, so we can just about afford it. We're teaching Sian to sail and she's taken to it like a natural. She's so bright. She asked me, how do we know the universe is infinite? Teddy said laughing, come on Uncle Zac, how do we know?

18 December 1962

I've been doing the form for my new passport. When it came to occupation, I thought, bugger it, and put down "writer". Who would have thought it would all turn out so well?

Zac brought home a Bedlington Terrier puppy for Christmas that year, a wriggling bundle of grey fur. We'd seen them on the Heath and laughed because they appeared so lamb-like but ran like whippets, like our Pip. It was Zac's turn to name him and he decided on Lamb Chop, for obvious reasons.

It started snowing the day after Chop came to live with us, and continued every day until the end of March. That winter was savage. The Thames froze – even parts of the sea. The milkman did his rounds on skis. I trudged through the Heath to the clinic in my wellies, sinking into heavy drifts. Zac and Chop would meet me under the copper beech and we'd crunch over the snow back home, our breath creating frosty palaces. We talked and read in front of the fire or played chess, Chop at our feet.

Sometimes, Zac would give me a contented smile and remark, 'We have everything we need inside these four walls, Teddy.'

I'd look at him, this man who filled and fills my heart, and say, 'Yes.'

The spy business and queer-bashing were still getting a lot of attention in the newspapers. They'd publish vituperative articles, such as "How to spot a homo". We had an uproarious dinner party over that one. Jordi acted out the "gay little wiggle", I was the man "too fond of his mother" while we all agreed Zac was the "over-clean man". But a deep anger stained our laughter.

Philby turned up in Moscow, publicly acknowledged as a spy. Zac gave a cynical laugh when he heard. Burgess died of liver failure not long afterwards. He was only three years older than Zac. I thought dolefully how Burgess had wasted his life and talents, as well as the destruction he'd brought to others.

15 March 1964

I turn 50 next month – bloody hell! I don't want presents. They're just things, possessions. I have everything I want. I told Teddy I want only one gift – to go sailing with him. We agreed we'll take four weeks in the summer and sail to Ireland.

Zac's third novel was published before we went to Ireland. He had established himself as an author of adventure and action stories, with a growing reputation for portraying complex characters. When I teased him about the absence of romance in his books, he gave an embarrassed laugh.

'Julia says the same thing. I don't want to write a heterosexual love story, and I'd cause a commotion if I put in a queer love interest. I'd rather leave it out.' He added, 'I do have a love story in mind, and I plan to write it one day.'

3 September 1964

Our last day on *Argo*. Teddy came as usual to join me in the cockpit with our mugs of tea. It was still dark with a finger of light on the horizon. Suddenly the sea was all fluorescence – as the waves came against the boat, sparks of light would fly out. It reminded me of those fireflies in Crete. What with this and the sky full of the Milky Way – God, it was exquisite. He said quietly, oh you beautiful planet. My joy was reflected on his face.

We joke that we have three good legs and hands between us, but we sail so well together. When we anchor up and retire for the night to our cabin, the sea gently rocking us – who could want for more?

28

When we had our New Year's party to see in 1967, I raised a glass to legality. Claude told me I was living in dreamland. But, after years of lobbying, an MP had agreed to take the Wolfenden recommendations forward in a private member's bill. This time, I told our friends, it would work.

That year felt momentous. The death penalty had been abolished and soon abortion would be legalised. Music and fashion were new and exciting. It was all wonderful as far as I was concerned. London really was swinging and seeds of revolution were sprouting like subversive triffids. We started hearing use of the word "gay" to describe us and I embraced the term. "Queer" had become too redolent of violence and abuse; it meant pursed lips and strangled diphthongs. "Gay" was open and friendly and put your mouth into a half-smile. I was glad to be gay.

Claude and Jordi agreed, while Anna shrugged, saying, 'I've always been called a "lesbian" and I'll go on with that. It doesn't change who I am.'

But Zac decided, 'Do you know, "queer" is part of our history. I'm damned if I'll let some idiots tarnish its meaning. After all we went through, all the hatred, I see it as a badge of honour. I'll stick with being queer, thank you.'

Francis was equally resistant to change. He made me laugh when he declared, 'Sweetie, I'm too ancient for these modern fripperies! Sometimes I'm gay, sometimes I'm sad, but always I'm queer.'

*

My friends wanted to throw a party for my fiftieth birthday, but I refused to celebrate before the Sexual Offences bill was passed. Claude teased, 'So, we'll wait for your eightieth?' After an all-night debate, the bill scraped through at the end of July.

Justice had arrived with a deadening, sloth-like creep. We knew how flawed it was. Men could have sex with each other in their own homes, but only over the age of twenty-one – and only in England and Wales. If we dared to make love when there was another person in the house – or if we went to stay in a hotel, or anywhere in Scotland or Northern Ireland – we could still be arrested. It didn't apply to men in the armed forces or merchant navy. Meanwhile, the penalty for consenting sex outside a private home had actually been increased. I was also angry about the patronising remarks by MPs. We were told we must not be "ostentatious" or "flaunt" ourselves too much in our victory, in case we made the sponsors of the bill regret their generosity. We had to stay quietly in our corner and be grateful for small mercies.

We all agreed my birthday party was fabulous – how could I not be happy, surrounded by my dearest people and celebrating life? Later, when just a few of us were left, we got into a discussion on the merits of the new law.

Miriam was optimistic. 'At least it'll make a big difference to the self-esteem of young men.'

Claude responded, 'That's if they can survive until they're twenty-one, having to be illegal and supposedly celibate.' We sighed and agreed.

'It's good for established couples like us. But young people who live at home or in college – how can they find somewhere private to meet?' asked Anna.

Zac argued, 'Yet it means we no longer have to feel like criminals. We don't have to fear being blackmailed or arrested in our own homes. Surely, that's got to be worth something.' We went back and forth on the subject.

But then Jordi, who'd been listening silently, exclaimed, 'You don't know how lucky you are! Gays in Spain are being tortured and murdered like dogs by Franco. They're locked up in prison or psychiatric hospitals. They can only dream of such a law.'

I was stilled at the memories standing before me. I wished Alan could be here for the change in the law, and to see his ideas about computers being developed. He'd been such a brilliant, good man – so ahead of his time, with so much to contribute. Daniel could have accepted his sexuality and found happiness. *This is for you, my dears.* Grief scoured my veins whenever I thought of them. They would forever remain young in my mind, but stuck in the past. I was now fifty, grey hairs were slyly infiltrating my hair, but I was happy and fulfilled. Zac pulled me close and kissed me. He knew what I was thinking.

Claude called out, 'I hope you two aren't ostentatiously flaunting yourselves!' We all laughed and I came back to the present.

Francis had the final word. 'From now on, if someone calls me a "disgusting faggot", at least I can turn around and say, "that's a legal disgusting faggot to you, darling".'

I lifted my glass, hesitated, then said, 'To full equality.' Everyone agreed and drank to that. I put the Kinks on then – we needed to remember this was a celebration. Everyone got up to dance, even Zac who could be a bit sniffy about pop music.

*

The world seemed to be imploding with student riots and demonstrations – against the Vietnam War, for black rights. Women went on strike for equal pay. Women's Liberation and Gay Liberation were born. And, in the midst of this, my mother died. She'd become increasingly frail. We were with her when she had the fall at home and stayed by her bed in the hospital while she grew weaker. The day of the funeral, I said to Zac, 'No one will ever call us "boys" again. We're the older generation now.' We mourned and comforted each other.

Life went on. And life was everything we wanted.

Our working pattern varied. We loved not being bound to regular office hours. We'd have weeks with long days, immersed in our work. Zac's fourth novel was published in 1969 and he was busy with writing commitments. I still lectured at King's College and the clinic was doing well. But we also had weeks with lighter commitments, when we'd go on short trips around Britain, or to our cottage to sail. Increasingly, we slipped over to the Continent – a few days in France, Italy. We took two months off in the summer of 1970, revisited Corfu and sailed around the Greek islands, an early celebration of our thirty years together.

We made new friends through our work, but always, the core of our circle remained the same. We went to plays and concerts, or swimming and picnics on the Heath in the summer. Anna and I often visited Irish pubs to enjoy the music. We had long, absorbing conversations over dinners or at our favourite gay pub. Sian was studying biology at university while David was finishing up at school. They were interesting, confident young adults.

Zac would sometimes say, 'These are our golden years.' So much had changed since we met – but always, in the still centre, was our bond. And that was unbreakable. We were determined not to live in each other's pockets, but we still delighted in each other, still loved best of all to be together, just the two of us.

30 April 1973

I turn 59 today. I just laugh. I don't mind getting older – it's better than the alternative! It's more that I still feel so young inside. Teddy and I are talking about the sailing trip we'll do next year for my 60th. We're going to take six months off and cross the Atlantic. I can't wait.

I'm engrossed in my new book. I've got the title already: *Violets of Pride*. The idea's been in my mind for a long time. I wake up in the night with the characters talking to me. This time, I'm going to write the love story I always wanted to do. Our love story. And I'll dedicate it properly to Teddy. No more being discreet. Bugger that.

14 May 1973

The more I research the so-called Great War, the more I see how the horror and needless suffering damaged a whole generation. As always, I discuss the book with Teddy. I love our conversations – they're like having a three-course meal. First, we nibble at a subject. That's the starters. We can get distracted, hop off onto other issues.

Then we get fully into the conversation and work through it. That's the main course. Today, it was about the nature of war. A few days ago, it was whether it's wrong to smack children. He always gives me a new angle to look at. We don't necessarily think alike – far from it. We've been disagreeing on capital punishment for years. But we respect each other's viewpoint and it would be boring if we thought the same about everything. Even when we argue, we just like each other too damned much.

Once we've thoroughly exhausted all aspects and come to some sort of a conclusion, we wind down into the dessert. Teddy will make a witty comment, or we'll remember some funny incident.

I can see us sitting here when we're old – holding hands, our bodies gradually crumbling. I suppose we'll be reduced to the occasional friendly fuck. But, above all, we'll always have our embraces and our conversation, the two essentials. Still so much to look forward to.

There's no doubt, when you get to a certain age, life does settle down. You fall into a routine and the years seem to pass more quickly. You don't have the excitement and turmoil of youth, the sense that anything is possible. But life is a series of phases. We were calmer and wiser and deeply contented. We were absorbed in our work and our interests. Our friends were our family. Zac and I swore we'd never take each other for granted. And yet – having survived our crisis, having overcome the hatred, having rebuilt our lives – we could only imagine a continuation of the same, sweet existence.

Then something happens that knocks you out of your cosy world and shatters all your certainties. You're left in the wreckage looking back at your old life, wishing desperately you could bring it back, knowing how inexpressibly precious it was.

1973-1977: The only thing that matters is that he should be all right

29

Soon after we buried our lovely Lamb Chop in July, Zac went to the States to report on the Watergate scandal. He looked fatigued on his return. 'It's just jet lag,' he said, dismissing my concern. I suggested we go to our cottage for a break. But when we went out sailing on *Argo*, the skies opened. By the time we got back to harbour, we were soaked. Zac caught a cold that lingered, along with a heavy cough. He picked at his food and would pause for breath on our walks.

Only weeks earlier, it seemed, he'd been striding up Parliament Hill, saying impatiently to Claude, 'Hurry up, slow coach!' I noticed he'd lost weight, which certainly wasn't needed. Zac told me he'd soon be fine. No, he didn't need to see the doctor. He hated fussing and never willingly admitted to any physical pain or problem.

One Sunday we had a picnic with Anna and Miriam, meeting as usual under our tree. Miriam regarded him thoughtfully. 'Zac, you really should see a doctor about that cough.'

Zac shrugged it off, but that decided me. I knew he wouldn't do anything about it, so I made an appointment for him.

I got home from the clinic at lunchtime to find him still in the study, caught up in his writing. 'Come on, Zac, I'm taking you to the doctor.' He sighed and tutted and expostulated, but walked with me down the hill to the surgery.

Once there, he grumbled, 'You don't need to come in with me, Mr Fusspot.'

I hung around outside, observing the changes in Hampstead village. When Zac emerged, he muttered, 'The doctor's booked me in for a blood test and x-ray. What a bore. It's just a cough.'

'I can go with you, Zac,' I offered.

He replied sharply, 'I think I can manage to do that on my own.'

I looked at him, then we laughed. We could never be cross with each other for long. I suggested we try out the new Italian cafe on the high street. He told me over coffee where he was up to in his book. Then we both went back to work.

A week later, Zac was in the study when Whittington Hospital rang to offer him an "urgent" appointment to see a specialist. I fixed a time at the end of the following day. When we went to bed, I could see he'd lost more weight. My uneasiness escalated to alarm.

Our conversation dried up as we waited outside the consulting room. I realised Zac was equally tense. When his name was called, I got up and stared him down. 'I'm coming in with you.' He just nodded.

The doctor was a balding man with an air of exhaustion, which I suspected was chronic. He looked up at us briefly, continued reading his notes and fired a few questions at Zac. He didn't bother to ask who I was. Then he said abruptly, 'It's not good news. You have advanced lung cancer.'

In the space of a breath, our world had collapsed. Everything seemed unreal. We stared at him, bereft of words.

As though from a great distance, I heard him spouting technical terms. The pancreas and the spleen – chemotherapy would just buy some time – new drugs coming onto the market in the future … I looked at him with nausea rising in my throat. I sneaked a glance at Zac then looked away, scared I would lose control in that room.

Zac cleared his throat and said, in a voice I didn't recognise, 'How long do I have?'

The doctor went off on another ramble: it's always difficult to make predictions; people respond differently to treatment. Finally, he came to a halt and said flatly, 'I'd say two to three months.'

I don't remember getting home. If I try, I can't call up a single detail about the journey.

When we got in, Zac said, 'I think we could both do with a drink.' He poured us a large whisky each. His face was blank, shocked. His voice was hoarse. 'The doctor's clearly an idiot. I'm perfectly all right. I just have a cough. Maybe I've got bronchitis, or fluid on the lungs, but the man doesn't know what he's talking about. He was probably reading someone else's results. Did you see how he barely looked at us?'

I made some sort of response.

'I want a second opinion.' There was more strength in his voice. He sounded more like Zac. 'I'm not going to take the word of this fool. What do you think, Teddy?'

His calmness astonished me. *Take a leaf out of his book.* I tried to sound confident. 'God, yes. I wasn't impressed by him at all. What about if we ring Claude and see if he can get you an appointment at the Royal Free?'

Zac got on the phone while I went to the kitchen. I stared out at the garden, bronze and amber in the dying light, knowing my life would never be the same again. Then I put the kettle on.

We got through the next couple of days. We didn't talk much about it. We didn't ring anyone with the news. We read, or watched mindless rubbish on TV. We were waiting for the appointment Claude had arranged for Zac. We clung onto the hopeless fantasy it might all be a mistake. When we went to bed, we lay close together, pretending we were sleeping.

The appointment was on a Friday afternoon. I went there from King's College and met Zac at the main entrance. Claude came out to meet us, his eyelids looking bruised, and I remembered there were others affected by this as well. He gripped our shoulders, then took us up to the clinic.

Dr Morgan had a clever face and sensitive hands. He said hello and asked who I was, which was a good start. When Zac replied, 'This is my lover, Theo,' he didn't bat an eyelid. He told us he'd gone through all the results and wanted to say right away there was no mistake in the diagnosis. Zac had terminal cancer. I felt the breath sag out of my body. I knew it was better to lose any stupid hope as quickly as possible, but that didn't lessen the blow.

The doctor waited as Zac stared out the window before asking, 'How can I have cancer when I don't feel too bad, just some tiredness and a cough?'

'I understand that must be confusing. You're obviously strong, if you have so few symptoms. But there's no doubt about the diagnosis.'

I managed to rasp out some words. 'How did Zac get this?'

'It's just supposition, but research is finding a strong link between smoking and lung cancer.'

We absorbed that in silence. Everyone smoked during the

war – it was often our only luxury. No one had told us it could be bad for our health.

Morgan asked Zac, 'I see you have an old burn injury. Was that from the war? Did you inhale a lot of smoke at the time?' Zac slowly nodded. I had a sudden recall of his intermittent cough during our early years together.

The doctor looked at him thoughtfully, then went on to say the cancer was advanced and had already spread to other organs. 'Chemotherapy might give you a few more months, but the treatment's brutal and likely to make you very sick. You need to decide if it's worth it.'

Zac's voice was a zephyr of air. 'How long do I have?'

'I'd say about three months.'

Morgan sat patiently and gave us time to absorb the information and ask questions. His manner was kind. He said, 'Come back any time you have questions. I'll leave the decision about treatment up to you.' I liked him. But it was all irrelevant. Does it matter if you like the person who tells you your beloved is dying?

When we got out, Claude was waiting. It was clear from his face that he knew the diagnosis. He came down with us to the street, his usual sardonic comments absent. As we were leaving, he said, 'Promise you'll ring me when you're ready to talk. I'll come straight over, any time.' We nodded and left.

When we got home, after a silent journey, Zac turned to me as if I were a stranger. His eyes looked out distantly from a face bleached and barren. Already, he seemed to be crossing the river Styx and reaching out from the underworld. He said, 'I need some time alone, Theo.' He went into the study, closing the door.

I waited outside for a while. I gathered all our cigarettes

and threw them in the bin. I went upstairs, shut the bedroom door and lay on the bed with the covers over my head. I wailed until I was heaving. When I thought I could cry no more, somehow my body found more tears. I heard Zac moving about downstairs once or twice, but he didn't come to me.

Around midnight, I knocked on the study door and went in. Zac was sitting at his desk, his journal open and a glass of whisky by his side. I shuddered at what I saw on his face. He was curt. 'I told you. I need to be alone.'

I wanted to howl at the world. I wanted to hold him and kiss the pain out of him. Most of all, I wanted to have the cancer instead of him. I said only, 'Let me know if I can do anything for you, Zac. Just call me if you need me. I'll always be here, darling.'

I spent the night staring into the abyss. That was a very bad weekend. Claude rang several times but Zac refused to go to the phone. Claude asked after me, his voice concerned, but I wanted only to speak to Zac, who remained secluded in the study. He rebuffed my attempts to talk, his eyes in some far-off Tartarus. I took him food and cups of tea, which he barely touched. All I could do was be there for him and wait.

21 September 1973

So that's it. I've bought it. I have months to live. This is how it ends. I want to scream up to the sky. I want to rip my clothes and beat my head on the ground. I'm so angry. And so fucking scared.

This bloody beautiful life – which once I accepted so carelessly – and which for many years now I've known is priceless. I have so much more I want to do. So many plans. Write more books, sail more oceans, have more conversations. Make love. Visit more countries. Most of all –

I just went for a walk up to Parliament Hill. No one was around.

For a few seconds I forgot and looked down onto the lights of London with delight. This beguiling, maddening city. Then it came back to me. All of this – no more. And the breath was knocked out of me.

I've been pacing in the study and getting through the whisky. I can't stop the thoughts any more. Because this is the worst thing. I want to live for so many reasons. But, above all, I want more time with Teddy. I want to grow old with him. I want us to be two old men looking after each other. His leg has been playing up recently and I know how best to massage it. We still have so much in front of us. I'm greedy for more of him. Every aspect of him. Even just sitting here talking – or knowing he's in the house somewhere. I can't bear to leave him, to think of him on his own. Without me to love him. It – kills me. Stupid expression, used so lightly. And so true here.

22 September 1973

I finally slept this afternoon. I dropped like a stone. I suppose my body couldn't take any more of the terror. And I need to remember it's riddled with cancer. My body has betrayed me. Always it was strong, it did what I wanted. No more.

It's the middle of the night now. I've been wandering around the house, looking at our things. Photos of our holidays, the blue and green rug that reminds Teddy of the Mediterranean, the little silver yacht he gave me for my 30th. All the things he's given me over the years. A seashell from that day in Crete. Mementoes of our life together. Wanting to bellow out my pain and rage.

I spent a long time watching him while he slept. He started moaning like a wounded animal. I put my hand on his shoulder and said shh Teddy, I'm here. When I think of my happy man who often sleeps with a smile –

I can't bear it. But I must. Somehow.

*

253

23 September 1973

I fell asleep on the couch. I woke up to find he'd put a blanket over me and a pillow under my head. He brought me a cup of tea just now, and I said thanks. Oh, his face –

I feel calmer now. I've been so angry at fate, raging around the place, snapping at Teddy. And the thought came to me: Zac Bonneval, you're acting like the worst sort of snivelling, selfish coward. I'm ashamed of myself.

Even in my worst times – when I thought he was dead, or I had that depression – I at least clung onto the fact that I face things head on. But where is that courage now? In my wandering years, I wasn't bothered about taking risks. When I found Teddy and realised how magnificent life can be, I became a lot more careful. But those were situations where I could mostly do something. Well, if bombs are falling on your head, or someone is shooting at you, you need bloody luck, but still. I can't ask for that now.

Teddy has sometimes told me, when talking about his work, that you may not be able to change a situation, but you can change how you react to it. So: I'm dying. I've got months left. I can't change that. But what I can do is make it as easy as possible for him and everyone around me. If I'm angry and full of self-pity, it doesn't change the outcome. It just inflicts misery on everyone. I've decided. I must go out of this life by showing the sort of man I hope I am.

Really, this is all about Teddy. He's the only important thing here. Because – Christ, how I love him. I think I was born loving him. At first sight, I was so drawn to him – as if my soul were calling out to his. I had to stop myself from staring. He was gorgeous, of course, but it was much, much more than that. It was – I don't know, his combination of sweetness and strength – his intelligence and integrity – the way he could be dreamy, then suddenly make some droll remark – the sense that he, too, was different and trying to find his way in life. From the time

254

I first kissed him, that chaste kiss 33 years ago – well, that was it. No one else counted. My destiny was sealed.

He fills my sky. I'm a better person, more myself, with him. He's all I ever needed or wanted. All those corny words in the pop songs – that's how I feel. I'd give up everything in the world to have him. So, how lucky that I've had this superb life with him. How miraculous that he's loved me as I love him – that it's been so mutual. I got the happy ever after. In every way, my life turned out to be more than I'd ever hoped or dreamed. I can't complain.

The only thing that matters is that he should be all right. I want to make this as easy as possible for him. I don't want him to suffer – that's all that counts. My lover Theo. My beloved Teddy.

30

Zac came to me when dusk was falling on the Sunday. I was in the garden, spiralling in a galaxy of grief foretold, when I heard him softly call my name. I turned and he was in the kitchen doorway. The setting sun had left his eyes – all I could see was his love. We embraced and kissed. We both cried and, somehow, we were smiling at each other through our tears.

He told me he'd come to terms with the news. He thanked me for giving him time. He said he'd been angry and scared, but not any longer. He accepted he was dying.

'I've had a good life, Theo. The best. There's no point being greedy. I've had thirty-three years with you when I barely hoped for one night. I've achieved everything I wanted. I've travelled the world. I've found work I enjoy. All I want now is to be with you and my friends, and to have a good death. The important thing is for you to be OK, darling. That's all that counts.'

He talked so calmly. He held me while I sobbed. He comforted me – he, the one who was dying. I'd always admired and respected him above all others. I always knew he was exceptional. But, that evening, I realised he could still surprise me.

We agreed it was time to share the news. The first call was to Ruth. We both spoke to her as she wept. Zac had a long conversation with Claude, then I rang Anna. She wanted to come straight over but I told her, truthfully, I was all right. When we went to bed, we made love in an instinctive affirmation. As I was falling asleep, I thought: *I need to be strong for him, too.* I was still desperately unhappy. We couldn't change the diagnosis. But, as long as we could talk and share the journey, we could make it as bearable as possible.

A subdued Claude came around the following evening. Zac was matter-of-fact. 'I need your help in managing this, Claude. I've decided I won't have any treatment. I think it'll be unpleasant and add little to my remaining time. Am I wrong?'

Claude looked at him unhappily. 'I can't deny it, my dear. You've always faced up to things. I don't want to waste your time being jolly, or giving false hope. I'll do whatever is needed to support you.'

Zac's face was set in determination. 'I'm not going into hospital. I want to stay at home till the end. Will you help me do this?'

Claude glanced over at me and I nodded. Zac and I had spent all day discussing this and we'd achieved a certain composure. He said softly, 'Of course, Zac.'

That was the first of many conversations we had with Claude about managing the way Zac would die. Life handed us a pyrrhic consolation because, apart from Claude, Miriam was an intensive care nurse and Huw had managed cancer cases. Zac would be under the care of Dr Morgan, but we all agreed we'd do our utmost to keep him at home.

Much later, Ruth told me that Sian had been distraught, then dealt with it in her usual rational way; but David had been badly affected. He'd recently come out, although Zac and I had quietly realised years earlier. He looked so much like Zac, but was quite different in character – gentle and dreamy, not sure where he wanted to go in life. Ruth had always felt such reassurance knowing that Zac and I would be there to guide David.

13 October 1973

The thing is – if you act a certain way long enough, it starts to feel natural. Teddy has a psychological term for it. At first, I accepted the cancer because it was the way he'd suffer the least. But I've discovered that, in fact, I have come to terms with it. And when I see how this helps Teddy, then it becomes easier. A sort of virtuous circle.

I have a strange euphoria. I've stopped thinking about the future. It's like in the war – we lived in the present, because we might be dead tomorrow. I don't worry about the outside world. I've pared down my life to the essentials, and it's surprisingly good. Colours seem so sharp and bright. When we make love, the pleasure is intense. I trail my fingers over his body, soft and silky. I lose myself in his eyes. I scrunch my fingers in his hair, the colour of dark straw with strands of grey. I look at the trees, all russet and gold, or the stars in the sky, and find them dazzling. Yesterday, we hung out of the window watching the full moon come up, pink-orange with wisps of cloud surrounding it like bridesmaids. It was just sublime.

I'm determined to get *Violets* finished, hopefully by Christmas. I know technically my three months are up then, but I don't feel too bad. Just I notice I get more tired and have these rotten coughing fits.

I'm making Teddy go to choir as usual. I don't want to let him out of my sight, but he needs to keep to his routines. That way it will be less of a shock once I'm gone. I know he's cutting down on his clients and spending more time at home. He's often nearby while I'm working. Sometimes I look over at him and the grief overwhelms me for a moment. Then it passes. I just look at him and love him.

Zac told me he wanted life to go on as normal. 'You mustn't

stop work, Teddy, it's important for you. I'm going to finish my book. Keep on as normal. See your friends.'

I looked at him doubtfully – but he was wise. Carrying on with our routine, having a structure, helped. I stopped taking new clients, but continued at the practice and gradually worked less hours over the following weeks. Zac worked on his book and came to meet me under the copper beech. We'd walk home, more slowly as the weeks passed, stopping for short breaks. We managed to keep that up until Christmas.

We went to Richmond most weekends, or down to the cottage. The last time we took *Argo* out was in November. We sailed out of the harbour and along the coast, but Zac was trembling with exhaustion, so we turned around. The next time, we sat on the yacht, watching pale sunlight glimmering on the water and talking about the trips we'd done. We knew his sailing days were over.

We went out in those first weeks. We saw plays in the West End and dropped by the pub for a drink. We wandered through the streets of London, found a decent coffee shop and watched the world go by. Francis popped around, sad dismay on his face, with cakes he'd baked.

As my clinic hours decreased, I stayed at home, reading or quietly playing the piano. I wanted to savour every second with Zac. I'd gaze at him while he worked at his desk, as if to imprint his face on my memory, feeling my heart could shatter. Every now and then he'd return my look with such love in his eyes. Then I had to go and give him a kiss.

Strange as it sounds, we were as entranced and absorbed in each other as in our first flush of love. We both agreed to live in the present and forget about the future. This helped us concentrate on what was important. We took pleasure from simple things, like our walks on the Heath, watching clouds race across the sky, or lying together, kissing and talking. We spent a lot of time revisiting the past, remembering our stories and adventures.

No one could have been braver than Zac, in the way he dealt with the cancer. We spent many evenings with our friends, meeting in the pub or over dinner. We gossiped about the latest scandal, or discussed literature, plays, gay life, our history together. If a stranger had seen us at dinner laughing and chatting, they would not have guessed that someone at the table was dying.

One evening, when I was seeing the others to the door, Anna said sadly, 'I've often noticed Zac has a special smile he reserves for you. I see that smile a lot now. People talk about "courage on the battlefield" – well, what he's doing now, making it so easy for us—' She stopped and swallowed hard, then added, 'I often have to bite my cheek to stop myself from bawling, but all I can do is try to follow his lead.'

I hugged her close, put on a smile and waved them off.

24 November 1973

This is a special day because I made it to our anniversary – 33 years. We'd talked about going down to the cottage, but I've been tired so we stayed here. Teddy got a bottle of champagne and cooked spaghetti for dinner, although I don't have too much appetite these days. We cuddled on the sofa and remembered all our other anniversaries, especially how it all started. The bathtub vow. We were so young, so madly in love, with so much to discover. We couldn't keep our hands off each other. I thought then I couldn't love him more. I was so wrong.

As December arrived, we were conscious we'd come to the

lifespan allotted to him by the doctors. Zac was weaker and needed regular breaks when we walked. But when I said I would give up choir he retorted crossly, 'Don't be a bloody fool, Teddy. What's the point of depriving yourself of something you love? Don't make yourself a martyr. That's the last thing I want.' Claude spent my choir evenings with Zac, and I was glad they had that time together.

We had a good turnout at the Christmas concert. All our friends joined in the carols and we ate mince pies afterwards. That was the last time Zac went into the West End.

Our trips outside the house declined to short walks on the Heath or to the high street. Zac was intent on finishing his novel. He spent hours writing and it took much of his strength. But I said nothing, because I knew how important it was to him.

22 December 1973

I've been plotting with Ruth to get Teddy another dog. Puppies are adorable, of course, but I want him to have company for when I'm gone. I wanted a whippet, the same as our Pip, and Ruth rang today to say she's found one.

I've finished *Violets*. I'm pleased with what I've done. Now I'll start revising. This is the love story I always wanted to write, and a way to work out my thoughts about war and the nature of courage.

It's three months now. I made it past the doctors' prediction. I wish to God – well, anyway, I just want Teddy to have a nice Christmas. He's being so strong. I know how much it's costing him.

I saw my last client on Christmas Eve – a young man who'd come far in our sessions and was ready to take on the world. We hugged and I sent him on his way with optimism. I felt guilty I wasn't taking new clients. There was so little out there to help gay men and women – still so much hatred and prejudice, so many destroyed and unhappy lives. Arrests for indecency had increased, in spite of partial decriminalisation. But I was being selfish. All my energy was reserved for Zac. He was the only thing that mattered.

Dusk was creeping in when I left the clinic. As I came to the first hill on the Heath, I looked up and saw a figure under the copper beech. Although I hadn't expected him, I knew at once it was Zac. When I reached him, I held him close and kissed him. A lifetime of being careful not to touch or stand too close in public – and it went in a second. We walked slowly over the Heath, stopping to rest on benches while he caught his breath. I pointed out a kestrel hovering overhead. We watched the clouds. I put his arm through mine for support and kept it there when we left the Heath.

As we passed by our local pub, a few men outside shouted, 'Poofs aren't welcome around here!' They laughed uproariously at their great wit.

Zac's voice was weary. 'Leave it, Teddy.'

But I couldn't. All my suppressed grief and anger came seething up. I crossed the road and went up to the men, who watched me with alarm – I suppose I had a wild look on my face. I said, 'He's sick. He's dying. For Christ's sake, show some basic decency.' I wanted to say more, but I was damned if I'd cry in front of them.

They stared open-mouthed, their atavistic impulse faltering before this glimpse of a shared humanity. One of them, eyes not quite meeting mine, mumbled, 'Sorry.'

I went back to Zac who was sitting, unmoving, on a wall. Memories slashed at my mind like shards of jagged glass. Zac striding energetically over the Heath – leaping up to change a sail on *Argo* – quelling a lout with one of his famous stares. I pushed them away. A silent acknowledgement passed between us.

'Let's go home, Zac.' He nodded. His face was nipped with fatigue. I settled his arm more firmly in mine and we resumed our slow progress while my soul keened.

But when we got in, I heard a bark and looked at him, wide-eyed. There was a flash of the old Zac in his grin. 'Happy Christmas, darling.' Ruth came smiling out of the sitting room, and a brown and white puppy came dancing up to us.

After dinner, I told Zac he should find a name. He replied, 'It's your turn, Teddy.'

I shook my head. 'No.' I couldn't say more.

I knew why he'd given me this present. This was to be my companion after he was gone. I wanted to use the name Zac had chosen, because it would be a link with Zac. We spent the evening playing with the puppy. It was sweet. Bittersweet, like everything then.

The next day, the family came around. Ruth and David cooked lunch. We pulled crackers. Sian talked about her plans to do a PhD in the States. David told us of his growing interest in acting. Huw mentioned the mess in Britain with all the energy shortages. Zac was on good form, with some colour in his cheeks, and he had an appetite that day. Afterwards, they cleaned up in the kitchen while Zac and I settled on the sofa with the puppy.

'Have you decided on a name yet, Zac?'

'What do you think about Plato?' We smiled at each other, memories of our adolescent confusions in our minds.

I said teasingly, 'Perhaps we could call him Phaedrus?'

Zac grinned. 'That would sound far too pretentious. Can

you imagine calling his name on the Heath?'

'Well, that rules out Epaminondas, I suppose.'

We started laughing while Plato jumped up, wagging his tail.

31

4 January 1974

I've made it into the new year. I have good days and bad days now, but fortunately I had one of my better days for our party. I spent most of it sitting down, but I got to talk to everyone and quaffed several glasses – not bad. We didn't talk about the future or my cancer. We just chatted and did a fair bit of reminiscing. And I got to dance to our song with Teddy. When we heard Big Ben on the radio we kissed and held each other tightly without speaking.

I got Plato so he'd be company for Teddy, but I gain a lot of enjoyment from him too. Who can resist puppy love – this warm, excitable bundle? He curls up on my lap when I have a nap. He does funny things to keep us entertained. It helps. And he did us a favour yesterday. I was telling Teddy I want him to find someone to love when I'm gone. He was nodding and saying all the right things, but the look on his face tore at my heart. I nearly lost my self-control – I wanted to wail at the injustice of having to leave him. Just then, Plato let off a fart, quite a stinker, so I pretended I thought it was Teddy. He indignantly protested his innocence, and we ended up having a laugh.

He's stopped work now and we're together all the time, although I want him to continue going to choir. I know he loves his music, so I mustn't be selfish. But I listen out for his key in the door. I feast my eyes on him. I lap up his presence, his conversation. We're not having sex as such, although there are many ways to make love. It doesn't have to be focused on the cock. We still lie skin to skin, kiss and hold each other. Always, we are lovers before everything else.

For the first week or so in January, we took Plato for gentle outings on the Heath. Zac was walking shorter distances and needed frequent rests. The day came when he said, 'Maybe I'll give the walk a miss today.' I just nodded. He didn't leave the house again.

We spent most of the day in the sitting room with short trips out to the garden. It was stormy, but a mild enough winter. The political turmoil in Britain meant that people were working three-day weeks. We had frequent strikes and power cuts and became accustomed to candlelight. It felt apocalyptic, and entirely appropriate.

Zac insisted I go back to choir after the Christmas break. Our next programme was Mozart's *Requiem*. Within minutes of starting the rehearsal, I knew I couldn't do it. My throat closed up; I couldn't get any sound out. The music affected me so much I thought I would faint. I went to the loo and put my head between my knees. Anna was waiting for me outside. 'Come on, Theo. Let's skip out.' We quietly gathered our things and went to the pub.

After that, we met every week in the Salisbury instead of going to choir. Anna said she wanted a break from singing as well, and I pretended to believe her. I disgorged my feelings over Zac, or we'd gossip about trivial things as a relief from the misery.

One night, I was in a bad way and she had her arm around me, hugging me close. A young man in tight jeans walked up to us and said loudly, 'This is a gay pub. Straights aren't welcome.'

Anna retorted, 'We were gay before you were born!' She glared at his retreating back before turning indignantly to me. 'What a bloody insult!'

I was laughing silently. After a stunned moment, she joined in. You know when you laugh so much you feel cleansed afterwards? That was how I felt.

I told her, 'That was better than hours of therapy.' But it was the last time I laughed for a very long time.

When I got home, Zac would ask after choir and I'd say, 'I had a good night.' I hated deceiving him, even a trivial lie like this, but I knew he'd be distressed if I admitted I couldn't sing.

Zac had lost a lot of weight and it gave him an ethereal beauty. He had this amazing sweetness. It was as though his personality had been stripped down to its core. I saw then the gentle and loving child he'd been before his parents, and life, had forced him to cover up.

Our friends took it in turns to visit every day. Anna and Jordi would bring us food or cook meals, not that either of us was eating much. Ruth would tidy the house. Sian or David took Plato for walks. Claude told me he was planning with Huw and Miriam to cover all Zac's medical needs. We couldn't have got by without their help. Zac wanted to have me around all the time. If I was out of the room, the others told me he was always listening out for me. When I returned, I'd see his face light up. His eyes followed me around.

13 January 1974

We spend all day at home now. My life has narrowed down to these few square yards, from bedroom to sitting room to kitchen and sometimes garden. Teddy doesn't want to hear music – he turns off the radio; he doesn't go near the piano. We read, we embrace and we talk. Sometimes we just lie silently in each other's arms. Other times, we talk endlessly about our life together.

He's been reading me *Emma*. I asked why he liked Jane Austen and when he explained I said, well, read me something. I thought she wrote romances about simpering young women looking for husbands.

Was I wrong. Such a clever plot and biting wit.

I get to lie on the sofa, Plato on my lap, watching his expressive face. There are so many Theo faces. Sleepy Teddy with a puzzled air – oh, am I awake? The sulky face, mulish obstinacy. Angry Teddy, eyes flashing. Happy Teddy with that sweet smile. Listening to music or watching nature, full of joy and something spiritual. The cheeky look when he says something funny, all dimples and irony. His sexy glance from under his eyelashes. His look of fierce concentration, eyes cloudy, when we make love. Or his look of love that turns my heart over, the best of all.

I'm proud of many things in my life. But my life with him is my greatest achievement. That doesn't sound at all manly. I should be thinking of the books I've written, what I did in the war or SIS, sailing the Atlantic – those are supposed to be the "proper" achievements. I'm glad I did these things. I delight in my friends and family. But to love and be loved by this man – that trumps all else. Anything good I've done, anything decent about me, has come out of the life we created together. Everything else is window dressing. I won the jackpot, I won the bloody lottery, with Teddy.

If only I could put an invisible cloak of protection around him. I never want him to be lonely, or unhappy, or scared. I just wish – but I mustn't go there.

It's taken me a while to write this. I get very tired now. I can see I'm getting near the end. I've said my goodbyes to my family and friends. I've done as much revising of *Violets* as I can. It's up to Teddy to finish it off.

24 January 1974

I ask myself why I keep this journal. It's been important for me. A way to explain the world or to understand myself, to tell stories, to work things out, express my feelings. I loved to write from a young age. I think my journals kept me sane at school, through those lost years. When Teddy gave me a notebook after the war and said you must write again – I wonder if he knew how that simple gift would give me so much?

I'm getting a lot of pain now. Pills just blunt the edge. I'm resisting the morphine. Once I do, that will be the start of the end. Claude tells me I'll get more confused, less alert. Like Teddy at Dunkirk. I want my wits about me. At least till we finish the book.

Towards the end of January, Claude arranged to take leave from work. Zac was getting breathless and I knew he was in pain. Claude and Huw arranged to get in morphine and oxygen. Miriam reduced her work hours and they agreed a rota.

Zac could just about walk down the stairs. I'd make up a bed for him on the couch in front of the fire, with pillows and a blanket. I read to him, we'd talk or I would hold him. He fell asleep every few hours.

Claude had explained what pain relief would mean. One day Zac said to me, 'I think I need morphine.'

I replied, 'Of course, darling,' although I was howling inside.

The drug gave him relief. For a while, he seemed to rally. But then he deteriorated rapidly. One day we realised he couldn't make it up the stairs. Claude picked him up in his arms – Zac was as light as a breath of air by then. 'Come on, my old cock, let's get you to bed.'

After that, he didn't come downstairs. He insisted on being in the back bedroom, saying he wanted to see the garden. I realised, afterwards, he'd done that so he wouldn't die in our bedroom. He didn't want me to have that association with the bed we shared.

I heard him saying to Ruth, 'Look after Theo. Don't leave

him alone, even if he says he's OK. Promise me.' Afterwards, I realised he'd said this to all the others.

Claude put some daffodils in a vase for me. Their silly faces are a streak of gold in the gloom. A promise of spring – but not for me.

We finished *Emma*. I said it made me think of us. Teddy thought Daniel was his love and I was his brother, just like Emma. He laughed and said, how true. And, like Knightley, I knew all along who I wanted.

It won't be long now. At least I'm not in pain. I feel quite dreamy, really. I just hope I can be brave to the end. I want so much to do that for him. Make it as easy as possible. A good life, and I hope a good end.

My darling Teddy. What a sweet nickname. Nothing like a bear. Never forget how loved you are. You always will be. My lover, my beloved. Be happy. Don't be lonely. I can't be here to look after you, but my love will be with you always. Any time you feel sad or scared, look inside yourself and you'll find the strength. My love has seeped into your bones, it runs like quicksilver through your veins. It will never leave you – "I shall but love thee better after death".

I barely left his side. The others would make me go and have a bath, stretch my legs, try to eat something. I'd be back in ten minutes. They took Plato out for walks, but he seemed to sense what was happening. He'd do his business then want to come home. He spent most of the time at Zac's feet, ears pricking up if Zac spoke.

I lay on the bed next to Zac. Always we were touching in some way – our legs or arms, or holding hands. I stroked his hair, kissed his face. I'd recall our adventures: sailing on the yacht, living in Italy or Morocco, our time as young lovers during the war.

For months, I feared he was dead. Life seemed hopeless. Then I walked into a hospital and found this pale man. A ghost, it seemed. My beloved ghost. In that moment, everything changed

During that last week, Miriam came every day. We made Zac as comfortable as possible. He drifted in and out of sleep. Claude and Huw made sure he wasn't in pain. Claude told me that higher doses of morphine might hasten the end, but I was adamant. 'That doesn't matter. He wants a good death, not to have his life dragged out in pain.'

On the last day, he was asleep most of the time. He woke up in the early evening. Claude came into the room and said, 'Hello, my dear.' Zac smiled at him. I kissed Zac and we spoke a few words to each other. He was looking at me so sweetly. He fell asleep soon after. Then I realised he was unconscious.

We spent all night in that room. Claude sat at the foot of the bed, stroking Plato, bearing witness to the final battle. Sometimes, he'd get up to moisten Zac's lips with a flannel. I lay next to Zac, caressing his face and talking quietly. Claude had explained that hearing is one of the last senses to go. I told Zac we were sailing on *Argo*. We were in the cockpit watching the sun come up. I described the beauty of the sunrise, the light on the water.

His breathing was rasping. Each time he exhaled, my own breath hung in a suspension of dread until he next took in air. There came a time when I put my lips to his ear and said, 'It's time to go, my darling.'

Soon after, there was a rattling sound then silence. I realised he'd stopped breathing. This was at dawn. His face was peaceful. *He's had the death he wanted. At home, in my arms, with as little pain as possible.* I hugged and kissed him.

Claude said, 'He's gone, Theo.'

'I know.'

We were both weeping but calm. Then we heard the doorbell. Claude went down to let in Ruth and Huw. Anna, Miriam and Jordi came over soon after.

The others took over all the arrangements. I refused to leave Zac at first, but they finally got me downstairs. Claude had taken Zac's ring off his finger, and I sat on the sofa holding that. Anna brought me a cup of tea.

Someone stayed with me each night. Everyone seemed amazed by my calmness. I heard them saying that Zac's courage really had made it easier for me.

The service was held at the crematorium three days later. There was a good turnout. So many people whose lives he had touched. They all mentioned the same things. How he energised a room when he walked in. His keen intelligence and humour. His integrity and honour. A steadfast friend, a loving brother and uncle. I didn't speak.

Everyone came back to the house afterwards. Miriam and Jordi had prepared sandwiches and tea. People started drifting away and it was just me with Anna and Claude. I went into the kitchen to put on the kettle.

And then – I lost it.

Everyone had said how well I was coping. But I wasn't, because I couldn't believe Zac had gone. I'd held him when he died. I'd just attended his funeral. His ashes were on the mantelpiece – but a bizarre denial had taken me hostage. I knew intellectually he was dead, but inside I had a running commentary. *When Zac gets back, he'll see how brave I am. He'll be proud of me.*

When I put the kettle under the tap and looked at the garden, a fox stared back at me in the dying light. *I must tell Zac.* And the words slammed into me: *Zac's never coming back. He's dead. You'll never see him again.*

The grief was so savage – I couldn't stop myself from screaming aloud. I collapsed on the floor, calling out his name. I was washed up on an alien shore, pulverised in a scorched landscape of loss. Anna and Claude were holding me and talking, but I couldn't respond. Terror eviscerated me and blockaded my tongue. I wanted Zac so badly, and I finally knew he'd gone forever.

Anna said, 'Come, my dear. Let's get you in front of the fire.'

They pulled me up and helped me into the sitting room. I was depleted, running on empty. Claude gathered me in his arms and put a glass of whisky into my hand. Then they put me to bed. Claude held me. 'Sleep now, Theo.'

The next morning, Ruth and Huw arrived and took me back to Richmond.

32

Ruth told me, 'You are my brother now', while Huw was practical, as always. 'You're far too thin, Theo. You're physically exhausted. We need to build up your strength.' They looked after me as carefully as if I were a helpless infant. They encouraged me to eat and sleep. David barely left my side. After a week, I started taking Plato out for walks. At the end of the second week, I decided to go home.

I didn't want my friends treating me like an invalid. I didn't want to be pathetic – I wanted to be strong for Zac. But I never anticipated how hard it would be. This thing had me in its grip, and it was violent. It was brutal. I'd experienced bereavement before, but this was something else entirely. Sometimes I wanted to crawl into a corner and die from the agony of his absence. At other times, cast adrift in a maelstrom of panic, I thought I was going mad. I would talk to myself in disbelief. *When was it I signed up to this world of pain?*

I went through the day with my face a frozen rictus, so consumed by the loss of Zac that simple transactions – walking down the stairs, following a conversation – took all my energy. A pain in my left chest paid intermittent visits. Instinctively pressing my hand to my heart, I realised how literal a broken heart could be. I would wake in the night with my heart banging away and wonder, *am I dying?* I felt quite calm about that. I didn't desire death but I would cross the road without looking, seemingly to tempt fate.

After that first breakdown, I did most of my weeping in private. I cried myself out, nothing left to give, until the next bout. I lay in bed poleaxed with grief, before falling asleep for a few hours. When I woke it would hit me – *Zac is dead* – and the blitzkrieg of loss resumed its cycle. I was flailing in a wild ocean, resurfacing to gulp in air before the next wave came crashing over me. I couldn't see an end to it.

Plato by my side, a link to Zac, gave me some comfort. Zac had been so wise in this. We went out walking every day. I must have covered hundreds of miles in those first weeks. It helped to keep moving.

My friends visited me regularly, unfazed by the rawness of my grief. Two conversations, in particular, made a difference. Claude explained that his mother used to tell him about certain death rituals. She'd described ceremonies held to mark one hundred, and one thousand, days of mourning. I decided I would set my sights on surviving to a hundred days. I knew I was incapable of going back to work – I couldn't help others when I could barely look after myself. This would be my allowance to give in to my grief, and a marker to aim for. I crossed off each day on the calendar in the kitchen. *Thirty-six, fifty days … I'm getting there.*

And Anna asked me one day, 'Would you change anything about your relationship with Zac? Do you wish you'd loved each other less, or that you'd been less happy?'

I looked at her, astonished. 'No, of course not. Never!'

'If you'd been less happy, you wouldn't be suffering so much now.' Her brown eyes were kind. 'Perhaps it's a trade-off? You had something so special, and now you're paying in grief. But there's a reason. You know it was worth it.' It didn't change what I was going through, but, for the first time, it gave some meaning to my anguish.

I went through a phase of dreaming vividly about him. I desired only to go back to sleep so I could resume our imaginary meetings. But you cannot command your dreams – you cannot go back to the same dream. When I woke to reality I would suffer greatly, but for a while I could retain the sound of his voice and our phantom embraces.

The hundred days were completed at the beginning of June. Claude and I walked to the Heath at first light and buried Zac's ashes. Afterwards I went down to the cottage with Ruth and the family, and we took *Argo* out. Huw and Sian did the sailing, while I trailed my hands in the water, gazing into the mutable depths. *I will survive this.*

The initial violence of my grief diminished to a lamenting dirge. I would stare listlessly at a dripping tap and move on. I would stand in front of Zac's raspberries then walk away, leaving them to rot. In an effort to knock myself out of this inertia, I decided to set myself tasks. I began to take on clients at the practice. By August, I was doing ten hours a week, by the end of September double that. King's College asked me to resume my tutoring role. I'd been anxious about counselling, fearing I couldn't withstand the pain my clients needed to work through. To my relief, it proved a welcome distraction from my grief.

I started sorting and giving away some of Zac's clothes. Each item was so perfectly folded – how I'd teased him about his neatness! I was incapable of singing, but I did go back to the piano, mostly Bach fugues. I resumed sailing, with Huw or Sian. It was a poignant reminder of something Zac and I loved to do together, but the physical activity helped. Afterwards, I would eat with a normal appetite.

In the autumn, I started working my way through Zac's desk. I'd never touched his journals and was hesitant, fearing I was violating his privacy. I'd been making steady, small steps until then. But when I read his private thoughts – his heartache over our crisis, his delight in our relationship – I plunged back into the most profound grief, as acute as the first day. Again, my friends reassured me it was part of the process. Again, I told myself to breathe in and out. Again, I concentrated on marking off the days on the calendar.

After a month, I started coming out of this second wave of grief. Anna and Miriam persuaded me to go to the theatre with them. I lost myself in the play and, for the first time since we got the diagnosis, forgot everything else for two hours.

One evening in November, a man approached me in the Salisbury and asked if he could buy me a drink. I politely turned him down. After he left, Claude said drily, 'Poor wretch. He has more chance of stealing the Crown Jewels.'

I laughed, and noticed the pleased expressions on my friends' faces. Jordi said, 'That is the first time we see you laugh for a long time, dear Theo.'

My initial reaction was guilt – how could I laugh when Zac was dead? When I thought this through, I knew it was irrational. Zac had told me many times he wanted me to be happy. Being able to laugh, enjoying the simple pleasures of life, was not a betrayal. I looked over at my friends. There were still many good things left to enjoy.

Soon after that, I returned to Zac's desk. I knew his manuscript, *Violets of Pride*, was there. Julia had asked hopefully if he'd left any work, and I'd given a vague reply. Now, I felt ready. We'd discussed it many times while Zac was writing.

I knew that it was a love story set during the Great War and the two main characters, Ross and Patrick, were based on us.

I was nervously bracing myself for another torrent of grief. But that was the start of my recovery.

I started reading in the early evening and finished around dawn, absorbed and deeply moved. It was not just a sensitive portrayal of love between men. His final work was a clear statement of pride in his identity. It gave me great solace, but also a clear purpose. His novel must be published.

It was only when I was putting the manuscript away, half-asleep, that I discovered he'd put a dedication at the front: "As always, for Theo. My one and only." Then I wept, but tears of joy mingled with those of loss.

I began typing up the manuscript. Zac's handwriting had deteriorated towards the end, and some of the text was sketchy, but I knew how he'd planned to finish it. My life became structured around his book. I'd walk home from the clinic with Plato, have something quick to eat, then settle down with the typewriter. My friends would urge me to come out with them on the weekends, so I'd go for a meal or a walk, then return to the study. I often looked up from my typing, lost in Zac's imaginary world, to find streaks of rain on the windows. Plato lay patiently at my feet. Every now and then I'd read him out a sentence.

A certain quietude was stealing into my body. I still had inconsolable days when I huddled in bed, mourning our interrupted cadence. The anniversary of his death was one such day. And yet, almost in spite of myself, I started to take an interest in the outside world. I joined in conversation with my friends and enjoyed walking in nature. Swimming or being by the sea helped provide a sense of peace.

By May, *Violets of Pride* was typed up into a respectable

draft. That was when I rang Julia and let her know Zac had left a novel. We spent hours going through the final proofs.

I cut out and read each review nervously. I expected criticism or ridicule, because it was a love story between two men. To my delight, reviewers praised the book, calling it "lyrical" and "important". Julia spoke to me regularly about how well the book was selling. In the winter, she rang to say it had been shortlisted for a literary prize.

The awards ceremony took place in March, not long after the second anniversary of Zac's death. Ruth, Claude and Anna accompanied me to the swanky hotel in the West End, while the others waited at my place.

There were speeches and a three-course meal. Occasionally, I looked down and thought of Zac. Just the fact he'd been nominated was enough recognition for me. I didn't for a moment expect that a gay love story with a happy ending, presenting us as integrated, normal people, would win an award. The few gay characters in books or films were either wicked, dysfunctional or cauterised by self-loathing. Always, they were doomed for a bad end. Homosexuality had only been removed from the list of mental illnesses the year before. The Foreign Office continued to ban homosexuals as unfit for diplomatic service. We were still being attacked and arrested; still objects of ridicule and hatred. At best, we were treated as pitiable or flawed human beings. Always we were "other", not part of mainstream society. Attitudes were changing so slowly, with such creaks of resistance.

When they announced the winner and I heard Zac's name, the breath was knocked out of me. My only conscious thought was: *if only you were here.* Anna and Ruth let out shrieks of delight. Claude picked me up off my seat and tightly embraced me. We kissed each other and Julia. I wasn't the only one crying. We didn't care what anyone else thought. For that hiatus, suspended in time and space, we were aware only of each other and our triumph.

Julia had said earlier that I should go up to accept the award if Zac's book won. I'd replied, 'All right,' not thinking for a moment this would happen. I had no speech prepared. Someone passed me a hanky and we all trooped up to the stage. After Julia said a few words, I stepped forward, knowing my speech was for Zac. *I must do him proud.*

Afterwards, we piled into a cab back to Hampstead and celebrated for hours. I got roaring drunk. I vaguely recall telling Claude I would always love him. I think I said that to everyone at some point. I remember hugging Anna and Miriam in the kitchen, and have another memory of lying with my head in Ruth's lap while Jordi held my hand. I was joyful one moment, and sobbing the next.

Claude and Anna came to my rescue, as usual. I was sitting with them in the garden while Claude had a cigarette. He held my hand. 'What's making you most unhappy, my dear?'

I had to concentrate to get the words out. 'Zac will never know he won this award. He'll never see the recognition he's achieved as a writer.'

Anna looked at me with her clever, sharp face. 'Do you think he cared about awards?'

My response was instinctive. 'Christ, no.'

'What was really important to him?' she asked.

I looked down in contemplation. I'd gone back to his journals many times, and they gave me such melancholy comfort. I still ached with his loss but, most of all, I felt such love and pride for my man.

I'll never forget that night. When I accepted the prize for *Violets of Pride*, I had this sudden clarity about what I should say.

'This award is so important. Not just because it recognises the beautiful story Zac left for us, but because it's a vindication of all gay men and women – our quiet courage and small triumphs, living our lives as best we can, carving out a small niche in a hostile world. We've been treated as second-class citizens. We've survived every type of persecution – and we're still here. We're not just clinging on. We contribute to society in every way and, somehow, in spite of the hatred, we make loving relationships and friendships. It's time to stop forcing us outside society. It's time to celebrate our differences and live together.'

An intrusion of emotions briefly engulfed me: thoughts of Alan and Daniel, of the tortured lives, the needless shame and misery. But it was as if I could hear Zac's warm voice telling me, 'You can do it, Teddy.'

I swallowed hard and went on, my voice steady. 'I'm proud to accept this award on behalf of Zac, the best – the bravest – the most beloved of men. He will never be forgotten.'

Everyone in the room stood. They clapped and cheered for a long time. Do you know what it felt like? For the first time in our lives – it felt like acceptance.

33

The thousand days were completed last November. I turned sixty last month. I'm older now than Zac. Never thought I'd say that. Writing all this down has helped – a way to keep his memory alive.

My friends insisted on holding a party to celebrate my birthday. It's never been that important for me, but I enjoyed it. So many people turned up: from Bletchley, the FO, choir. Monica and Julia, Hannah with her family, Huw's and Jordi's families as well. Francis, rather frail now but resplendent in a purple velvet suit. Diane brought Daniel's two children. I noticed David and Theodore deep in conversation, and smiled wistfully to myself.

In many ways, my life continues as usual. I'm back singing in the choir. I work in the clinic, still trying to make a difference for gay men and women. I swim in the pond and meet Anna and Miriam for picnics after. I spend time at the cottage and go sailing with Huw and Ruth, or Sian if she's back. I go to the theatre or exhibitions with my friends.

Anna, Claude and I meet up every week in the pub. We set the world to rights and laugh at Claude's jokes. Sometimes Ruth comes along, a fourth musketeer. Claude told her she can be an honorary gay and she laughed, saying, 'Well, as the sister, friend and mother of gays, that's fine by me.'

Anna has declared, 'Let's all age disgracefully together,' so that's what we plan to do.

I'm a proud uncle. Sian often stays with me on her visits back to England. She's a scientist doing research, a confident and brilliant young woman. David came to live with me while he attended RADA. He's touring with the RSC and writes me funny letters. We all agree, acting is the perfect occupation for him.

Plato is my constant companion. I take him out for long walks, although my old injury sometimes gives me trouble. He seems to know if it's aching in the evenings and sits that much closer. Ruth noticed me rubbing my leg the other day and asked, 'Is it paining you, Theo?'

I shrugged and said, 'Oh, it's all right', then smiled at her. 'I suppose Dunkirk will always be with me. But I don't complain. It brought me Zac.'

I sometimes get a sharp pain in my chest. I'm sure it's emotional. When it comes, I press my hand to my heart and think: *I know, my darling. I'll never stop loving you.* It passes off after a few minutes. Otherwise, I am well.

There's much to look forward to. Huw and I are planning a long sailing trip, hopefully with Sian. I'm going to Italy soon with Anna and Miriam. And Hannah and I plan to write a book together for young gays. I want it to be a manual for how to feel good about yourself – how to be happy and gay. Hannah will cover the family aspect. There's more open discussion now about homosexuality. It's less of a shameful secret than when I was young. But still far too much ignorance and hatred. Too many people are still suffering.

I'm not unhappy. I love to be with my friends. I think life is a gift. We should try to make the most of it. Try to be better human beings – make this world a kinder place. My work gives me satisfaction. I still take great pleasure from music and swimming, or from nature. I was listening to a blackbird in the garden the other evening and, for a moment, I felt such joy. Then it goes. But I don't mind, because I was deeply happy for such a long time. I had all the happiness in the world.

They say time is a great healer. Sometimes my grief flares up and it's as bad as the first day. But it's like living with my bad leg – you just get on with it. I'm lonely, but in a specific way. I'm lonely for Zac. I still yearn for him, but mostly it's just there, a background hum. Otherwise, my life is busy and full.

My friends ask me: When are you going to find someone, Theo? When are you going to stop being on your own? I know they worry about me, so I joke, 'Oh, I'm far too fussy', or I'll say, 'I'm waiting for a sexy millionaire to come along.' I did meet someone last winter, a good man. We went out a few times, but in the end, I sent him away. I knew he wouldn't get a good deal with me. I would just have compared him with Zac and he would always be found wanting.

The truth is, Zac spoiled me for anyone else. He was everything for more than thirty-three years – my lover and companion, my philia and my eros. How could another man match up to him? Maybe I'm made to love just one person in this life. Or perhaps I'll feel differently one day – who knows?

Claude, in particular, seemed to worry about me being alone. It all came out in the spring, when we met for coffee in Soho. Soon after arriving, he said, 'Theo, you've got an admirer. Did you see that man staring at you?'

I was dismissive. 'Oh, that's all behind me.'

'Really, you can be bloody stupid sometimes.'

Claude sounded cross and gave me this oblique look. I sensed he was debating with himself and wondered, surprised, what was going on. He said abruptly, 'You never guessed, did you?'

'Guessed what?' Images rampaged through my brain like violent intruders. *Zac had a secret lover – he'd planned to leave me ...*

Claude's voice was quiet. I had to lean close to catch his words. 'For a long time, I was very much in love with you.'

I looked at him, speechless.

'I thought no one knew, apart from Zac and Jordi. But it turns out everyone guessed, apart from you. I never wanted you to know. You would have just felt sorry for me in your sweet way.'

'But – I had no idea, Claude. When did this happen?'

'Perhaps that night you came to the gay pub in Bristol to meet Zac, and I thought: God, he's gorgeous. Or perhaps the day after Zac's place was bombed, when you gave me that kiss in the hospital. Or maybe it began when I first met you. I was fed up with Gordon's stupid jealousy, but he was no fool, in spite of his foolish behaviour. I think he picked up on something I wasn't aware of myself.'

I had a sudden memory of Gordon's spiteful behaviour that night in the pub.

'It was the last thing I wanted, Theo. If it had been anyone else but Zac ... I don't believe in this romantic crap about there being just one person for us in this world. You know, the "twin soul" and all that nonsense. I think we can get along fine with a number of people. You and I are well suited in many ways. But once you and Zac found each other, well, that was it. No one else counted. You had this bond, this love story that lasted all your lives.'

His usual sardonic manner was gone. He looked me in

the eyes and spoke simply. 'The first years were the worst. Zac soon guessed. He knew me so well, and he had a heightened awareness of anything to do with his darling Theo. One evening, when you were at Cambridge, we went out for a drink and he tactfully let me know. I was mortified, but he was very kind. We sometimes talked about it over the years. Funnily enough, it was a relief. He'd always listen sympathetically.'

'He never said a word to me.'

'No, he wouldn't. He was a man of his word. Well, I decided I needed to get away, so I moved to Liverpool. When I saw you again towards the end of the war, I knew my feelings hadn't changed, but Zac said he'd hate our friendship to end over this. He was right. Cutting myself off didn't change the feelings. It just made me lonely. You two were always so important to me …'

I covered his hand with mine. He gave a rueful shrug.

'So, I told myself, just deal with it. This will fade. It was hard for a few years. There were times I'd snap at you or have to take myself away for a while. You'd look at me with hurt in your beautiful eyes and say, "I'm sorry if I offended you," and I'd want to scream. None of my boyfriends liked you. But it all changed when I met Jordi. Darling Jordi! He guessed as soon as he met you. Thank God, he was so wise.'

A lot of things were falling into place for me. *Call yourself a psychologist, Theo?* 'Go on, Claude.'

'After that, my feelings faded to a manageable level. I'd look at you and find you lovely – I still do. But I'm so happy with Jordi, it's just something minor I live with. Like having an allergy or something,' he added with a sudden mischievous smile. 'It did get difficult when you two had your crisis and you started sleeping with other men. I'd like to say I did nothing because of Jordi, or because I'm some sort of saint – but really, it was for Zac. Before he left, he said to me, "Please look after Theo. I trust you." He said that deliberately. He knew I'd understand the message. I couldn't break my word. Not to my dearest friend.'

'Thank you for telling me this, Claude. I'm sorry I was so stupid over the years. I couldn't bear to lose our friendship. It means a great deal to me. I hope—'

'Don't worry, my dear. Nothing will change. We're friends for life. It's just a part of our story, that's all. No regrets.' I gripped his hand in relief.

And he was right. Our friendship continues unchanged, although with an added closeness. Now that Franco is dead, I plan to visit Barcelona with Claude and Jordi. I did worry Jordi might want to move back permanently. Luckily, he says he loves London too much now to leave. I'm glad. I'd miss them very much. This is our home. We are family.

I often sit here in the garden, or under the copper beech, with my memories. They are glorious memories. He wrote in his journal about loving my different faces, and that's how I remember him. The man of action and decision, so charismatic and vital. The way he took command, although he could be bloody overbearing at times. His angry face, eyes narrowed and glaring at me. His sexy grin. He would give me one of his looks and I'd feel weak at the knees. Making love with him, the passion and intensity on his face. And only I knew the private Zac – his softness, his vulnerability. Sometimes I'd have a love attack and hold him tightly, telling him how beloved he was – and the delight on his face … oh, my Zac.

But I think my favourite memories are from our sailing

trips, especially the way we saw in the dawn. Zac was so free, in his element, on the water. We'd lean together in the cockpit, our arms around each other's waist, often silent for minutes at a time while we watched the sky lighten, the stars fade, and the red glow on the horizon. Sometimes a dolphin would jump out ahead of us, or we'd see a falling star. We'd kiss and smile, in perfect communion, wordlessly celebrating this life. Those images help me now. They keep me company.

Maybe I sound like a miserable, lonely sod. It's not like that – well, not to me. I'm not saying his ghost haunts me. I believe there is nothing after death. But, although Zac has gone physically, his spirit is still here with me. We were together for so long, we were so close, that I can feel his energy inside me. That gives me strength. I wear his ring on a chain around my neck and I will die with it.

I remember our years together with joy. We were true to ourselves and to each other. We did good work. We loved each other. And you can't say better than that.

CPSIA information can be obtained
at www.ICGtesting.com
Printed in the USA
LVHW102237220422
716981LV00005B/319